Dear Reader:

It is my pleasure to present yet another captivating novel from bestselling Allison Hobbs. A "Queen of Erotic Fiction," she is the author of *Double Dippin,'* *Dangerously in Love, Insatiable* and *Pandora's Box*; all published by Strebor Books. She took on the genre of "paranormal erotica" with *The Enchantress*.

Now with her sixth novel, *A Bona Fide Gold Digger*, Allison spins a seductive tale about the alluring Milan Walden, her secret sex life and her quest for wealth.

I first met Allison at the Baltimore Book Festival several years ago and was immediately impressed with her talent. Not everyone has a natural writing ability but Allison was born to create masterpieces such as the one you are about to read. She is ever positive and determined, much like myself, and will go far in this industry as her next three books are already scheduled for publication.

Thanks for supporting Allison's efforts and for supporting my imprint, Strebor Books. I am overwhelmed by the legions of avid readers who genuinely appreciate not only my personal work but the works of the dozens that I publish. For a complete listing, visit www.simonsays.com/streborbooks.

Now sit back in your favorite chair or, better yet, chill in the bed, and be prepared to be tantalized by yet another great read.

Peace and Many Blessings,

Zane

Zane
Publisher
Strebor Books International

D0802070

ALSO BY ALLISON HOBBS
Pandora's Box
Insatiable
Dangerously in Love
Double Dippin'
The Enchantress

ZANE PRESENTS

a bona fide

GOLD

digger

ALLISON HOBBS

STREBOR BOOKS

NEW YORK LONDON TORONTO SYDNEY

Strebor Books
P.O. Box 6505
Largo, MD 20792
http://www.streborbooks.com

This book is a work of fiction. Names, characters, places and incidents are products of
the author's imagination or are used fictitiously. Any resemblance to actual events or
locales or persons, living or dead, is entirely coincidental.

© 2007 by Allison Hobbs

All rights reserved. No part of this book may be reproduced in any form or by any means
whatsoever. For information address Strebor Books, P.O. Box 6505, Largo, MD 20792.

ISBN-13 978-1-59309-119-4
ISBN-10   1-59309-119-2
LCCN 2007923508

First Strebor Books trade paperback edition July 2007

Cover design: www.mariondesigns.com

10 9 8 7 6 5 4 3 2

Manufactured in the United States of America

For information regarding special discounts for bulk purchases,
please contact Simon & Schuster Special Sales at 1-800-456-6798
or business@simonandschuster.com

dedication

In Loving Memory Of My Sister,
Rhonda Hobbs

acknowledgments

I wish to thank Monique Ford and the Circle of Sistahs Book Club for hosting the *Double Dippin'* ice cream-themed book event. It was a unique idea; I had a lot of fun.

Special thanks to cover model Logan Steffon. I appreciate your support and all the extras you do to promote the authors of Strebor Books.

Extra special thanks to Dante Feenix, author of *Black Butterfly*, and the boss's right-hand man!

J.B. This is late, but thanks for the flowers. Bringing roses to my book signing made me feel sooo special. Thank you very much.

Many thanks to my Strebor friends: Nane Quartay, D.V. Bernard, Harold L. Turley II, Lee Hayes, Tina Brooks McKinney, Rique Johnson, Shelley Halima, Jonathan Luckett, Michael Baptiste, J. Marie Darden, William Fredrick Cooper, Naleighna Kai, Suzetta Perkins, and Shonda Cheekes.

Very special thanks to my webmasters, Cory and Heather Buford.

As always, much love and appreciation to Karen Dempsey Hammond and Aletha Pauley.

Thanks for holding it down, Charmaine Parker.

And thank you, Zane, for being the absolute best publisher in the world.

chapter one

Had her guard been up, Milan Walden would have sensed something was amiss. She would have noticed while gliding into her reserved space that there were more cars than usual in the company parking lot. But, seduced by the unseasonably springlike weather and still basking in the afterglow of a succession of mini orgasms and one major, body-quaking orgasm the night before, Milan felt lighthearted and carefree. It was February, but her mind was already on a new summer wardrobe, a new hairstyle with bronze highlights, and perhaps a new car. Something sleek and elegant—a Jag or a Ferrari. And breast implants.

Smart, competent, and accomplished, Milan damn well deserved a bigger set of boobs. But with her low tolerance for pain, she doubted she could suffer through surgery or the agonizing healing process afterward. So, on second thought, she decided to forgo breast augmentation altogether. She'd start wearing bras with more padding to give the illusion of a bigger bustline. Her extra dollars would be spent on something totally unrelated to pain—like the pricy anchor pendant, with its brilliant round diamonds that swung from a delicate platinum chain, that she'd been coveting at Tiffany.

After a successful nine-month stint as the executive director of Pure Paradise Renewal Center and Day Salon, twenty-six-year-old Milan Walden was earning a six-figure salary and would soon be eligible for a substantial salary increase. The board of directors was decidedly pleased with Milan's inventive ideas and vigorous campaigns to promote the spa's beauty and wellness services. They were particularly impressed with the quarterly profits.

Under Milan's helm, profits at Pure Paradise had tripled in nine short months. Business was booming! Though the wealthy elite were the target market, Milan had innovatively devised beauty renewal and well-being programs to fit the budgets of women from all economic brackets.

Of course, Milan had the good sense not to integrate the well-to-do with the hopeless bottom feeders. No, no, no. The streamlined programs for those of modest income were scheduled on specific days and time slots, and upon arrival, the less fortunate were herded down to the lower level—unseen by discriminating eyes.

Milan looked forward to her performance review. Certain that her salary would more than double, she smiled wistfully as she envisioned indulging herself with all the fabulous material things money could buy.

Not bad for a gangly black kid from the Raymond Rosen housing projects, she thought with smug satisfaction as she breezed through the automatic sliding glass doors. She caught a glimpse of her reflection as she passed the mirror that hung above the security station and had to admit that she looked damn good.

Impeccably swathed in a textured well-cut pantsuit and a pair of beaded mules, carrying a colorful trendy leather briefcase, and sporting an expensively coiffed hairstyle, Milan had used her fashion and beauty sense to change her ugly duckling status to that of a beautiful swan.

She was brimming with pride and absolutely pleased with her life as well as the glorious sunny day, which she perceived as a divine design to complement her charmed existence. She failed to notice the serious expression of the usually smiling and solicitous security guard as she whisked past him.

When she approached the company's reception area, the woman who sat behind the desk greeted Milan with a strained smile and a weak "Good morning." The woman was Milan's exact age. She had a nice figure and appealing facial features, however, being a lowly receptionist was probably as far as she aspired. The poor envious creature would never come close to reaching Milan's level of success. Feeling superior, Milan smirked at the receptionist as she briskly walked past. *Don't hate!*

A few moments later, as she floated toward her secretary's desk, Milan couldn't imagine why, though she could smell the overpowering and sick-eningly sweet fragrance of potpourri that always wafted throughout Pure Paradise, she was unable to detect even a hint of the wonderful aroma of her morning cappuccino.

Her secretary, Sumi, who also served as the center's tour guide for prospective clients, was completely incompetent, but being a young and flawless Eurasian beauty, Sumi was excellent advertising for Pure Paradise. Desperate women in their forties seeking to stave off the destruction of time flocked to Pure Paradise, where they were promised youth and rejuvenation with massage therapy, aromatherapy, yoga, Pilates, facials, seaweed wraps, colonics, and even journaling sessions, for pity's sake! What a crock!

Thankfully, a sucker had been born every minute during the wild sixties. Bless those grungy, down-with-the-establishment hippies for prolific breed-ing and for producing such materialistic and narcissistic offspring.

"Sumi," Milan hissed, banging her chic, lime-colored Italian leather brief-case on Sumi's desk. "Where's my cappuccino grande? You know I can't begin my day without my caffeine fix."

A look of extreme discomfort crossed Sumi's pretty face. "Someone snatched it," Sumi explained, her voice an apologetic whisper.

"Someone snatched it?" Milan echoed. "Who?" she screeched. In search of a cappuccino thief, she whirled around and assessed her secretary's work area in anger and disbelief.

Sumi pointed toward the executive office—Milan's office. Just as Milan cut her eyes in that direction, the door flew open. A stern-faced board member emerged from Milan's office and beckoned her.

Utterly surprised, Milan's jaw dropped. "Good morning, Mr. Billings," she said, quickly composing herself. "What a wonderful surprise," she continued in an unnaturally high-pitched voice.

"Yes, good morning, Milan." He gave her a tight smile and then with a pompous lift of his chin, he said, "We'd like to have a word with you."

We? Milan mouthed the word as she turned her head to meet the wide, doe-shaped eyes of Sumi. She grasped the handle of her briefcase and glared at her secretary, willing the frazzled girl to enlighten her.

"The board," Sumi finally responded. "They're all in there."

"All of them?"

Sumi nodded gravely.

What the hell? With panic mounting, Milan cleared her throat, donned a twitchy smile, and walked woodenly toward Mr. Billings. Wheels turned quickly inside her head and then it dawned on her—the board wanted to reward her for her amazing accomplishments. They probably wanted to present her with a monetary bonus a few months before her scheduled performance review. A genuine smile now replaced the painful spastic grin. With a feeling of great relief, Milan traipsed inside her spacious office and offered a cheery "Hellooo," animatedly waving a hand at the board members as if they were all the best of friends.

⁂

Six entirely caucasian Pure Paradise board members were convened. They all sat stiffly on the sofa, settee, and two chairs. The board's chairperson, Dr. Kayla Pauley, an attractive and fashionable, forty-something dermatologist, sat behind Milan's desk, wearing a classy Norma Kamali jacket and sipping the stolen cappuccino. Milan was reminded of how much she disliked the sickeningly self-assured Dr. Pauley. Still, she gave a delighted smile that welcomed the insufferable woman to her desk—and to her badly needed morning java.

Milan cast a hopeful glance at a male board member who sat in one of the cushy chairs. Not only did he refrain from offering her a seat, the man had the gall to give Milan a look of contempt and then fixed a pleasant gaze on Dr. Pauley.

Irritation coursed through her body and threatened to make an appearance on her face, but she shook off the feeling and graced the board members with another forced smile. She supposed their solemn expressions and the stifling doom and gloom atmosphere was merely a façade, a necessary preface to glad tidings.

Dr. Pauley set the container of cappuccino upon the desk. "Good morning,

Milan. I guess you're wondering why we're here." Dr. Pauley leaned forward in Milan's executive chair and began shuffling papers.

Milan nodded absently as she glanced disapprovingly at the bloodred lip prints left on the cup. *Her* cup! Despite the monetary compensation she was about to receive, Milan couldn't help feeling violated. Why did Dr. Pauley have to ruin the moment by brazenly guzzling her cappuccino and sitting at her desk?

"It's been brought to our attention," Dr. Pauley began slowly, "that you haven't been...how should I put it?" She paused briefly and then exclaimed with an extravagant wave of her hand, "Milan, we've discovered you haven't been forthcoming."

Say what? Milan kept her bright smile frozen in place, for surely she had mistaken the word *forthcoming* for *rewarded*. Of course the board was gathered to show how much they appreciated her. Her performance at Pure Paradise was stellar. They couldn't possibly have convened to accuse her of—what? Theft? Embezzlement? Why did white people always think blacks were prone to steal? How dare they even suggest that an intelligent, attractive, polished, and educated woman such as she would take something from Pure Paradise?

Hmm. On second thought, she had pocketed dozens of those cute little pastel-colored bottles of Hawaiian hand lotion. Sudden fear made her heart pump a trillion beats per second. *Oh hell!* she thought with relief and calmed down. The product was included in the gift bags—giveaways for new clients. *You can't steal something that's being given away.* She had a notion to inform the stuffy board members of that fact, but held her tongue. In Milan's opinion, the real thief was Dr. Kayla Pauley, the coffee-snatching, desk-stealing hussy.

Without a doubt, the board had made a mistake, and Milan was prepared to loudly protest any wrongdoing on her part. "Exactly what are you trying to say?" Milan inquired. Her broad smile morphed into a don't-mess-with-me-before-I've-had-my-coffee scowl.

Taken aback by Milan's sudden intimidating presence, Dr. Pauley drew back and nervously reshuffled the papers.

"Milan," Mr. Billings said, rising from his position on the settee. "It's come to our attention that you falsified your credentials."

Milan's mouth went dry. Her rising panic escalated to full-blown terror. She swallowed and took a peek at the papers on her desk. She squinted at her resume, scrutinized it as if there was some kind of mistake. But her name was right there in bold letters as well as her educational background. There were other papers on the desk. One was embossed with the University of Pittsburgh logo and another boasted the Temple University logo.

"There is no record of your ever receiving a bachelor's degree from Pitt or an MBA from Temple." Now emboldened, Dr. Pauley leaned forward. "Milan, your position requires a degree from a four-year college at the least. Our records indicate that your education is limited to a high school diploma," Dr. Pauley said, shaking her head and scanning the papers in annoyance. "Unless you can provide the proper documentation, we're going to have to terminate you immediately."

Dr. Pauley's words were chilling. Milan's knees, damn them, knocked together uncontrollably. She hadn't heard what she thought, had she? She definitely needed a moment to process the information. She stammered, "I know I don't actually have a degree, but obviously I'm a strong, dynamic leader. My experience speaks for—"

Before she could utter another word, Royce, the security guard, appeared. He glowered at Milan briefly and then said gruffly, "Come with me, Ms. Walden."

Milan's jaw dropped. "You're kidding!" She twirled on her heels and faced the group of six. "Is this necessary? My accomplishments here have been huge," Milan said, fighting for survival, trying to reason with the board. "I put in thirteen-hour work days and I've made this company a small fortune." She paused to catch her breath. "And now you're treating me like a common thief."

"Please leave the premises, Milan, or security will have to forcibly remove you," Dr. Pauley said, unmoved by Milan's outburst. Slowly and gracefully, she picked up the phone. "Sumi, please pack up all Milan's belongings."

Milan opened her mouth to further defend herself, but she felt faint. The words necessary to halt this travesty of justice escaped her.

Smiling wickedly as she swiveled toward Milan, Dr. Pauley said, "We'll forward your belongings to your current address. Hopefully, that isn't a fabrication as well."

The next three minutes were a blur of embarrassed gasps, chuckles, and outright slurs from subordinates who apparently felt Milan had it coming. A minute or so later, she sat inside her car, stunned and trembling, but very reluctant to leave Pure Paradise. Driving away obliterated her chance of being available should the board come to their senses and reconsider their absurd decision to fire her. As far as Milan was concerned, keeping her around—college degree or not—made good business sense.

Royce had brusquely escorted Milan through the sliding doors and returned to his station. From his vantage point, he could see that she was making no attempt to vacate the company parking lot. The once-friendly security guard stepped outside. With an angry expression, he motioned for Milan to get moving.

Could the day get any worse? Her mind was spinning, her head throbbed, and she felt queasy. She really needed something to calm her down. She imagined Dr. Pauley and realized that what she needed was a goddamn cup of coffee!

Blinking back tears, she pulled herself together, turned on the ignition, and careened out of the lot. The car, seemingly on automatic pilot, was pointed in the direction of the nearest Starbucks.

chapter two

"**D**id you get ghetto on that heifer?" Milan's sister, Sweetie, wanted to know after Milan related her harrowing ordeal. Dropping batter-covered wing dings into a pan of sizzling oil, Sweetie spoke with her back to Milan.

"No, I didn't get *ghetto*," Milan spit out the last word. As her sister damn well knew, Milan had long ago redefined herself and had shed the skin of a person who resolved issues by behaving in a manner as abhorrent as *getting ghetto*. She now possessed well-honed sophistication and was a savvy businesswoman. Her mother and her sister still embraced their ignorance and lack of sophistication, but in no way did the word *ghetto* apply to Milan.

Sweetie tossed in the last wing ding and turned around. "Well, what did you do? I'm waiting to hear how you whipped that ass." With her face screwed up and clearly exasperated, Sweetie folded her arms as she waited for Milan to respond.

"What could I do?"

Sweetie gawked at Milan. "Please tell me that you at least grabbed that wench by the collar and smacked your coffee out of her hand."

"Get serious, Sweetie. You know I wouldn't disgrace myself like that."

"Hmph! If that heifer had come at me like that, her ass woulda been wearing that damn espresso."

"Cappuccino," Milan corrected.

"Whatever! Did you whip that ass?" Sweetie repeated.

Milan sincerely loved her sister, but Sweetie had to be the most hopelessly ignorant and thoroughly ghettoized person she knew. The two sisters were like night and day. They had nothing in common.

Sweetie had no ambition. She was out of shape and her wardrobe was a fashion disaster. How her sister could walk around in a pair of low rider jeans with a roll of flab hanging over the waistline was beyond Milan. Sweetie was satisfied being a sloppy-looking, stay-at-home wife and mother. She and her husband, Quantez, had two bad-behind boys spaced only ten months apart, and judging by the way her sister loved to brag about her sex life, it wouldn't be long before baby number three was conceived.

In Milan's opinion, the only thing Sweetie had going for herself was her pretty face. She didn't need a drop of makeup, not even lipstick. Her glamour routine was simple: moisturizer and lip gloss. Milan had to work hard to be glamorous and couldn't help thinking that God had given the wrong sister the natural beauty.

Breaking off her thoughts of envy, Milan said, "Sweetie, I just lost the best job I've ever had and all you can think about is whether or not I retaliated with physical force. I need to focus on finding another job. A good job that pays as much or even *more* than I earned at Pure Paradise." Milan fell silent briefly, and then looked at her sister intently. "Sweetie. There's a possibility that the board might spread malicious rumors about my education."

"Rumors?"

"You know what I mean. After all the energy I put into my career, I could end up blackballed. The board could inhibit my earning power; they could prevent me from ever working again."

"Oh, please, how can a few people stop you from ever working again?"

"Those few people have a lot of power. They're well respected in the spa industry. But besides that, I don't know what I'm going to tell Mom. I need you to help me come up with a story." Milan shook her head mournfully. "She's going to be absolutely distraught when she finds out I lost my prestigious position."

Sweetie nodded in sad agreement. "Yeah, she's gonna miss all those freebies. Did you grip up some gift bags for us before you split?" she teased, making light of Milan's situation.

"I don't give Mom just the free gift bags. Ever since I've had the job, I've showered both you and Mom and your kids with expensive gifts."

"And we appreciate it, but Mom gets a big kick out of getting all that free stuff," Sweetie explained, giggling as she spoke.

Not seeing any humor in being unemployed and possibly having her future earning power opposed, Milan grabbed her briefcase and stood. Stepping over several Fisher Price toys she recognized as part of the plethora of Christmas gifts she'd purchased for her nephews, Milan announced, "I'm leaving! How can you be so insensitive? I can't think of any reason why you'd think it appropriate to poke fun at a time like this." Pointing a French-manicured finger around Sweetie's disorderly living room, Milan confronted her sister. "What's the problem, Sweetie? Are you jealous because I didn't screw up my life the way you screwed up yours? Two kids back-to-back, living in low-income housing—"

"Excuse me!" Sweetie said, interrupting Milan. "My life is not screwed up. I have a hard-working husband who loves me enough to pay all the bills, including the day care bill for our two kids so I can have some free time for myself."

"Your husband earns—what? Thirty...thirty-one thousand a year?" Milan tsked at the absurdity of such a meager salary. "You sound like a fool bragging about the pittance Quantez is bringing in. You should be out looking for a job so you can help make ends meet around here." She looked around her sister's house with her nose turned up. "And you shouldn't be bragging about sending your children to that subsidized, ghetto day care center while you're sitting on your butt, not even making an attempt to elevate yourself or your family."

"My husband does not want me to work. And anyway, Miss High and Mighty, what the hell do *you* have?" Sweetie asked, her face scrunched up in hostility. "I'll tell you what you have— a bunch of nothing, that's what! Nice clothes and an overpriced apartment and that's it. But you know what your problem really is?"

"No, but I'm sure you think you're in a position to tell me."

"You need some dick," Sweetie said in a deadly calm voice. "How long have you been humping that fifteen-hundred-dollar penis?" Sweetie asked and then gave a burst of loud, malicious laughter. "Girl, I remember when you called me to brag about the price you paid for a damn vibrator." Sweetie's shoulders shook from laughter. "Anytime a woman brags about the amount of money she spent on some battery-operated dick, you know her life is fucked up. *My* life, however, is just fine. Let me remind you, I have a fine-ass husband and two gorgeous kids who *looove* me."

Milan inhaled sharply.

Sweetie's dark eyes sparkled with mischief. "With all your important *this* and expensive *that*, how come you don't have a man? How come you're sitting up in my crib, crying on my shoulder? Oops! I forgot. Unlike me, you don't have a man to hold you tight. There's nobody at your crib to take your troubles to. You wanna know why? Because there's not a man on the planet who would find you loveable enough to even listen to your bullshit."

Milan realized her sister's words were designed to cut deeply, but she honestly did not feel any pain. No, there wasn't a special man in her life—her choice. With her all-encompassing career goals, there was little time left to emotionally invest in a man. Yet, her sex life was completely gratifying. But how could she expect someone as closed minded and unsophisticated as Sweetie to understand her hedonistic lifestyle?

"It's not like I *can't* get a man; but honestly, emotional attachment is the last thing on my mind. And marriage?" she said with a scornful snort. "You know my career comes first. I don't have time for a relationship with a man or anyone else for that matter. As you well know, I don't even have time for girlfriends."

Sweetie folded her arms. "Well, that's a damn shame, 'cause now you don't have nothin'. No job, no man, and not one even one girlfriend. Umph!" Sweetie screwed up her face and shook her head.

Ow! Now, Milan winced. Damn shame that she didn't have a single friend, male or female. But at what point during her rise to the top was she supposed to take the time to cultivate friendships? In her current predicament, she could use some meaningful advice from a cultured and educated best friend. Instead, she had to listen to Sweetie pontificate about life lessons—how Milan should take this setback as a lesson in knowing one's place in life. Sweetie droned on and on as if it were the perfect time for Milan to embrace an existence similar to hers, with a poorly paid husband and a couple of snot-nosed brats hanging on to her skirt tail. *No thanks!*

Milan shook her head. She should have thought twice before she spoke disparagingly of Sweetie's husband. Sweetie became a monster over the slightest criticism of Quantez. Now on a roll, Sweetie viciously continued to cut Milan to shreds.

"You were married to that damn job and now you ain't even got that. I hate to tell you this, Milan, but every time you said the words *executive director*—which was about a thousand times in every conversation—me and Mommy wanted to throw up. I'm sorry those people kicked you out the way they did but at least now I don't have to hear about Pure Paradise every day of my life. Without your job and snooty job title, you ain't shit. So, whose life is really screwed?"

Being informed of her worthless status was jolting and the only thing she could think to say was, "You and Mommy talk about me behind my back?"

"Every day!" Sweetie said with a vindictive grin.

"How could Mommy talk disapprovingly of my carefully planned lifestyle when you and Quantez live like *this*?" Milan looked around the cramped and untidy quarters with an expression of revulsion.

Offended, Sweetie sucked her teeth. "We got a roof over our heads and food—" Sweetie closed her mouth abruptly. "I don't have to explain my life to you. You said you were leaving, so get the hell out." She walked to the door, twisted the knob and yanked the door open.

"You don't have to tell me twice." Milan moved toward the door with her nose turned up. When one last insult formed in her mind, she turned around suddenly. "By the way, since you have so much *free time*, how come your place smells like pissy diapers?"

"Get out!" Sweetie shouted at her sister and held the door wide open.

Milan huffily obliged. Sweetie slammed the door behind her.

Being thrown out of the upscale Pure Paradise was extremely humiliating, but being ejected from Sweetie's little shack of a home was degrading as hell. Her own sister's rejection seemed to foreshadow the coming of terrible times, as if this was an ominous warning that dire circumstances loomed close by.

chapter three

"How could you talk about me behind my back with Sweetie?" Milan complained to her mother.

"Honey, we say the same things to your face," Milan's mother, Bernice Walden, said in an irritatingly pleasant tone.

"But you never say a word against Sweetie. No matter what I accomplish, I'm still the black sheep and Sweetie's still your favorite child."

"That's not true. My favorite is the child who needs me most. And right now, you need me more than Sweetie does, so I guess that makes you my favorite."

"Sure, Mom," Milan said sarcastically. "So, what did Sweetie tell you?"

"She told me what happened at work."

Milan let out a sound of surprise. Despite their little tiff, she was surprised that Sweetie would betray her trust and disclose her shameful predicament. She hated that her mother was now aware of her degrading dismissal from Pure Paradise.

"I hate to admit it, but you act more like your father every day," her mother said disapprovingly, as if any traits her sperm donor father had passed down were Milan's fault. It didn't matter that she was speaking of a person Milan had never met, a man who, according to her mother, hustled everything from stolen property to drugs and women. A man whose name was considered worse than mud in the Walden household.

The untimely death of Earl Walden, Bernice's husband and Sweetie's father, led to Bernice's involvement with Milan's unsavory sperm donor.

Earl Walden was a handsome man and a loving husband, according to Bernice. He was killed in a car accident just a month after their marriage. Seven months later, Sweetie's birth was a bittersweet celebration, but a celebration nevertheless.

Milan, however, made her unwelcome appearance a year later. Her grief-stricken mother, masking the pain of losing a husband, had engaged in a brief period of loose living. She claimed she'd fallen into the hands of Milan's no-good, silver-tongued father while under duress.

Besides the physical similarities (she'd seen a faded photo of him and thought he was nothing to brag about) Milan felt she had nothing in common with the man. Thank God she'd discovered that expertly applied cosmetics, a good rapport with a top-notch hair stylist, and designer clothing could disguise bad genes.

"What could *I* possibly have in common with *that* man?" Milan inquired pleadingly. Her father, a man known simply as Slick—no real first or last name—was considered scum by the family. Having a father who was scum was a great deal to overcome and Milan felt she'd done a fine job. Again, she inquired, "How am I like *him*?"

"For one thing, you're always looking for shortcuts. I told you not to accept that job at that hotel spa—what was it called?"

"The Velvet Touch," Milan said wearily.

"Yeah, that place. You let those people build up your ego. They had you thinking you didn't need to finish school."

"I didn't!" she yelled.

"But all you needed was a few more semesters to get your college degree."

Milan sighed loudly. The conversation with her mother was aggravating and exhausting, but she managed to tone down her irritation and speak in a calm voice. "I was more than qualified for that position, Mom. I proved myself. Obviously, I can run a day spa without a stupid degree."

"But not having that piece of paper is going to keep coming back to haunt you," her mother said with a rush of irritation. "Sweetie told me that you had those board members at Pure Paradise thinking you had a college degree *and* a master's degree. Why'd you go and tell a big ol' lie like that?"

Milan silently cursed her jealous-hearted, big-mouthed sister.

"After all this time," Bernice Walden continued, "you could have gone back and finished a couple of semesters. Why do you always feel the need to hustle people?"

"Hustle? Mom, you're confusing me with that man you had indiscriminate sex with. Don't try to put me, the executive director of an upscale day salon, in the same boat with a small-time con man."

"*Ex*-executive director," Bernice reminded her daughter, "of a glorified beauty parlor," she added. "That place sure had some fancy names for the same mess you can get at Hilda's Hair Palace over on Twenty-Third Street." Bernice let out a loud guffaw. When she finished laughing, she said, "Seriously, Milan. You need to go back to school."

"If I need to go back to school, your other daughter needs to start using birth control before she brings another innocent child into a life of substandard housing. You also need to tell her to start working out and lose some weight because she looks a sloppy mess."

"Milan, your sister has a beautiful face and her husband loves her just the way she is."

"Hmph! After she drops a couple more babies and blows up to the size of a house, we'll see how much he still loves her," Milan said with a snort.

"I hope that's not wishful thinking on your part, Milan. I wish you weren't so jealous of Sweetie."

"Jealous!" Milan repeated, her voice shrill. "Of what? She lives in a hovel and her husband flips burgers at a fast-food restaurant!"

"He's the manager, Milan," Bernice Walden reminded her.

"So what! A grown man should have higher aspirations than..." Remembering that her mother staunchly supported anything and anyone involved with Sweetie, Milan sighed wearily. She'd been trying her entire life, but she'd never been able to please her mother. For the life of her, she couldn't fathom why her mother refused to take her seriously.

It seemed her mother viewed her as being haughty and pretentious. And to not get her mother's respect or approval, hurt. It hurt badly. "Look, never mind, Mom." Milan's voice caught, her eyes welled with emotion. "I'll talk to you later." She pressed the off button, terminating the conversation before she broke down and cried.

Years of resentment prevented her from having a healthy relationship with her mother. Her mother and her sister were two peas in a pod; they'd been teaming up against Milan for as long as she could remember. No matter what she did, no matter how many gifts she bestowed upon her mother, she still wasn't good enough. She just couldn't win and she was through trying to earn her mother's approval. To hell with her mother, she thought, as the back of her hand reflexively smeared tears across her cheek. *And to hell with my freakin' loser deadbeat dad, whoever the hell he was.*

Self-pity quickly turned to self-preservation. She was in a terrible predicament, but Milan was a survivor. Refusing to accept defeat, Milan resolved to call some of her old connections. She'd schmooze it up with some of the people who were in a position to help her and in no time, she'd have a new job paying three times the salary she earned at Pure Paradise. And she'd be damned if she'd ever give her ungrateful mother and sister another freebie for as long as she lived!

The anxiety she felt after arguing with both her mother and her sister on the same day felt similar to the high stress level she experienced at the end of a particularly hectic workday. She needed a quick remedy. She needed a shot of freaky sex. As she did during terribly tense times in the past, Milan picked up the phone and scheduled an appointment at Tryst, an upscale, private sex club where pleasure seekers like herself indulged their primal urges. Tryst was a place where Milan could go and have her darkest desires satisfied, anonymously. Membership at Tryst was ridiculously expensive—more than her rent and her car payment, but her next payment wasn't due for another week, so she decided to take advantage of her current up-to-date status.

chapter four

I t had taken over a year for Milan to get accepted into the exclusive sex club, which she'd stumbled across on the internet. The club preferred couples membership. Single females were eligible to apply only once a year during open enrollment. Single males, however, were not permitted to join the club nor were single males permitted to enter the premises as a guest. Married men, Milan presumed, did not appreciate the competition.

Because of the rigid rule, Milan's prearranged sexual encounters were always with a couple. More often than not, the wife played the role of lesbo slut, commanded by her husband to tongue Milan's pussy until it was warm and slushy enough for him to slip his dick in with ease. Every so often, an occasional wife would select limited involvement and opt to watch, voyeur-like, through the glory hole—a circular opening in a wall that separated adjoining rooms.

Wives who liked to watch didn't bother Milan. Her only concern was getting hers. Getting, *not* giving, were the terms she'd agreed upon when she joined Tryst. She paid exorbitant monthly dues to be matched only with people willing to accept her conditions: she would not give a blowjob, or cunnilingus, or even lift a finger to give pleasure to another. Whenever she engaged in an erotic interlude at Tryst, the connection was made for the sole purpose of releasing stress—not to exhaust herself with the arduous task of sexual reciprocity.

Inside a dimly lit room, Milan waited. Apart from dark sunglasses and a golden blonde wig to disguise her identity, Milan lay naked on a large bed.

Positioned on her side with her back to the door, her head resting on an outstretched arm, she felt her pulse race with anticipation when the door opened.

The anonymous married couple she'd selected from a database of dozens of potential sex partners had arrived. Although Milan had her head turned away from the door, she expected the pair to be naked, as she'd instructed on the sex club's request form.

"She's lovely," a female voice whispered.

"Quite," a husky male voice agreed.

She sensed the couple approaching the bed, and then felt the mattress sink on opposite sides as the man and woman knelt at the foot of the bed. The sudden sensation of two pairs of lips placed softly on the sole of each foot caused Milan to release a muffled gasp.

A warm tongue kissed and sucked each toe, and then licked the space between her toes. Her upper torso tensed, and she began to twist involuntarily at the waist. Her body seemed to make an unconscious attempt to thwart the shivers of pleasure that were shooting straight to her passion center.

While focused on the glorious dual stimulation occurring between her toes, Milan's attention was drawn to the tickly sensation of a mustache that grazed the bottom of her right foot, nuzzled her ankle, her leg, and quickly traveled upward, tickling the back of her thigh. A tongue, thick and warm, licked the flesh of her thigh while the mustache hairs teased her, sending a series of quivers up and down the length of her spine.

The triple sensation of two tongues and a teasing mustache was decadent pleasure. When the woman's mouth abandoned her foot, Milan, desiring more, moaned in desperation. Her anguished cry quickly turned to a breathy murmur of contentment when female hands began to lightly, tantalizingly fondle her buttocks. Next, the anonymous woman placed a flurry of soft kisses and light flicks of her tongue on Milan's smooth brown ass.

With her eyes tightly closed, she fought against the heat that was slowly building inside her pussy. Involuntarily, her hips moved in a circular motion. Needing to do something to take the edge off, she couldn't help rubbing her clitoris. Slowly at first, and then her finger started to circle the distended clit faster, creating a friction that was so stimulating, her pussy ached with desire.

The mustache pulled away. "Honey," the man said, sounding concerned. "I think our chocolate princess is ready for some cock now."

The wife withdrew her lips. Seconds later, she had made her way to the head of the bed. "We want to please you," the woman whispered seductively, her mouth pressed against Milan's ear. "I'm holding my husband's cock in my hand. Do you want me to stuff it inside your hot pussy?"

Stirred by the sexy low tone of the nameless woman's voice, aroused by the feel of large breasts brushing against her own, and tempted by the thick penis that rubbed against her flesh, Milan's pussy went into panic. It began pulsing rapidly, secreting syrupy fluids.

But fighting her carnal urges, Milan shook her head vigorously. "No, not yet," she murmured. She needed more foreplay—more titillating whispers, caressing hands, probing fingers, prodding tongues.

In an instant, strong male hands eased her body over and two sets of lips put suction holds on the nipples of her small, firm breasts. "Mmm," Milan murmured. The encounter enticed all her senses.

Female lips disengaged and were replaced by a moist tongue. Quick, wet, circular motions around her areola caused Milan to jump as if she'd been hit with electrical currents. The woman bit Milan's nipple lightly and then increased the intensity until Milan's head lolled from side to side in a curious combination of sexual pleasure and mild pain. Male lips sucked softly, yet intently, as if extracting nectar from a delicate flower.

Suddenly, the couple stopped sucking. Alarm coursed through Milan's system. Was she being abandoned by the twosome? She was immediately reassured when a strong, hairy arm lifted her upward and placed her back against the headboard. The man sat on the side of the bed. He cupped both her breasts with his large hands. Hungrily, his mouth went from one nipple to the other, while the woman's soft hands caressed her legs, gently encouraging Milan to spread them apart.

The anticipation of having someone whose face she'd never seen cater to her pussy while another person sucked her breasts was enough to make her cry out as if in pain.

Instead of performing cunnilingus, as Milan eagerly expected, the woman inserted the tips of two slender fingers inside Milan's well-lubricated vagina, twisting them in a spiraling motion as she delved deeper and deeper inside.

Hit with waves of almost unbearable pleasure, Milan arched her back. She clamped her thighs shut with such force, the woman reflexively removed her fingers. She examined her fingers, and after determining they were unharmed, she began to suck each finger, making a loud slurping sound.

She inhaled Milan's vagina. "Mmm. Smells as good as it tastes. Honey, come down here for a minute," the wife said to her husband. "You really have to eat some of this; she has the sweetest cunt I've ever tasted."

"No!" Milan raised her head from the pillow, but avoided making eye contact. "Just you," she told the woman, forcibly.

Promptly doing as she was told, the wife used a finger to delicately part Milan's wet spot and began giving the moist opening a superior tongue bath.

The husband stopped sucking to observe his wife's performance. Stroking his penis, he exclaimed, "My cock is getting so hard, I can't wait any longer; I gotta fuck." He sounded tortured and completely miserable.

Again, Milan shook her head. The husband returned his lips to her hardened nipples. His wife was giving such magnificent head, Milan couldn't help clamping her thighs around the woman's face. With her head trapped between Milan's thighs, the wife, a willing captive, drank from the over-flowing fountain of lust, slurping, sucking, and swallowing as if she was in desperate need of hydration and dying of thirst.

Milan shuddered. Her nerve endings felt exposed and raw. She tightened her grip on the wife's head. At this heightened point of arousal, Milan was beyond caring if the woman smothered to death.

Finally, the warmth—the heat—started spreading up her thighs and swirled into the pit of her stomach. She parted her legs to free the wife from her pussy choke hold, but, declining her opportunity to escape to freedom, the woman remained in the confines of Milan's thighs and continued to suck and slurp.

A fire raged inside, weakening Milan's resolve, but she was determined to maintain control of the encounter. "Switch positions," she demanded in a forced authoritative voice.

The husband scrambled to the position his wife had held below. Milan felt him aiming for admittance. She relaxed her pussy muscles, rotated her pelvis, exhaled contentedly as she welcomed him inside.

Meanwhile, the wife crept upward. She cupped Milan's face and began tongue kissing her. The taste of her own juices on another female's tongue was an added stimulant, prompting her to thrust her twitching pussy forward and rub her clit against the base of the man's dick. "Tell your husband to fuck me harder," Milan implored.

"Give it to her harder, honey," the wife said urgently. She rushed to his side, cheering him on. "Give it to her hard, you fuckin' stud. Fuck that cunt; make her cum." Fueled by decadent passion, the wife gripped her husband's ass and pressed him into Milan, assisting him with each thrust.

Close to cumming, Milan stiffened. The woman slipped her hand between Milan's legs and stroked her husband's dick as well as Milan's engorged clit. Milan instantly exploded; her body shook from tiny quakes. A few moments later, the husband shot a load, groaned loudly, and then rolled onto his back.

"You're a great fuck, honey," the husband told Milan as he panted and gasped for breath.

Too exhausted to speak, all Milan could manage was a lazy smile.

The wife, still hungry with passion, took advantage of Milan's incapacitated state. She parted Milan's thighs and sipped her husband's semen until she had Milan's pussy revitalized, clenching and throbbing with desire. Finally, the woman straddled Milan and ground her clit against Milan's. Together, their bodies convulsed and jerked until they were both completely satisfied.

chapter five

Three weeks had passed since her dismissal—her unfair and improper dismissal, as far as Milan was concerned. She faxed ten to twenty resumes daily, but it seemed that every potential employer insisted upon having a copy of her college transcript before even agreeing to grant her an interview.

The companies to which Milan sent her resume were all familiar with her. If they didn't know her personally, her reputation of being a dynamic leader should have preceded her. It was puzzling why she was being given such a hard time.

Undoubtedly, the board had put out the word. It was absurd that some-one with Milan's experience and successful track record was being railroaded into returning to college. It made her nauseous to even imagine sitting in a classroom with a pack of pimply faced teens, being forced to listen intently while an asshole professor talked endlessly and expected her to take copious notes on the theory behind a profession about which she already knew every-thing there was to know. Hell, she could write a book about the business.

Write a book! Hmm. Now, that's a damn good idea! She'd write a how-to book. Women were so vain and gullible. They loved to be told how to enhance their beauty and improve their lives. She'd call her book, *Weekend Escape: Your Spa At Home.* Suddenly excited, Milan started jotting down notes. She'd use a pen name since she'd become such a pariah in the field. Her ego didn't require having her cocoa-colored face on the back cover, either. Concealing her identity—her African-American heritage—would ensure a mainstream readership. She'd keep her identity a secret until she appeared on the cover of *Fortune*. That would be a real shocker to the power mongers, who'd never intended for more than one black woman, Oprah, to reach the pinnacle of success.

Taking another gulp of wine, Milan happily envisioned herself making so much money she could not only buy out Pure Paradise, but also open an international chain of spas. Ah! It was such a delicious fantasy.

She felt so elated; she was ready to share the news with her mother and her sister. But no, she decided. She was feeling much too energetic and inspired to have them burst her bubble with negativity and warnings of disaster if she didn't return to school. She was battling for survival and couldn't afford to hear any unsupportive words. To hell with school; she'd never go back. She didn't need a formal education. She had skills and she'd make sure all those who opposed her, especially Dr. Kayla Pauley, would regret their harsh treatment of her.

Where should I start? Although she possessed a vast knowledge of beauty and lifestyle services offered by day as well as weekend spas, putting it all together in a book could be a daunting task. But she was up for it. She took a long swallow of wine and happily began to outline her future bestseller.

Her euphoria was short-lived, however. A phone call from the bank that had provided her favorite Visa platinum card—the corporate card from Pure Paradise with the unlimited balance that they had forgotten to repossess when they fired Milan—disturbed her peace.

"Is this Milan Walden?" asked the nasally voice of a bank representative.

"Yes, this is she," Milan said boldly. She'd known it was just a matter of time before the card was deactivated, but she hadn't expected it to be so soon. She'd thought the board had forgotten about the damn card. Her rent was due and she'd planned to use the credit card instead of dipping into her badly needed savings.

It seemed only fair to use the company credit card since the board claimed that the falsification of her credentials had rendered her ineligible for severance pay, or payment for her accrued vacation and sick time. She didn't get squat from Pure Paradise and felt a small measure of satisfaction every time she used the company card. As soon as she pulled herself together, found a new position, and got her bearings, Milan intended to sue Pure Paradise for discrimination and any other kind of lawsuit a good attorney could slap them with.

The woman rattled off the numbers of the credit card and then informed Milan of what she'd already presumed—the card was cancelled. What Milan wasn't prepared to hear was that practically all of the purchases she'd made with the card were considered fraudulent.

Intense fear clutched her insides. "Fraudulent?" she asked in a shaky voice.

"Yes, you'll be billed for numerous suspicious purchases made during and after your employment. A list of those purchases and the amount owed will be FedExed tonight."

Milan swallowed. *Could they really make her pay back the expenditures on a company card?*

"I have to inform you that if you don't pay the balance within ten days, you'll be prosecuted to the fullest extent of the law," the bank rep said, sounding as if she derived immense pleasure from scaring the hell out of Milan.

Milan hung up the phone with an unsteady hand. *Calm down and think!* How many purchases had she made since she'd left her job? *Car note, groceries, hair salon.* Okay, she had enough in her bank account to cover those. Then she remembered her wild online shopping spree at Bloomingdale's the very day she was fired. And the in-store shopping rampage at Neiman Marcus the day after her argument with her mother. She'd spent thousands in the store. Oh Lord! What else had she bought with the damned card? She searched her memory, terrified of the additional damning information her mind could possibly retrieve.

So far so good. She had some money in the bank and she'd pay off the purchases ASAP. But damn, she hadn't expected to spend her nest egg paying for things she already possessed.

❧

The next day the bank sent a stack of papers that was so thick it filled a FedEx large box. The "suspicious" purchases went back nine months. Unwilling to pore over every item, Milan searched for the balance due. *Twenty-seven thousand dollars and eighty-one cents!* No way! They had to be out of their minds. Surely, their system was flawed. Now she had no choice but to scrutinize the voluminous computer-generated accusations.

Mentally rolling up her sleeves, Milan went over the detailed purchases. To her chagrin, there it was in black and white. Thousands and thousands of dollars spent on personal items. Jewelry, designer clothes, furniture, electronic equipment, perfume, a slew of expensive small kitchen appliances that looked good in her kitchen but had gone unused since Milan never, ever cooked. The list also included luxurious bed linens, beauty accessories, designer fragrances, and damn—she paused when she discovered she'd spent over three thousand dollars at Pier 1 Imports. She shook her head in amazement. *Did I really need so many candles?* Further down the list was a shocking nineteen hundred dollars' worth of items purchased at Toys "R" Us and seven hundred dollars spent at Gap Kids. She sucked her teeth, thinking about all she did for her ungrateful sister and her two bad-ass kids.

She scanned her online purchases. Her jaw dropped when she saw the company name, Freaky Pleasure Zone. Why, why, why had she bought the gold-plated vibrator with the company credit card? Now, the conceited and self-righteous Kayla Pauley was privy to one of Milan's most intimate predilections.

After an hour or so of investigating, she had to concede that she'd gone buck wild with the company credit card and hadn't realized it. Beads of sweat began to pop out on her forehead, under her armpits, and on her neck.

She knew there was a little over nine thousand dollars in her piddly little personal checking account, but she picked up the phone to check her balance just to be sure of the exact amount. She stabbed the telephone buttons to input her account number but kept getting a ridiculous mechanical message that stated the account had been closed.

Frustrated, Milan turned to a different source of information and tried to log in to her checking account online. Instead of pulling up the page she was familiar with, an official-looking page appeared with a threatening red headline that boldly announced her account was unable to be accessed. She gasped in horror. The bank had frozen her checking account—put a hold on the only money she had to her name.

While she tried to make sense of the catastrophe, she noticed there was more information in small black letters. Leaning forward, Milan squinted at the screen. *To obtain more information on this account, please visit your local branch.* The small black-print letters had a more chilling effect than the glaring red print. There wasn't a chance in hell she'd visit *that* bank, which happened to be the same bank that she owed the money for the credit card purchases. For all she knew, she could walk right into a trap. The board could be trying to lure her out of her safe place so they could have her arrested for fraud.

Safe place? Milan looked around her apartment; she wasn't safe here. The board had her current address.

Oh God, what am I going to do? She felt queasy and, like the actresses of the golden era, Milan actually swooned. Her knees gave out and she collapsed into a bedroom chair—a hand-woven rattan armchair that she'd adored on sight and hadn't hesitated to purchase while browsing a few months ago in Pier 1 Imports.

In a burst of anger, Milan jumped up and kicked the accursed chair, toppling it. Working off more anger, she kicked it again harder, this time putting a hole the size of her foot in the back of the chair.

Breathing hard, Milan flopped down on her bed. The thought of making an emergency appointment at Tryst flitted across her mind. She needed to relieve the tension with an impromptu freaky sex rendezvous. Then disappointment caused her shoulders to slouch. Her critical financial situation had caused her to forget to make a payment and the monthly fee was now a couple of weeks late. Not too bad, she'd pay the fee and whatever penalty.

Feeling kicked in the gut, Milan suddenly remembered she no longer had access to her bank account or funds. Her membership, she sadly realized, was in poor standing and would soon be revoked.

But she had a back-up plan. Excitedly, she felt beneath the plump pillows, her hand seeking the object of tension release—the golden vibrator. *Oh damn!* It was inside the top bureau drawer on the other side of the room. Wound up with sexual tension and too badly in need of release to make the short jaunt across the room, she decided to pleasure herself the old-fashioned way—using her hand.

Milan pulled off her outer clothing and quickly shed her panties and bra. She lay back and caressed her breasts, pinched her small nipples, applying pressure until they became sensitive to her touch. Aroused, she felt a rush of sensation between her thighs that was so intense, she moaned and drew up her knees, allowed them to part. Her right hand ventured down past the thatch of thick pubic hair, her longest finger leading the way. She massaged the bud of her clit until it throbbed and her finger became moist. Then, with two fingers of her left hand, she gently spread the dewy petals of her vagina, creating an opening that ached to be filled. Desiring instant gratification, she worked the longest finger inside, slid it in deeply, while simultaneously pressing her clit with a finger of the other hand.

One finger caressed gently, the other probed deeply. It never took very long to get what she needed; she knew exactly how to make her pussy purr. Solo sex was the only way she could achieve a really strong orgasm.

She had such an powerful pussy explosion, she cried out in ecstasy—a long, strident sound. The cords in her neck protruded as she jerked and shuddered and seemed to vibrate. When her heart rate slowed down and her breathing returned to normal, she withdrew her sticky fingers and reached over to the nightstand and yanked out a tissue to wipe them as well as the creamy smear left on the bedspread.

Then, temporarily forgetting her troubles, she basked in the afterglow of self-administered satisfaction, slipped beneath the covers, and dozed off blissfully in the middle of the afternoon.

chapter six

Milan awoke from her midday nap feeling refreshed. For a scant few seconds, she felt serene and at peace. But when she adjusted a pillow and snuggled into it, she caught a glimpse of the over-turned chair from the corner of her eye. The gaping hole in the back was a disconcerting reminder that something wasn't quite right. She groaned as her mind peeled away the shadowy layers and revealed her life, in shambles.

Distressed, she recalled the bank officer's threatening words—*prosecuted to the fullest extent of the law. Oh God, my life is ruined!*

She sat up, grabbed the phone, and called her sister. The instant Sweetie picked up, Milan launched into a hysterical rambling. "They're out to get me!"

"Who?"

"The board," Milan shouted. "If I don't pay off the balance they're threatening to have me arrested. In ten days," she added in a high-pitched wail.

"Well, pay off the damn balance. How much do you owe?"

"Twenty-seven thousand."

"Dollars?"

"Yesss," Milan whined.

"How the hell did you put that much—"

"I don't know."

"Well, do you have enough saved to pay those people back?"

Milan shook her head as if her sister could see her.

"Milan?"

"No, Sweetie. I had nine thousand dollars saved, but the bank froze my money. I can't write a check, I can't get cash from the ATM…" Distraught, Milan covered her face. "What am I going to do? I think the police are going to come knocking if I don't pay up."

"Milan, calm down. Why would the police get involved in credit card fraud?"

"Oh, you don't think they'll get involved?" Milan asked, sounding hopeful.

Sweetie became quiet. "Um …don't hold me to my word," she stammered. "It doesn't sound like something the police would be interested in. The company will probably just take you to court."

"Are you sure?"

"No," Sweetie admitted. "I said don't hold me to my word."

"Well, then stop giving me bad information. That bank official made a horrible threat. She told me that if I don't pay back the money, the board will have me prosecuted to the fullest extent of the law. Now, that sounds serious, don't you think?"

"Yeah, it does," Sweetie admitted, "real serious," she added gravely. "Especially coming from someone who works at the bank. I mean, you don't want to commit fraud and involve a bank. That's like a federal offense, isn't it?"

Milan sighed. "I don't know anything about crime. But thanks a lot for making me feel better," she said, her voice dripping with sarcasm.

"Look, Milan, in my opinion, you should pack your things and just bounce. Get the hell outta there as soon as possible."

"And go where?"

Sweetie quietly mulled over the question. "I guess you'll have to come over here for a while," she offered with a loud sigh.

"That sigh sure makes me feel welcome."

"You know you're more than welcome, but you're so high maintenance. My place is too small. It's too small and too cluttered, according to you. And you always say the kids get on your nerves…"

Everything Sweetie had said was correct, but what other choice did she have? Milan interrupted her sister with a sigh. "Sweetie, I think I can survive a couple nights at your place. I should be able to come up with some sort of plan in a day or so."

"Okay, sounds good. Now, go pack everything that can fit inside your car."

"What about my furniture and the rest of my things?"

"Milan! Stop worrying about material things that you can't use. I think it'll look really suspicious if you try to drag furniture out of there without notifying the rental office. Is that furniture worth your freedom?"

"No."

"I didn't think so. Now, get moving. I would never forgive myself if I gave you bad advice and the po-po showed up at your door."

"I'm on my way," Milan said, her voice shaking.

❦

Two hours later, Milan burst through Sweetie's front door, talking a mile a minute.

"Slow down, stop talking so fast," Sweetie chastised her younger sister.

"I swear to God, Sweetie. Somebody was following me while I was driving here. I'm scared to go back out to get the boxes out of my trunk," Milan ranted as she yanked off her black Christian Dior shades. She untied the silk scarf that was draped over her head and wrapped around her neck.

Sweetie held up her hand. "Before you open your mouth and say another word, I have to know…"

"What?"

"Why the hell are you looking like Whitney Houston in *The Bodyguard?*"

"I didn't want, uh," Milan stuttered. "I didn't want anyone to recognize me. I'll have to travel incognito until this misunderstanding is cleared up."

"Well, if somebody followed you here, I guess the cover-up didn't work," Sweetie said with a snicker.

"Sweetieeee," Milan griped. "This is serious."

"I know. I know. I'm just trying to make you laugh. I don't like seeing my baby sister all scared like this." Sweetie opened her arms.

Milan fell into them. "Oh, Sweetie—" The words caught in her throat and tears began to trail down her face. "Sweetie, I'm in so much trouble."

"It's going to be all right, Milan." Sweetie patted her sister's back. "We'll figure out something. Those board members hated the fact that it took a young, talented sister to get that place on track. If they gave you the credit you deserve, they'd have to look at their own sorry butts and admit a black woman is smarter than all of them put together."

Milan pulled away, wiped her eyes, and gave Sweetie a look of surprise. "You know, you can be so wise sometimes, you amaze me. Your insight is astounding. Sweetie, I just wish you'd live up to your potential." Milan was instantly sorry she'd opened her mouth. Her words definitely sounded more like criticism than praise and judging by Sweetie's expression, she was none too pleased with the lopsided compliment.

"Don't start. I'm not the one in trouble. Like I told you before, my life is just fine."

"I know, Sweetie, but I just wish—"

"Milan, you better wish your butt doesn't end up behind bars. This is not about me, so don't start trying to fix something that's not broke."

"Broken," Milan corrected her sister.

"Watch it, lil' sis," Sweetie cautioned. "Don't make me change my mind about letting you stay here awhile. I'm trying to help you out and here you go trying to change the way I talk. If you wasn't frontin' all the time and acting like you forgot where you came from, you wouldn't be in this big mess in the first place."

Milan didn't view her desire to forget her North Philly roots as being a character flaw, but she kept her opinion to herself. Being on the run and in dire need of a place to hide did not permit her to voice an opposing point of view.

"So, I guess I get to bunk out here on the sofa?" Milan asked, trying to sound as if sleeping in her sister's living room was as pleasing as a night at a four-star hotel.

"Hell no! I'm not letting you tear up my new couch. You're gonna have to squeeze in with the boys. Dominic and Diamonte won't mind sharing their beds," Sweetie said with a snicker.

"Okay," Milan said in a meek voice that expressed her feeling of help-lessness. For the time being, she was at Sweetie's mercy.

"How many boxes did you bring? Now, you know you can't be crowding up my kids' room with a whole lot of unnecessary stuff," Sweetie said, jok-ingly. She and Milan both knew the children's room was already filled to capacity with the abundance of toys Milan had bought them.

While she really wanted to throw a tantrum at the very suggestion that she share personal space with two snot-nosed kids, Milan attempted a smile, pretending to enjoy her sister's humor. She'd never be able to think straight, let alone write a book in Sweetie's wild household. Without a doubt, she had to resolve this atrocious situation, pronto!

❧

Sleeping on the floor inside Sweetie's ancient Strawberry Shortcake sleeping bag, the one her sister had taken to the horrible city-run summer camp the two sisters had attended when they were kids, seemed a better choice than trying to sleep comfortably on a twin bed that reeked of urine. Sweetie was too lazy to toilet train her two heathens and insisted on pur-chasing the cheap generic brand of Pull-Ups for three-year-old Dominic and two-year-old Diamonte. Suffocating from piss fumes that were as strong as ammonia, Milan seriously doubted she could last another night. There was nothing she could do except borrow some money from her mother so she could get a hotel room. *Oh God!* Enduring her mother's freakin' interrogation might be worse than being confined inside a pissy bedroom.

But paying for a hotel room with cash wouldn't work. The desk clerk would want to see valid identification, which would blow her cover and possibly have law enforcement hot on her trail. *Oh Lord, what am I going to do?*

A black streak darting across the semi-darkened bedroom caused Milan to bolt upright. Then a rustling sound in the children's closet caused her heart to pound. *Damn, Sweetie has mice*, she thought disgustedly as she lay down, zipping her body including her head inside the sleeping bag. Being encased inside a sleeping bag was bad enough, but the continuous squeaking made her terrified that the mice inside the closet would become bold and scamper across her body. Resignedly, Milan dragged the sleeping bag on top of Dominic's smelly bed.

It was beyond her comprehension how her sister could bear to live in such an appalling housing development. Before finally falling to sleep, Milan made up her mind. She would not spend another night in Sweetie's funky, mice-infested hovel!

When Milan woke up the next morning, she was pleasantly surprised that Sweetie's household was fairly quiet. The only sound she heard was her sister's voice. Somehow, she'd managed to sleep through the early morning chaos as Sweetie got her husband and two boisterous children fed and dressed and out the door to work and the day care center.

As Milan sleepily stumbled to the bathroom, she heard Sweetie's loud laughter as she yakked on the phone with one of her numerous unproductive, unemployed girlfriends. When Sweetie spotted Milan, she waved a hand and motioned her inside the kitchen.

Milan sucked her teeth and continued her trek to the bathroom. Whatever idle gossip Sweetie wanted to share would have to wait until she relieved her bladder. When Milan came out the bathroom, she tried to slip past Sweetie. She really wasn't interested in hearing any of the latest neighborhood rumors that Sweetie and her circle of idiot girlfriends found so fascinating.

Sweetie muffled the phone. "Come here, Milan. Girl, I just found the answer to your prayers."

Yeah, right! Had she not been addicted to caffeine, she would have ignored Sweetie and gone back to her nephew's smelly twin bed, but the strong desire for coffee motivated Milan to move toward the kitchen. She grimaced when she remembered that Sweetie did her grocery shopping at the neighborhood Sav-A-Lot, a grocery store that sold mostly generic brands of food items. *How did I forget to pack a bag of Starbucks? Damn, life sucks!* Doomed to ingest an abominably bad cup of java, Milan poured the weak-looking coffee her sister had brewed and flopped wearily into a kitchen chair.

"I'll call you back after I talk to my sister," Sweetie said and hung up the phone. She gave Milan a devilish grin.

"Who was that?" Milan asked, not really caring. She frowned as she sipped the terrible-tasting coffee.

"That was my girlfriend Tookie. Guess what?"

"What?" Milan murmured, disinterestedly.

"I know you don't wanna sleep in there with the kids and I think I've found you a perfect place to hide out while you're untangling this mess you're in."

Milan seriously doubted that Sweetie had an appropriate solution, but she arched a brow, indicating a half-hearted willingness to listen to the undoubtedly ridiculous plan Sweetie and her friend, Tookie had concocted.

"Tookie's mom, Miss Elise, works for this rich dude. He's sick with some kind of illness that requires around-the-clock care."

"I didn't know Tookie's mother was a licensed nurse," Milan said, wondering how she could possibly fit into what was already sounding like a half-baked plan.

"Miss Elise isn't a nurse. She's the old dude's companion. She sits there with him reading the paper, playing music, and whatnot for him. He has a registered nurse who takes care of him, but he's rich enough to afford a cook and a companion, too."

"So how do I fit in?" Milan asked skeptically.

"Well, Tookie said the old dude's nurse is real bossy and she's starting to get on Miss Elise's nerves. But the shit hit the fan when she started bugging Miss Elise to put in more hours. She wants her to stay overnight but Miss Elise said that heifer can kiss her ass. She's planning to quit but she doesn't wanna leave old boy hangin'."

"A companion!" Milan scoffed. "It's absurd for you to think I'd even consider such a ridiculous job." Milan grimaced and then shivered with disdain. "You know I'm over-qualified for that position. It's totally beneath me."

"All right, Miss High and Mighty, go ahead and turn your nose up at a good opportunity. Hell, I was just trying to look out for you, but I forgot how ungrateful and snobbish your ass can be."

Milan's indignant expression softened. "I appreciate your effort, Sweetie," she said gently. "But I'm looking for a real job that pays real money. Besides, you know how squeamish I am. I wouldn't last a second trying to baby-sit some sick old man." *Eeew!* Milan wanted to barf at the very thought of playing nursemaid to an old geezer in failing health.

"Last I heard, you were on the run. I didn't know people in your predicament went out looking for *real* jobs," Sweetie snapped. "The only reason I even brought up the subject was because Tookie said her mom could get you the job and you wouldn't have to give up your social security or any information that would put the po-po on your trail. You could hide out!"

Milan flinched. Being reminded that she was a fugitive was jolting. She really had to quickly gather her wits and get out of this insane situation. She cradled her chin thoughtfully. If she could endure Sweetie's two little barbarians she could put up with a feeble old man. Merely reading the newspaper and playing music for an old man would allow her plenty of free time to think straight, and an added benefit would be the peace and quiet necessary to work on her book. The companion position suddenly sounded quite promising.

"Okay, Sweetie. I guess I can handle it. Call Tookie and get the details."

"Thank God," Sweetie uttered. "Dominic and Diamonte complained about you all morning."

"About me?" Milan asked in shock. "Diamonte can barely talk."

"Actually, it was Dominic."

Milan snorted. "Dominic needs to learn how to go to the bathroom before he voices a complaint about me. What did he say?"

Sweetie laughed. "He said you made them sleep with the light out."

"So what! It was bedtime. Children don't need a light—"

"Milan, I let them sleep with the night-light on. They're scared of the dark."

"Well, I can't sleep—"

"That's why I was up early trying to find you another situation. Mom reminded me that Tookie's mother was planning on quitting her job."

"You discussed this with Mom before you even spoke to me?" Milan asked, her face twisted in horror. "Sweetie, that's not right." Milan shook her head, deeply wounded. "Isn't anything I tell you sacred? Why can't you keep your big mouth shut?"

"Me and Mom talk about everything," Sweetie said in a matter of fact tone. She punctuated her indifference with a shrug.

"Yeah, tell me something I don't know. Seems like you and Mom had to put your heads together to figure out a way to kick me out."

"Aw, come on, Milan, you know I'd never throw you out in the street."

"Whatever," Milan muttered. "Call Tookie and get the details. You don't have to put up with me any longer."

"Stop being so sensitive, Milan. I'm just looking out for you."

"Yeah, thanks. And make sure you tell Mom I said thanks for sending me off to look after a half-dead, disgusting old man," Milan shouted and slammed down the coffee cup. She pushed back the chair and stood. "If I'm lucky, maybe I can get a decent cup of coffee at the old man's house!"

chapter seven

Most of her possessions had been put in storage. Her remaining belongings were packed in boxes inside the trunk of her car and stacked along the backseat, the floor, and there was even a large box sitting in the front passenger seat. If Milan had the nine thousand dollars the bank was holding, she wouldn't have felt like such a nomad. But she was penniless.

Taking a deep breath, she approached the massive wooden front door and lifted the burnished brass door knocker.

Tookie's mother, Elise Corbett, ushered Milan into the marble-tiled foyer. The tiles were so shiny, Milan could see her reflection.

"You made it," Elise said cheerfully. "Come on in." She wore a welcoming smile.

Milan stepped inside the stately dwelling and followed Elise into the great room. Awestruck, Milan appraised the place. There were oil paintings in gilded frames, floor-to-ceiling French windows, a dazzling butterfly staircase that overlooked the foyer and the grand family room, a fireplace, and expensive area rugs scattered tastefully upon a shiny parquet floor. Sure, she knew that Radnor, Pennsylvania, was part of the collection of wealthy Main Line suburbs situated west of Philadelphia, but she was completely unprepared for the exquisite abode of Mr. Noah Brockington.

Though the heavily carved antique furnishings admittedly didn't suit her modern taste, her eyes had never beheld such opulence, such grandeur, such lavish abundance.

Being on the run and not wanting to draw unnecessary attention to herself, Milan had dressed down for the interview. Elise had assured her that she was already hired. The interview, she'd told Milan, was just a formality.

Wearing a fleece jacket, a plain pair of brown wool trousers, and an unimpressive beige sweater, Milan felt suddenly shabby. Old memories of feeling unworthy reclaimed her. Once again, she was the skinny little dark-skinned girl from the Raymond Rosen projects. *Big feet...crooked teeth...stinky stink Milan*, cruel children used to chant. Humiliated and broken hearted, Milan would burst into tears, inciting the children to taunt her with even more enthusiasm. But then her sister, Sweetie, taught her to stand up for herself. Taught her to be tough. Fight the jeering kids. Whip their asses.

But when she reached her teens and yearned to be perceived as refined and sophisticated, physical fighting was no longer an option. Getting her crooked front teeth straightened had been a top priority when she reached adulthood. Cosmetic dentistry had cost her a small fortune, but having even teeth and a boosted self-esteem made it worth every dime. Focused on her expensive Jimmy Choo or Gucci footwear, people didn't make comments about the size of her feet anymore. The part of the malicious rhyme that alluded to bad hygiene had never been true, but nevertheless, Milan splashed herself daily with only the best perfume.

But today, she'd toned down everything and the lack of embellishment made her feel impoverished and exposed.

"Give me your coat," said Elise. "I'll show you around before I introduce you to Mr. Personality. Let me warn you. That man is a doozy, but don't let him get on your nerves. Put your foot down and remember, you're the boss. He's just a cranky and very sickly man. You can't please him, so just do your job and go on about your business."

As Elise had promised on the telephone, an application and formal interview would not be necessary. Elise had already secured the position for her. Milan was so elated that she wouldn't have to provide a resume or even suffer through an interview, she hardly heard a word regarding Mr. Brockington's character traits. Who cared? She was only concerned with having a place to hide and to write her book with minimal distractions.

Inside the exquisite French manor home, Elise, a small and energetic woman in her mid-forties, briskly walked Milan from one picturesque room to another. "All total, this house has nine bedrooms, seven full bathrooms, two half-baths, a guest house in the back that has three bedrooms and just as many full bathrooms. There are all types of athletic facilities around here, but not a soul bothers to use any of it. Such waste," Elise said. She shook her head and sucked her teeth.

Quite honestly, Milan didn't share Elise's disgust over waste for she truly didn't give a damn whether any of the inhabitants of the French manor used the facilities or not. However, feeling she needed to appear to be on the same page as Elise until she was officially hired, Milan shook her head disapprovingly also.

"You can look around on your own later. There's a two-story gym, an indoor and outdoor tennis court, a pool house, steam room, and a hot tub." Elise thought for a moment. "Oh yeah, there's a musty old wine cellar with a bunch of dusty bottles of wine. Girl, everything in this house is just for show. A bunch of nonsense. How come the Lord doesn't know who to give good money to?" Elise asked with another somber headshake.

It was amazing good fortune that she'd secured such a luxurious hiding place. In a state of astonishment, the only response Milan could muster was a tight smile.

"It's too cold to go out on the grounds, but there's supposed to be fourteen or so acres out there. What Mr. Brockington needs all that yard for is a mystery to me. It ain't like he puts it to any use. Chile, do you know how many barbecues me and my family could have out there? We could hold our family reunion right here at the Brockington place and have rooms to spare." Elise broke up laughing.

Milan cracked a polite smile. "So, how many people live here?"

"Oh, just Mr. Brockington. But his nurse, Greer..." Elise's voice trailed into a whisper. "She calls herself a traveling nurse. Whoever heard of such a thing as a traveling nurse?" Elise muttered disgustedly. "Anyway, she's been Mr. Brockington's nurse for, oh, I guess about six months or so. But honey, you can't tell that woman she ain't Mr. Brockington's personal physician. When she whips out her stethoscope or blood pressure gadget, you can't tell her nothing. She swears she runs this place, but she ain't nobody, so don't let her boss you around."

"Well, who is Mr. Brockington's doctor and where's his wife?"

"He never married," Elise answered, shaking her head. "He's a strange bird. As far as I know, he's never even been to a doctor's appointment."

Milan crinkled her brow. "You said he's terminally ill. What's he dying of?"

"Don't get me to lying. Something to do with his heart—I think." Elise scrunched up her face and searched the ceiling for an answer. "Or is it cancer? I'm not sure. He's very secretive about his illness. I think he's ashamed."

"Does he have HIV?" Milan inquired, her eyes wide with concern.

"No, I asked Greer right out because I wanted to make sure it was safe to take care of his...um, personal needs," Elise stammered. "Greer showed me a recent report of his blood work. She said she drew his blood and sent it out to a lab. He's HIV negative."

Milan sighed in relief.

"So, like I was saying, Mr. Brockington doesn't trust doctors. Greer is the only person allowed to take care of him. Look, I've only been here about four months and that's long enough for me. Every time I turn around, Greer's asking me to put in more hours. She wants me handing out pills, monitoring his blood pressure, and mess like that." Elise rolled her eyes.

Milan shook her head, pretending to commiserate with Elise, but she had too many problems of her own to give a damn about Elise's troubles.

"I told that bossy heifer my job don't have nothing to do with nursing." Elise made a clucking sound. "So, a word to the wise. She'll probably ask you to give him his medicine at night. I figured that wouldn't be a problem for you since you're going to be living here and all."

"Not a problem," Milan chimed in, though she seriously doubted that she was qualified to administer medication. But since Mr. Brockington was already at death's door, could she do the man any real harm?

Elise scratched her head. "Maybe it's just my nature to be suspicious. But I think Greer is trying to figure out a way to get Mr. Brockington's money.

Being that he doesn't have any kids or anything, I think she feels entitled to it. If she didn't have a husband and a family to go home to, I swear that greedy heifer would set up shop right here while she waits for him to die."

Wheels started spinning fast inside Milan's mind. If the dying old man didn't have any heirs, maybe she could get a cut, too. She made a mental note to treat him extra nice. "So, if Mr. Brockington refuses to seek qualified medical care, who told him he was dying?" Milan inquired. She needed to make sure her employer's death was imminent before she started doting on him. She certainly didn't want to waste her energy if he was going to be among the living for any significant amount of time.

"I don't know who told him," Elise responded. "But I'll tell you something—Noah Brockington might be sick and all, but he ain't nobody's dummy. I'm forty-five years old and when you've lived as long as I have, you start to get a handle on folks. Mr. Brockington knows that Greer is just pretending to be his devoted nurse. He knows she can't wait for him to kick the bucket so she can get her grubby hands on his money. She probably thinks she's gonna move her own poor white trash family in here. Hmph, I wouldn't be surprised if Mr. Brockington leaves every penny of his money to some charity or to some distant relative nobody knows about. You know how rich folks do. They love stringing greedy people along. They get what they want out of folks and then turn around and leave them something worthless like a book or a picture frame." Elise made the clucking sound again.

Lines of worry began to form on Milan's forehead. She hoped Mr. Brockington lived long enough for her to get an opportunity to become included in his will. It would be nice if he left her some money. Just enough to comfortably tide her over until she finished her book and was able to acquire a hefty advance from a publisher. With the publisher's advance, she planned to pay off the credit card debt and any other restitution she was required to pay for her freedom, and then she'd open her own day spa. An exclusive day spa that would put Pure Paradise out of business!

The companion position was starting to sound really good. It was a stroke of unbelievable good luck. Once she got her bearings and was comfortable, she'd put the neglected athletic facilities to good use. She'd worked so hard at Pure Paradise she hardly ever got a chance to enjoy any of the perks. They worked her like a damn horse. It was no wonder she took comfort in using the company credit card. Who could blame her? But here at the Brockington estate, having only to read a daily newspaper and play music, she'd work out in the gym, relax by the pool, and enjoy the hot tub during the day. At night, she'd sip the rare and expensive aged wine from the cellar while working on her book. This job would be a piece of cake!

"Where did Mr. Brockington get his money? What business is he in?" Milan was suddenly quite curious about her new boss. She wanted to be able to engage him in topics of interest when they spent quality time together. She'd be a complete idiot if she failed to make a favorable impression on a wealthy man. A wealthy man without kin, whose days were numbered. Yes, she'd deserve to be left penniless if she didn't jump on this opportunity.

Elise shrugged. "I think Mr. Brockington inherited his money, but to be honest, I don't know anything about his family history. I know he's richer than God, but he can be mean as a snake sometimes...and he's a very lonely man." Elise paused thoughtfully. "Oh, yeah, let me tell you something before I forget." She pointed a finger for emphasis. "The maid, Irma, comes every day from six in the morning 'til around three or four in the afternoon. Irma cooks too, so don't listen to Greer if she tells you to cook or clean something around here." Milan nodded.

"Mr. Brockington doesn't have much of an appetite," Elise continued, "so Irma only fixes him soup and some kind of half-cooked eggs. Poached something or another." Elise wrinkled her nose. "Real nasty-looking eggs, if you ask me. You're supposed to fix your own meals, but if you want Irma to fix something special just for you, take her to the side and ask her. Just don't let Greer know."

The thought of being asked to cook or clean made Milan instantly queasy. She would have probably fainted from shock had this Greer person approached her with the demand that she perform such menial and demeaning tasks. Milan gave Elise a knowing look and nodded appreciatively for the heads-up.

"Elise," called a white woman who stood at the top of the staircase. She wore a nurse's uniform. "I gave Mr. Brockington a sedative," the woman added. "He'll be napping soon."

"That's Greer," Elise whispered, then gave a snort.

"Do you want to introduce the applicant before he dozes off?" Greer had a Southern drawl, she obviously wasn't from the area.

Applicant? Milan ascended the stairs and extended her hand. "Milan Nelson," she said, giving a fake last name to conceal her true identity. Elise, aware of Milan's temporary problems with the law, went along with the ruse. "I'm not applying for the position. Mr. Brockington told Elise to hire me." Having already claimed the French manor as her temporary hiding place, Milan couldn't risk having her safe haven snatched from her before she'd even moved in.

"Nice to meet you," the nurse replied dryly. Looking past Milan, she spoke to Elise. "Elise, you've overstepped your boundaries. You should have cleared this with me. Mr. Brockington isn't well enough to—"

"I ain't overstepped nothing," Elise said with hostility. "And I don't have to clear anything with you."

"Lower your voice," the nurse hissed at Elise. "Mr. Brockington is resting."

"Then don't come down here starting with me," Elise said, practically shouting. "I don't have to explain myself to you, but since you tryin' to be all up in my business—for your information, I already cleared everything with Mr. Brockington. He still makes his own decisions, you know. You should stick to your nursing duties. He doesn't need you to pick out his companion." Elise gave a snort, rolled her eyes, and huffily pushed past the nurse. "Come on, Milan," she grumbled. "Some people always minding other people's business."

Just in case the nurse had the power to have her fired from her cushy position before she'd even gotten it, Milan gave the woman an ingratiating smile that was intended to convey her apology for Elise's bad behavior. The nurse sucked her teeth in return. Milan shrugged and hurried behind Elise. A few moments later, Elise led Milan to the master bedroom suite. It was an enormous bedroom with ankle-deep carpeting that showcased a shimmering crystal chandelier, built-in dark mahogany cabinetry, an eye-catching mosaic tile fireplace with mahogany mantel, and a dropped ceiling with mahogany inset. Pillars separated two sitting areas and a large rectangular silk rug was displayed in the dressing room.

The appearance of the man lying in the bed propped up by what seemed like a dozen pillows was so shocking Milan covered her mouth to stifle a gasp. Her eyes bulged as she looked back and forth from Mr. Brockington to Elise.

Noah Brockington was a light-brown-complexioned black man. He had caucasian features and straight, thinning hair, but he was most definitely an African American. Being sickly and gaunt, he gave the impression of an aging man; still Milan could tell that he was somewhere in her mother's age range—between forty-five and fifty years old.

"I'm pleased to introduce you to your new companion," Elise said with a dramatic flourish. "Mr. Brockington, meet Milan. Milan, this is Mr. Noah Brockington."

"Does Milan have a surname?"

"Uh, yes. It's Nelson. Milan Nelson," she said.

Milan had never even entertained the thought that her employer was a filthy rich African-American man and she wasn't entirely certain if his being black would be beneficial or a thorn in her side.

chapter eight

Noah Brockington's eyelids fluttered open, revealing sharp brown eyes that were alert and appeared wise. Though frail, he did not appear to be close to death. Maybe he was having a good day. Milan hoped so; she had no intention of allowing his improved health to interfere with her free time. She hadn't planned on reading to a fully alert person who might expect to be engaged in meaningless chatter for hours at a time.

But looking on the bright side, Milan decided that a longer life span for her employer gave her more time to work on getting her name mentioned in his will.

"I'm sorry to see you go, Elise," Noah Brockington said, his voice strong and clear. He didn't sound sickly at all. "However, I couldn't be more delighted with my new companion. Elise, you missed your calling, you should consider going into the employment recruiting business," he said with a pleasant laugh. "You're a marvelous headhunter and you've certainly earned your finder's fee."

Finder's fee? Milan turned to Elise with eyes widened as if to say, *He gave you money for me?* Elise looked back blankly. There was something terribly fishy going on. Elise had not told her the entire story and Milan was deeply offended, but being in a particularly sticky legal situation, she was in no position to huffily leave the French manor.

As if he possessed a sixth sense and was aware that Milan had silently acquiesced, Mr. Brockington said, "Welcome to my home; I hope you'll be comfortable here." He gave her a brilliant smile.

There wasn't a trace of illness in his tone, Milan noted again. And that twinkle in his eye—was he flirting? She gave him a closer look. He winked! He actually winked at her. *How disgusting*. She shot Elise an accusing look, which Elise, blinking innocently, chose to ignore.

Elise turned her blinking eyes to Mr. Brockington. "I thought you'd like Milan," she said proudly.

Milan looked at Elise in bewilderment. She'd thought being a companion to a doddering old man would be a breeze, but Mr. Brockington was not senile and appeared to be in complete control of his mental faculties.

While he was by no means a young man, he wasn't as decrepit as Elise had insinuated. He was wizened and gaunt by ill health, but Milan couldn't consider him elderly. Sure, he looked old enough to be her father, which was old as hell from Milan's perspective. But he wasn't the grandfatherly type she'd expected.

He spoke in an articulate and formal manner. There was a hint of a British accent, which she found curious. He was probably one of those black people who used a fake accent to give the impression of being worldly, as if he'd lived abroad for most of his life. His crisp and direct manner of speech gave Milan the distinct impression that her employer was accustomed to giving orders and would most likely be difficult.

And hanging in the air was the ominous hint that Mr. Brockington was not only hard to please, but was also lecherous. She wondered what the hell Elise had gotten her entangled in. Was this some sort of practical joke?

"You look perplexed, my dear," Mr. Brockington said. "Despite the sparkle that's no doubt in my eyes after seeing you, I'm extremely ill." He coughed, cleared his throat, and continued. "My time on this earth, I'm afraid, is coming to an end." He gave a regretful sigh. "Six short months—that's all I have left. But I've accepted that fact," he continued, nodding solemnly as he spoke.

Milan nodded in return and offered as sympathetic a look as she could manage.

"However, as my last day draws closer," he said, "I find that I'm not as brave as I'd hoped to be. You see, I'm without family and I now realize that

I'm afraid to die alone. I'd like someone by my side when I take my last breath. And I don't mind paying for peace of mind," he added in an upbeat tone, as if discussing pleasant weather conditions instead of his imminent demise.

"Elise, did you discuss Milan's duties and responsibilities?" he inquired drowsily.

Milan felt a sudden dread at the sound of the words *duties and responsibilities*, but was greatly relieved when Mr. Brockington closed his eyes and slumped into the mountain of pillows.

"Yeah, I told her about the job." Elise seemed perpetually defensive. Her words, spoken in a boisterous tone, echoed inside the spacious bedroom.

Milan sensed that Elise hadn't told her everything about the position. She had a sneaking suspicion that she would be expected to do more than just read boring books and play music. Feeling vaguely troubled, she wondered what other irritating tasks she'd be required to perform.

Mr. Brockington was silent. The sedative the nurse had administered was obviously starting to have the desired effect on the eccentric older man.

Suddenly, his eyes popped open, startling Milan. "Did you speak to her about the soothing?" he asked Elise.

"I didn't get a chance to bring it up," Elise snapped.

"Well, don't dawdle. It's time for my soothing," he said, agitated.

Soothing! The word suggested something calm and gentle, but there was something unsettling in the way he said it. The word *soothing* held a creepy ring when spoken from the lips of a sick and cranky man.

Under her breath, Milan cursed Elise. She cursed Sweetie for getting her involved in this lunacy. She cursed the board members and she cursed her insufferable new charge, Noah Brockington, for causing her to feel so uneasy. She shuddered at the thought of whatever the hell this so-called *soothing* entailed. What did the old boy want her to do? Bring him a glass of warm milk and cookies every night at bedtime? Sing him a freakin' lullaby?

"I forgot to mention that Mr. Brockington likes to be rubbed down right before he goes to sleep," Elise explained in an uncharacteristically soft voice.

Milan shot a glance at Mr. Brockington's bony shoulders and grimaced. *Eeew! I'm not touching him.*

"It doesn't take very long to soothe him," Elise said. Her voice carried an apologetic tone. "A couple of strokes and he's a goner. Sleeps like a baby," she chuckled, her expression sheepish.

"What are you talking about? Giving a massage sounds like a nursing duty. I'm not qualified to—"

"Get another companion, Elise," Noah Brockington barked. "Show Milan to the door and hurry back upstairs. I need my soothing!"

"I'm so sorry, Milan. You're gonna have to leave." Elise put an arm around Milan's shoulder and steered her toward the doorway. "I'll be right back, Mr. Brockington," she told the ailing man.

"I don't understand," Milan said, looking over her shoulder at Mr. Brockington for clarity. He abruptly closed his eyes, refusing to look at her. He sank down into the pillows with his eyes shut tight and his bottom lip poked out.

Elise escorted Milan out of the room. She apologized profusely as they descended the stairs.

"I don't get it. What just happened?" Milan asked.

"Mr. Brockington's such a weirdo. You're probably better off. Look, it didn't work out, so don't even worry about it."

"You don't understand, Elise. I *have* to worry about it. I thought this job was a sure thing. I don't have anywhere to go." Milan was frantic. "Please tell me what's going on. Whatever Mr. Brockington wants me to do, I'll do it. Now, what's the deal with this soothing thing? What's he want—a back rub or something?" Milan tried to sound calm but she was quite distraught. Using her precious hands to soothe anyone other than herself went completely against her grain. But she was desperate. She needed this plush hiding place, she needed the extra money, and dammit, she'd just have to get over herself and give the sickly old fart a freakin' rubdown.

Elise motioned Milan toward a rose-colored antique sofa. Feeling as if she were about to sit upon a delicate museum piece, Milan lowered herself gingerly. Elise, however, flopped down on the dainty sofa and quickly explained the manner in which she soothed Noah Brockington.

chapter nine

When Elise finished giving the disturbing details, Milan could only stare into space with her mouth hanging open. She didn't shut her mouth until Elise passed her a wad of money so thick, Milan couldn't close her hand completely around it. "That's your cash bonus for coming on board as Mr. Brockington's companion," Elise said pleasantly.

"How much?" she asked tonelessly, playing it cool—pretending that the feel of the money didn't give her an adrenaline rush.

"Three thousand. Count it, if you don't believe me."

Milan's hand tingled. The delightful feel and smell of paper currency reminded her of how she loved everything about money. That was another trait her mother attributed to her infamous sperm donor father.

"Mr. Brockington's gonna pay you two hundred and fifty dollars a week."

Milan almost choked. "Two hundred and fifty dollars! To live here full time?" Milan asked, astonished.

"Well, there's room and board included and use of the facilities."

"I understand, and I appreciate having access to the amenities, but two hundred and fifty dollars hardly seems fair for…"

"Listen, Milan," Elise said patiently. "Mr. Brockington is very generous. Like I said, he's lonely…and he loves to play harmless little games."

Milan raised her brow. "Games?"

"Sex games," Elise said, nonchalantly. "Nothing major. Besides, you'll get a surprise bonus every couple of weeks."

"Elise, what kind of sex games?" Milan asked in a strident tone. "I can't rely on surprise bonuses; I need to know what other freaky pleasures this pervert has in mind and I need to know exactly how much he's going to pay me. I'm in a hell of a financial jam, you know."

Elise nodded.

"I have a twenty-seven-thousand-dollar debt to pay and Mr. Brockington could keel over and die before I can save enough money."

"Just play his little games and you'll have that money in no time, Milan."

Milan curled her lips doubtfully.

"Do you think I'd get you involved in something like this if I didn't know it was a sure thing? I know the tight spot you're in right now; that's why I'm trying to help you. Like I told you, I've only been working for him for a few months, why do you think I'm leaving?"

"Because you're tired of him and that revolting soothing thing you do for him. God only knows what other sick games he's into."

"The games aren't that bad, all you have to…"

"Don't even tell me," Milan interrupted, holding up her hand. "I've heard enough for one day."

"I know it sounds weird. And I agree, he's one strange bird, but I would stay here and stick it out if I wasn't already set for life."

"Set for life? Are you serious?"

"Do I look like a fool? As long as I don't try to live above my means, I have enough money to live off for the rest of my life. I don't have to worry about holding down nobody's job ever again." Elise gave a satisfied smile. "Mr. Brockington is a very generous man, Milan. And if you soothe him the way he likes it, you can become a very wealthy young woman. Not everybody's cut out for this type of work, but you can do it."

Milan frowned at Elise. "But, it's so nasty…and perverted. It seems like prostitution."

Elise sucked her teeth. "So what? What isn't prostitution? One way or another, everything you do for money is prostitution. It seems to me, you were prostituting yourself over at the spa place."

"I was not," Milan protested. "That was legitimate employment. I had a prestigious position, I might add. I had the respect of my colleagues and there was nothing shameful about my work."

"Whatever," Elise said, rising. "Mr. Brockington is getting antsy. Come on upstairs and I'll show you how to soothe him."

❧

The combined fragrances of lavender and chamomile were purported to have a calming effect, but when Elise uncapped the bottle of massage oil, the scent made Milan want to puke. The floral scent along with the knowledge of the intended purpose of the essential oils caused Milan to cover her mouth to keep from heaving.

When Elise pulled down Mr. Brockington's pajama bottom, Milan reflexively closed her eyes. Elise cleared her throat, indicating that Milan should pay attention. Reluctantly, Milan opened her eyes as Elise gently turned Mr. Brockington over. He lay on his stomach, his bare ass exposed. With his face buried in the pillows, his discontented grunting was muted and in an effort to hurry Elise along, he impatiently wiggled his backside.

Elise quickly squeezed a generous amount of the potion into her palm and smoothed the aromatic concoction onto his deeply wrinkled behind.

Eeew. Eeew. Eeew. Milan recoiled at the repugnant sight. Barely able to contain her revulsion, her hand instinctively covered her mouth. Three thousand dollars wasn't nearly enough. She needed an additional bonus just to endure this display of depravity.

Then it occurred to her, the voyeuristic aspect of this dirty deed should be the least of her concerns. Elise turned to her, holding the massage oil. Shaking, Milan had to conjure an image of the money inside her purse to keep herself from fleeing the bedroom. Breathing deeply, she dutifully extended her arm and then bravely opened her tightly closed damp fist.

She wiped her sweaty palm on her pant leg. Unable to hide the grimace on her face, she unenthusiastically cupped her hand. Elise squeezed a few oily drops. Mr. Brockington lay prone as he waited for the soothing.

"He likes for you to rub in circles," Elise explained, sounding somewhat embarrassed.

Mr. Brockington, apparently losing patience, jutted out his behind. "Hurry up," he implored Milan.

A middle-aged ass had to be the worst sight she'd ever beheld. Additionally, Milan had major issues with touching anyone intimately; still, she courageously took over for Elise. His ass was soft and mushy, but she persevered, making circular motions as Elise had instructed. In a matter of minutes, Mr. Brockington was snoring contentedly.

Elise nodded knowingly. "I told you it wasn't nothing to it. Now, that's an easy day's work, so stop complaining and let that money pile up."

Milan rushed to Mr. Brockington's private bathroom. She had to wash—no, sterilize her hands. She ran hot water and pumped about an ounce of hand soap into her palm.

As she dried her hands on Noah Brockington's monogrammed cream-and-coffee-colored handtowels, she looked around the exquisite suite. The luxurious bathroom was actually a fully equipped spa, complete with a six-jet whirlpool tub, a separate steam shower, a double vanity with expensive sinks, and oak cabinetry that spanned an entire wall. So lavish, so utterly beautiful. What a pity it was being wasted on a despicable, degenerate, dying man.

"Well, I guess you got the hang of it. I have a hot date with a new man I met at the Post, so I have to be on my way." Elise giggled girlishly.

The Post was a veteran's club where a bunch of old fogies hung out. Anyone going there to have a good time deserved to be pitied. Milan refused to give Elise a "you go, girl" smile. "Have fun," she said dryly and gave a mental head shake.

Elise checked her watch. "Listen, you'll have to give him another soothing tonight at ten."

"Tonight!" Milan shrieked as she followed Elise back into the master bedroom.

"Yes. Three times a day. Eleven in the morning, four o'clock in the afternoon, and ten o'clock at night. He likes a different type of oil with each soothing, so switch it up. All the bottles are on the top shelf of the armoire." Elise nudged her chin toward the ornate mahogany armoire.

With disgust contorting her features, Milan regarded the elegant piece of furniture as if it contained deadly toxins or a colony of cockroaches.

The sympathy she'd felt for Elise a scant few moments ago abruptly shifted to herself. How many times, she wondered miserably, would she have to rub the sickly man's horrible buttocks before she had a complete nervous breakdown?

"In addition to the bonus he gave you, you'll get your weekly pay and you'll get five hundred a day extra for soothing him."

Five hundred a day extra? Milan couldn't argue with the money she was being offered. She'd have to grin and bear it. Let the money stack up, get her affairs together, and get on with her life.

chapter ten

The leather-bound collector's edition of *Great Expectations* by Charles Dickens was heavy. The embossed front cover gave it an elegant and distinctive look, but Milan was certain that the unexciting text inside the impressive covers would have her yawning before she got through the first few pages. Now, if she were reading something hot by erotica author Zane, she'd really be able to stay alert and put her heart into the story. But then again, reading Zane's spicy prose might not be such a good idea. She didn't want the old geezer getting any sex tips from Zane; his own naughty notions were quite enough.

Clearing her throat, Milan began reading. Mr. Brockington's luminous eyes were riveted on her as if the main character, a boy named Pip, was an incredibly fascinating lad. Some of the paragraphs were outrageously long and so dreary, she wanted to hurl the miserable book against the wall. But when she thought of the primary role she played for her employer—a tawdry, live-in masseuse—she forged ahead and poured her heart into the reading of the Dickens classic. Perhaps Mr. Brockington would doze off from all the excitement of the reading and miss his eleven o'clock session.

"My dear," Noah Brockington said at exactly ten minutes to eleven. Milan cringed. Then, bracing herself for the dreaded words her employer would soon utter, she marked the page with the sewn-in red silk ribbon and closed the book.

Noah Brockington did not speak another word. He casually pointed to the armoire. Trying desperately to repress hysteria, Milan took several deep breaths. Then, in a carefully controlled manner, she placed the heavy leather-bound book on the bedside table.

"Be sure to return that to the collection downstairs," he reminded her. She rolled her eyes up to the ceiling. If she could have gotten away with it, Milan would have used the book as a weapon and clunked Mr. Brockington upside his head with it, but of course, she couldn't. She nodded an agreement to return the boring book to its designated spot in the maple-paneled library downstairs.

With mounting trepidation, she opened the armoire and randomly selected a container of massage oil. When she turned around, Mr. Brockington had sneakily lowered his sleepwear and lay poised on his stomach.

Having to rub an old man's ass for pay was an all-time low and an extreme stretch from Milan's perceived dignified persona. In order to survive this humiliation she instantly retreated to a vacant place in her mind. Now, successfully crossed over into an emotionless zone, Milan kept her eyes unfocused as she mechanically rubbed the sweet-scented oil in the prescribed circular motion.

"I enjoy your technique, my dear. You're much better suited for this work than Elise."

Earlier, Mr. Brockington had been silent during this procedure. His unexpected comments snatched Milan from her safety zone. *Thanks a lot for bringing me out of my trance, asshole!* Now, emotionally present and discomfited by the compliment, she responded with a curt "Thank you." She began rubbing again urgently, as if the speed of her hands would hasten the session.

"Would you be kind enough to slip your finger inside; I enjoy having my anus caressed."

Milan's oily hands skidded to a stop. Surely her ears deceived her. "Excuse me?" she asked, shocked, prepared to puke and then take off running.

Mr. Brockington cleared his throat and spoke with his face turned away from Milan, his head rested upon several pillows. "I'm rather ashamed to admit it, but I allowed Elise to introduce me to something that many would deem unnatural and pervasively taboo." He sighed. "Unfortunately, now that I've developed a penchant for anal play, I find it extremely diffi-cult to drift off to sleep without the benefit of my naughty little pleasure."

His request was more than troubling; it was absolutely revolting! Milan immediately envisioned herself running down the staircase, but when Mr. Brockington followed his expressed desire with "Of course, there's a one-thousand-dollar cash bonus for you. It's in the top drawer of the armoire," Milan's physical body did not cooperate with her fleeing mental image. Her feet remained in place.

"Please continue rubbing while you consider my offer," Mr. Brockington said. There was a smug self-assurance in his tone that told Milan he expected her to bite the bait.

She'd been employed by Noah Brockington for a little over a week and her money was accumulating faster than she'd imagined. But her growing nest egg gave her little comfort. Never, ever had she touched anyone's ass-hole, it was a despicable thought. But she needed to pay off her debt and get back on her feet. Short of murdering someone, there wasn't much she wouldn't do for money.

Expecting an unpleasant whiff when she spread Mr. Brockington's squishy butt cheeks, she pursed her lips and scrunched up her nose. Fortunately, the man was clean and the only thing she smelled was the scent of the papaya massage oil she'd randomly selected. Her middle finger tensed in objection as she directed it toward the ridged flesh—the outer ring of muscles that surrounded the anal opening. After stroking the area for less than five minutes, she heard the familiar sound that was music to her ears—the hum of Mr. Brockington's snoring.

After retrieving a hand towel from the bathroom, she wiped the oil from his behind. The gesture was not an act of kindness or even consideration. Milan was removing evidence. She'd die of mortification if Mr. Brockington's private nurse discovered his oily backside and became enlightened to how Milan really earned her keep.

She pulled up his pajama bottom. The snap of the elastic waistband against his skin caused him to wince in his sleep. Milan smiled, satisfied by the small degree of discomfort she'd caused her perverted employer.

She held her hands under scalding hot water and scrubbed them until she could no longer endure the pain, but her hands still didn't feel clean enough. They never would. With that realization, Milan used a clean mono-grammed towel to pat her defiled hands dry and rushed to the armoire. She pulled open the top drawer and scooped up the crisp, neatly stacked bills—her thousand-dollar bonus. For a fleeting moment, the money delight-ed her, but a flash of the pages and pages of credit card debt brought her back to reality. She felt like an indentured slave.

Ravenous after showering, Milan returned Dickens to the library and then trekked to the kitchen. She wasn't much of a cook, but she intended to put together something for lunch.

Irma, the maid-slash-cook, was at the stove, stirring something in a pot. The compact, round woman turned to Milan. "Hungry?" she asked kindly.

"Yes, I was going to make a sandwich. Do you have sliced turkey?" Milan asked, pulling open the fridge and snooping around inside.

"You need to eat more than a sandwich; you're still a growing girl," Irma fussed playfully and fixed her face in a thoughtful scowl. "Let me see…" She looked at the pot on the stove. "I'm a good cook, but something tells me you don't like pea soup."

Milan wrinkled her nose. Though appreciative for Irma's interest in her appetite, she couldn't hide her disdain for pea soup.

Irma wiped her hands on her apron and began opening cabinets. "You're gonna have to order some take-out. There isn't much to work with right now, but if you let me know what you like, I'll pick up the ingredients when I do my grocery shopping tomorrow."

Milan was thrilled that Irma was amenable to shopping and cooking for her. "That's really nice of you, Irma. Thanks. I'll make a list. What's the food allowance here? How much does Mr. Brockington allow me to spend on food?"

"The sky's the limit, sugar. Put anything you want on that list," Irma said excitedly.

"Great. Are you sure you don't mind cooking for me?" Since Milan had no talent or patience for culinary undertakings, she wanted to be absolutely sure Irma intended to prepare the items she listed.

"I'm a good cook. I used to have my own restaurant, but that's a long story. Mr. Brockington pays me good money to clean and cook but all he wants me to do is fix him a couple poached eggs in the morning and a variety of soups with pumpernickel bread for the rest of his meals. He eats like a bird and his menu bores me to tears. It'll be nice to show off my skills in the kitchen while that nurse is away on vacation," Irma told her.

"Greer's going on vacation?"

"Uh huh. She's going back to Alabama to visit family. She'll be gone for two weeks."

Milan smiled inside. She was surprised Greer hadn't mentioned something as important as being away from the household for two whole weeks. It would be nice to be out from under Greer's scrutiny for a while. So far, she hadn't enjoyed any of the amenities of the Brockington estate. She hadn't even worked out in the gym. After all the dirty work she'd been doing, she definitely deserved a taste of the lifestyle of the idle rich.

"Speaking of Greer, where is she?"

"Your guess is as good as mine. She's probably taking her tennis lesson. She gets paid for eight hours, but all she does is give him his pills, walk him up and down the hallway a couple times a day, and the rest of the time she's out getting facials, taking all kinds of lessons and whatnot."

"You're kidding."

"I'm not kidding. Greer's preparing herself for the good life. She has every intention of moving in here when the old man dies. She thinks he's going to leave all his money to her."

"That doesn't make sense. She's only been with him a few months. How did she get so much power?"

Irma shrugged and said scornfully, "She's a foxy ol' girl. By the way," she added, her tone suddenly cheery, "did you get that money he asked me to put up in that armoire for you?" With a twinkle in her dark brown eyes, Irma gave Milan a wink.

It hadn't occurred to Milan that someone other than Mr. Brockington was handling her earnings. The thought should have crossed her mind since he had to get around with a rolling walker and the assistance of his nurse.

Suddenly sickened that her dirty little secret was out, Milan narrowed her eyes in feigned indignation. "What money?" she asked, her voice nervous and high-pitched.

"Sugar, you don't have to worry about me running my mouth. Elise told me all about it. She didn't tell me any details, mind you," Irma blurted. "But I have a general idea of what goes on up in that room. The thing of it is," she said, pausing in thought, "Elise used to give me extra cash after I picked up the groceries I needed to fix her those fancy meals she liked."

"I thought you said the sky was the limit."

"It is for the groceries. Mr. Brockington has an account at the market. The grocery bill comes right out of his bank account. Nobody even pays it any attention. I buy food for me and my family on his account. The thing of it is…" Irma paused. "Me and Elise had a nice little arrangement. She paid me five hundred a week."

Milan gave Irma a long, significant look. It now occurred to her that the seemingly kindly, stout little woman was trying to hustle her. She wanted Milan to pay her to keep quiet about her sessions with Mr. Brockington. But five hundred a week was a bit steep for hush money. And though it wasn't the type of information she'd want Greer to be privy to, besides turning up her nose and looking at Milan as if she were pure scum, there wasn't a damn thing Greer could do about Milan's arrangement with Mr. Brockington. She certainly couldn't fire Milan. Mr. Brockington wouldn't hear of it. Irma had to be out of her mind if she thought she was going to extort five hundred a week to keep the secret from Greer.

"With ol' Brock leaving all his money to Greer, that leaves us in a hell of a pickle," Irma said with a snort. "A black man leaving all that money to a white woman! Now, that's a damn shame. Excuse my language," Irma said, shaking her head. "So, sugar, as you can see, we have to milk that old man for all he's worth while we still got a chance. Yes, indeed. Black women have got to start sticking together."

Milan was silent as she tried to figure out how forming an alliance with Irma would benefit her.

"That man got a big ol' steel trunk full of cash money. It's his secret stash. Greer doesn't know anything about it."

Milan looked at Irma with renewed interest. Now Irma held Milan's undivided attention.

"That's how he pays you, with the money from that trunk. Greer withdraws your weekly pay out of the regular bank, but I'm the one who counts out anything extra he decides to give you." Irma paused, lifted the lid from the big pot on the stove and stirred the soup. After stirring, she placed the green gook-covered wooden spoon on a wide ceramic spoon holder.

"I don't know exactly what Elise was doing," Irma continued. "And Lord knows I don't want to know. But she made out like a fat rat. That woman won't ever have to hold down a job as long as she lives. Now me myself," she said, pointing a finger at her chest. "I'm not the lazy type. I'm not looking to retire and sit around on my tail all day watching TV. All I want to do is open up another restaurant, be my own boss. I want to make some real money so I can leave something behind for my children and my grandkids."

Milan considered Irma's words but was still confused as to why Irma, who dusted and polished a few items and served the old man poached eggs and a couple bowls of soup, felt entitled to more than she was already being paid. She'd already admitted she received a generous salary.

With her brow furrowed, Milan said, "So, enlighten me, please. Why exactly should I give you five hundred a week?"

"I know where he keeps the key to the trunk," Irma said with a trace of pride in her voice.

Milan's eyes locked on Irma's. Her nerve endings tingled with excitement.

"While Greer's gone, you and me are gonna get all that money in the trunk."

"How? Taking money from the trunk is stealing. And stealing is a crime. And believe me, I don't need that kind of trouble."

"Sugar, there's well over a million in that trunk. Probably a couple million. There's more money in that trunk than I've ever seen in my life."

Milan's heart started beating wildly.

"The only time I can get my hands on that key is when he wants you to do something special during your private time."

Stunned by the mention of tons of money hidden in a trunk—money that she could possibly possess, Milan was rendered speechless. Then she began to worry at the thought of the seedy role Irma intended her to play. Milan swallowed nervously.

"It's up to you to keep him interested."

Milan peered at Irma uncomprehendingly.

"You have to keep it interesting," Irma explained. "Whatever it is you're doing, you have to do it better. It's all just a game to him. Raise the stakes. He can afford it. He'll just tell me to take out more money. The way I see it, instead of getting a bonus every now and then, you should be getting a bonus every time you're in there with him. That's the way Elise worked it and that's why she's sitting pretty right now."

Milan appreciated the information and intended to make good use of it. Who would have thought that such a pleasant and sweet-looking woman could be so calculating? Still, there was no way Milan would allow herself to be pimped by a cleaning lady or anyone else for that matter. The thought was insulting and absolutely out of the question. She'd get that money in the trunk but she didn't intend to share with either Irma or Greer.

chapter eleven

A few days later, Milan noticed Greer's appearance had changed. With her eyebrows raised to the rafters, the nurse looked ridiculously startled. Judging by the red areas on her face, her complaint of a headache, and her unchanging expression of frightful surprise, Milan quickly assessed that Greer had not been taking tennis lessons at all, but had instead been spending her time pursuing the ever-elusive fountain of youth with Botox injections.

In Milan's opinion, Greer would have done better with the tennis lesson. At least her body would have benefited from the exercise. It was hard to look at the nurse without bursting into laughter, so Milan was greatly relieved when Greer announced she'd be leaving early. She asked Milan if she'd be kind enough to give Mr. Brockington his medication.

"Sure, no problem," Milan said indifferently.

"I forgot to mention it, but I'll be off for two weeks," Greer said, waiting for a reaction from Milan.

"Oh, really?" Milan assumed a look of worry that suggested she didn't know what she'd do without Greer.

"Don't worry. The agency will be sending a replacement," Greer assured Milan.

"Oh, okay." Milan allowed her speech to falter as if she weren't quite sure whether the agency employed a nurse with qualities that matched Greer's. "Good for you," Milan said after appearing to have tossed the idea around and finally coming to reluctant acceptance. "Enjoy your vacation," she exclaimed happily. *Now hurry up and get your scary-ass face out of here. I have serious business to handle.*

Irma had left a half hour ago, so after walking Greer to the door while assuring her that she could handle things, and yes of course she'd make sure the agency nurse walked Mr. Brockington twice a day, Milan practically clicked her heels in celebration of her sweet freedom. She now had the house all to herself. She checked her watch. Two forty-five. An hour and fifteen minutes before she had to deal with Mr. Brockington.

Instead of relaxing in the Jacuzzi for an hour as she'd planned, Milan spent forty-five minutes hunting down the million-dollar trunk. She had no plan of action, no specific knowledge of what she'd do if she found it, but she considered knowing the whereabouts of the trunk as useful information.

But she'd wasted her time. The freakin' trunk was nowhere to be found. Winded and perspiring badly from the fruitless treasure hunt, she dashed to the bathroom to take a quick shower. She intended to add some flair to her appearance with heavy makeup, provocative attire, and a brazen attitude. It was entirely possible that acting like a slut in addition to getting her employer tipsy might garner the key to the trunk. But Mr. Brockington demanded promptness and, with no time to apply makeup, style her hair, or make a trip to the wine cellar, Milan rushed into Mr. Brockington's bedroom, breathless and five minutes late.

Clean-faced, with her hair pulled back into a boring ponytail and wearing a plain denim skirt, she felt drab and unattractive, but there was nothing she could do. She'd have to wing it.

"My dear," Mr. Brockington greeted her cheerfully. "You look like a schoolgirl. A very tardy schoolgirl," he added, noting the time.

He was sitting up, propped against his mountain of pillows. Surprisingly, despite her lateness, Noah Brockington smiled at Milan delightedly. "How ingenious," he said. "I must say, the schoolgirl look becomes you. You've made an old man's failing heart flutter." With a glint in his eyes, he readjusted himself against the pillows and straightened his shoulders. "What a shock. I didn't think that I was still capable, but the heart doesn't lie...I believe I'm quite smitten."

Oh, cut the crap, she wanted to shout. But she humored the old goat by bashfully lowering her eyes. She covered her mouth and pretended to try to stifle a giggle, and then she blushed in the manner of an innocent young girl.

"Little girl," Mr. Brockington exclaimed and patted the side of the bed. "Come, sit next to me and tell me all about your day at school."

The shame of being so callously fired from Pure Paradise and the humiliation of being hunted down like a dog for making use of the company credit card, something she felt entitled to…well, the entire tragic affair had broken Milan's spirit and caused her to stray from her true nature of skillful survivor until now. Sick and tired of playing the role of cowering victim, her well-honed survivor skills suddenly kicked in.

The ability to change like a chameleon in order to make a favorable impression on those in power was one of her many talents. Making money was another. Hmm. Maybe she was just like her father. Oh well, she'd think about their shared characteristics at another time. Meanwhile, if this multi-millionaire sleazebag wanted her to prance about and pretend to be a nubile preteen…so be it.

Feeling as victorious as she would if the key to the steel trunk was already in her hand, she climbed upon the sick man's bed with the sense that there'd been a shift in power. "I don't want to wear this stupid uniform to school anymore," Milan said in a pouty, childlike voice.

"Why not? You're required to wear the mandatory attire while you're at school," Noah Brockington stated sternly.

Milan folded her arms stubbornly. "I'm in the seventh grade now and I don't want to wear this silly skirt anymore."

"What do you want to wear?"

"Pants," she said, poking out her lip.

"Pants! That's outlandish and out of the question. You have to wear a skirt to school."

"Then, I'm not going back. Not ever!" Milan folded her arms defiantly.

"Did something bad happen at school today?"

"Yes," she whispered and dropped her head. "During math class, I caught Tommy Alston trying to peek under my skirt. He's such a bad boy; he has to sit next to the teacher's desk. I was working hard on the class assignment and I forgot to keep my legs closed." Milan's voice was tiny and filled with remorse. "The counselor says when little girls are seated, we should make certain that our legs are tightly closed, both knees should be touching."

"And how were you sitting, my dear?" Mr. Brockington said excitedly. "Go sit over there." There was a chair nearer to the bed but he pointed to a high-backed chair across the room. "Reenact the scene, my dear. Show me exactly what transpired in the classroom."

Milan felt awkward as she walked over to the chair. At five feet, eight inches, pretending to be a little girl didn't feel quite as comfortable while standing as it had while she sat on Mr. Brockington's bed.

As daintily as she could manage, she eased herself into the chair. Getting into character, she sat primly with her hands placed on her lap, her back straight and her knees pressed together. After a few moments, Milan began to slowly part her legs. To keep the scene interesting, she improvised and began to stroke her inner thigh.

"Oh, you naughty, naughty little girl," Mr. Brockington said with delighted mischief dancing in his eyes. "Were you actually touching yourself like that? Right there in the classroom?"

Milan concurred with a regretful nod. "But I didn't mean to. I didn't realize I was touching myself."

"Do you always touch yourself?"

"Yes."

"Just your thigh?"

She shook her head.

"What else do you touch, Milan? Remember, you can tell me anything." Mr. Brockington's voice quivered as he spoke.

"Sometimes I rub my secret place."

"Show me your secret place, Milan."

"I can't—boys aren't supposed to see it. And I really didn't mean to touch myself in school. I only do it in bed at night…" She paused and bit her lower lip nervously. "It helps me fall asleep."

Stimulated, Mr. Brockington's breathing became labored and erratic. "Come and sit with me, Milan."

After crossing the room again, she climbed back on the bed.

"You're a bad girl; you provoked little Tommy What's-his-name. It's no wonder he couldn't take his eyes off you."

"Are you going to punish me...*Daddy*?" she asked, testing to see how her employer reacted to his new title.

"I'd never punish you; you're my darling little girl. Now, close your eyes, sweetheart. I have a surprise for you."

"Okay, Daddy," she squealed. Grinning, Milan squeezed her eyes tight as she waited for her surprise.

Noah Brockington took her hand in his and placed it on his private part. Milan jerked her hand away. "What is that? It's so big and hard. Can I open my eyes?"

"Yes, go ahead and open your eyes, my dear."

When Milan opened her eyes, Noah Brockington flung off the bed cover. Sticking through the slit in his pajama bottom was a very rigid, russet-colored penis.

Shocked, Milan covered her mouth, her eyes genuinely wide in amazement. She thought an erection like this was unheard of for someone terminally ill.

"I can scarcely believe this myself. It's a miracle," he said. "You've raised the dead." He smiled as he reached for her hand. "Now, don't keep me waiting. Touch it, dear girl, let's see if it still works!"

Twenty minutes later, after being informed that she'd officially stolen his heart, she washed the sticky white fluid from her hands while Brockington emitted satisfied snores. Before pleasantly drifting off to sleep, he'd promised her nirvana and more.

chapter twelve

"**D**id you make out your shopping list?" Irma asked Milan the next morning as she prepared Mr. Brockington's poached eggs and buttered pumpernickel bread.

"No, I didn't," Milan said snippily. She was comfortably garbed in a long bathrobe and soft terrycloth slippers.

Taken aback, Irma regarded her with an indignant sidelong glance. "Sounds like somebody got out of the bed on the wrong side this morning," she retorted as she brushed past Milan. Carrying Mr. Brockington's breakfast tray, Irma muttered discontentedly about having to carry the heavy tray and climb the long flight of stairs.

Briefly contemplative, Milan watched the overweight woman huff and puff as she ascended the stairs. Narrowing her eyes, Milan tilted her head and cradled her chin between her thumb and index fingers.

When Irma returned to the kitchen, Milan sat perched atop a stool in front of the island in the middle of the room. Hunched over the granite countertop, Milan wrote furiously on a piece of Brockington monogrammed stationary. Her hand moved rapidly across the page. Despite the thickness of the expensive stationery, the thuds of the pen hitting the paper in quick succession sounded like an explosion of small caliber bullets fired by a trigger-happy gunman.

Milan finished writing and sat up straight. "Here," she said holding out the paper. "This is my list for today."

"You must have lost your mind. Listen up, Milan. I don't take my orders from Greer and I'll be damned if I'm gonna let you start bossing me around," Irma yelled, worked up to the point of erratic breathing. "You can forget about that little arrangement I was willing to share with you," she said, waving an admonishing finger as she spoke.

"Are you finished?" Milan asked calmly.

Irma rolled her eyes, took a deep breath to collect herself, and began puttering around the kitchen. She ignored Milan's presence as she tidied up the kitchen.

"You attempted to take advantage of me yesterday. In fact, it seemed like you were trying to pimp me."

"I did nothing of the sort," Irma protested. "How could you even attach a nasty word like that to a high-moral woman like me? You better take a look in the mirror before you start calling names; you're the one doing unnatural things with that sickly man upstairs."

"I'm going to pretend I didn't hear your unkind remarks because Noah—"

"Noah!" Irma repeated, astonished that Milan had the audacity to refer to their employer by his given name.

"Yes, you heard me correctly," Milan said, smirking. "I call *your* boss Noah. He enjoys those awful-looking poached eggs you make, so I guess I'll have to suffer keeping you around. Now, get yourself together and go out and get my breakfast." Milan held the paper at arm's length and shook it tauntingly.

"The hell if I'm going to take orders from you," Irma said, stubbornly.

Milan walked over to the kitchen intercom and pushed a button.

"Yes," said Noah Brockington. The single word was spoken with a happy lilt.

"Noah," said Milan, in a whining girlish voice. "I want you to speak to Irma. She's being mean to me."

"Send her up, my dear," Mr. Brockington said. His voice was warm with affection.

Milan twisted toward Irma, folding her arms in front of her chest. Her eyes gleamed victoriously.

Looking stricken, Irma left the kitchen to climb the exhausting flight of stairs once again. After a few minutes, she huffed back down to the kitchen. Sighing, she ripped off a paper towel and wiped perspiration from her forehead. "Do you want me to pick up your groceries from Genuardi's?" Irma's lips stretched into an embarrassed grin.

"No, I prefer Whole Foods," Milan said in a taunting sing-song manner, her tone very much like that of a petulant child. "Now, please hurry." To speed the woman along, Milan clapped her hands twice. Looking shell-shocked, Irma grabbed her pocketbook and bustled off to do Milan's bidding.

During Irma's absence, the new nurse arrived with a clipboard and other medical documentation that concerned Noah Brockington. "Good morning, I'm Ruth Henry," the woman said cordially.

"Milan," she offered, deliberately leaving out her surname. Ruth Henry had dark hair mixed with gray. With her slightly stooped posture and what appeared to be the beginning of a very unattractive hump just below her neck, the woman had early signs of osteoporosis, Milan determined with lips pursed in condemnation. Aging was so unattractive and Milan believed it was a woman's social responsibility to keep the process at bay. The beauty industry went to great lengths to keep women looking their best, and this woman, a nurse no less, hadn't even bothered to take calcium supplements. Milan had no respect for Nurse Henry, she decided. "I'm in charge here, so please direct all inquiries to me," Milan said, keeping her tone impassive.

She escorted the nurse to Mr. Brockington's master suite. "Noah, this is Ruth Henry, your temporary nurse."

"My dear, will you sit with me awhile? New nurses tend to be a bit rough."

Ruth Henry's cheerful expression instantly distorted. "I would never—"

Milan interrupted the nurse's objection. "Noah, your nurse is here to help you, not hurt you. I want you to be cooperative," Milan coaxed. "I'll be in to see you in a few hours. Now, behave yourself." With Noah's sad yet adoring eyes trying to hold her captive, Milan turned and whisked out of the room.

The winds of fate had shifted in her favor. Though she was swathed in a fashionable, clearly adult robe, she had sense enough to put her hair in a ponytail, replete with a big girlish bow. She had a few more innovative ideas that were sure to have Noah eating out of the palm of her hand, and turning all his money and possessions over to her. Milan laughed wickedly at the thought of Greer's reaction when she discovered she'd been disinherited.

But she had to work fast; Greer would be back in two weeks. A short time to accomplish a life-altering goal.

❧

While the nurse tended to her charge and Irma puttered about doing much of nothing, Milan decided to go shopping for costumes. Greer had always used Mr. Brockington's personal vehicle for running errands, and now Milan had the key to the old man's vintage car as well as the key to his heart. But she thought the antique BMW was as old and ugly as Noah Brockington and she wouldn't be caught dead inside the car. So she chose to drive her own year-old Nissan Altima to the nearby Suburban Square Shopping Center.

Undoubtedly, she would be replacing her moderately priced car very soon for something that screamed money. Her taste had suddenly shifted from the sleek European cars she once coveted and now veered toward the Hummer. It was a big, bad, and bodacious piece of machinery and absolutely appropriate for a gutsy woman such as she.

She arrived at ritzy Suburban Square armed with Mr. Brockington's credit card. Milan yearned to explore and invade all the posh shops, especially Coach. The scent of leather shoes and handbags called her name. But she was forced to exercise restraint. There'd be plenty of time for pleasure shopping once she'd secured her position; her mission today was to pick up an assortment of girly items and accessories to add authenticity to her role of pubescent schoolgirl. She intended to throw herself fully into the character of Noah Brockington's darling little girl.

The salesperson at a high-end little girls' specialty shop greeted Milan with a sunny smile and offered her a trendy little shopping carrier. Milan immediately began to gather and toss heaps of satin hair bows, barrettes, and headbands adorned with silk rosettes into the carrier. A table filled with oodles of colorful panties with ruffles and frilly edges caught her attention. When she spotted a pair of white cotton panties with three rows of eyelet lace in the back and *DADDY'S LITTLE GIRL* embroidered in pink, Milan felt reassured that in a very short while, she'd be the sole beneficiary of all Noah Brockington's worldly goods.

chapter thirteen

Milan burst through the front door loaded down with shopping bags, including two with the Coach logo. Unable to resist going inside Coach after completing her girly shopping, she'd bought a pebbled leather shoulder tote and a signature metallic outline large hobo.

Irma was in the kitchen thumbing through a food magazine. Clearly, the woman had too much down time.

"Take these to my room," Milan instructed Irma. Then, remembering that she didn't want Irma to have an opportunity to snoop through her bags, she gave her a scathing look and said, "Oh, never mind," as she rushed toward the staircase. On her way up, she called over her shoulder, "I'll have a baby spinach salad Niçoise with pan-seared halibut for lunch. Bring it to my room. On a tray. Hurry, I'm famished!"

Irma sucked her teeth.

"I'm going to pretend I didn't hear that!" Milan yelled as she ascended.

When she reached the landing at the top of the stairs, she noticed Noah's bedroom door was wide open. Damn! She'd hoped to creep past her aging paramour and slip into her own bedroom to gaze adoringly at her new purchases.

Begrudgingly, she stuck her head inside Noah's bedroom and formed her mouth and facial expression into what appeared to be a caring smile. As instructed, Ruth Henry was reading *Great Expectations* to the patient. The nurse smiled back, closed the book, and nodded toward Noah, who was snoring softly.

"He's taking a little snooze," Ruth Henry said, her voice a cheerful whisper.

"Thanks for reading to him. He loves those awful classics," Milan said, shaking her head and rolling her eyes as if offering condolences.

"Oh, it was my pleasure. I enjoyed reading *Great Expectations*, it's one of my all-time favorites," the nurse squealed, much too loudly, and hugged the tome to her chest.

Milan shot a quick look at Noah. "Be quiet," she snarled at the nurse.

"Sorry." Ruth Henry cast a cautious glance at Mr. Brockington who, thankfully, was still sleeping soundly. "I didn't mean to. It's just…," the nurse stammered excitedly, "well, I'm such an avid reader and to have reading included in—"

"Whatever!" Holding up her hand, Milan wouldn't let the nurse finish gushing about her love of reading. She eyed Ruth Henry disdainfully, shook her head, and without another word, continued walking past the room. *What an idiot!* Striding down the long hallway, she curved around the bend that led to the staff accommodations, which included her own bedroom. She was, after all, still just staff. But that didn't bother her. She was glad to be far, far away from Noah's perverted den.

She haphazardly dropped her purchases, closed the door, and hastily locked it. Spared from having to interact with her lustful benefactor, she let out a long sigh of relief. But the feeling was short-lived as Milan listened to her stomach growl. She pushed the intercom. "Is my lunch ready yet?" she asked irritably.

"A few more minutes," Irma said, slowly and calmly. Too calmly. She was obviously monitoring her tone and refraining from sucking her teeth.

"How many freakin' minutes? I'm famished."

"Uh, I had to go through a stack of gourmet magazines to hunt down those recipes, but I found them. I'll have everything ready in another thirty minutes or so."

Milan bristled. *Some caterer! Shouldn't a real caterer have a collection of recipes committed to memory?* "I thought you said just a few minutes," Milan asked, agitated. "Since when does a half hour equal a few minutes?"

Irma responded by breathing into the intercom, then she stammered a half-hearted apology. Pissed off, Milan flopped down on the bed. Who knew how long it would take a woman who showcased her culinary skills with an assortment of soups and soggy eggs to put together an elegant meal? Milan hadn't had any good food since…well, since she'd gotten the axe from Pure Paradise. Her face felt hot as she remembered her humiliating exit from the day spa. Unable to push the distressing thought from her mind, she began to feel tense and extremely angry. Needing a target to unleash her fury, Milan reached for the intercom, prepared to fire a barrage of insults at Irma, the so-called cook.

But struck by a better idea, she withdrew her pointed finger, hopped up and traipsed over to her lingerie drawer and rifled through wads of silk, satin, and other soft fabrics until her hand wrapped around the object of pleasure—her eighteen-karat-gold-plated vibrator. Now smiling, she slipped out of her clothing and under the coverlet. The next twenty minutes were a multi-orgasmic blur as she relieved her tension with the vibrator.

When Irma finally rapped on the bedroom door, Milan was in a tranquil post-orgasmic state. "Come in," Milan said dreamily.

Irma entered the room. A scrumptious aroma that boasted Irma's familiarity with gourmet cuisine wafted from the wicker bed tray she carried.

Milan smiled delightedly and sat up straight. After shifting into a more comfortable position, she reached for the tray. At that moment the golden vibrator rolled from beneath the sheets and onto the coverlet.

Irma looked startled and then turned crimson. Clearly uncomfortable, her blinking eyes wandered everywhere except in the direction of the offensive rolling object. Milan glanced at it, then shrugged, totally unconcerned that her secret pleasure had been exposed. "Oh, this looks absolutely divine," Milan said, digging a silver fork into the halibut and not even bothering to throw the coverlet over the usually bright gold vibrator, which was now dulled by the light film of her feminine juices.

"Will that be all?" Irma asked, not looking at the vile thing on the bed and instead taking a sudden interest in the pattern of the Persian rug.

Milan swallowed. "I'm impressed, Irma. You're quite the chef when you have a recipe on hand and when you put your mind to it." Milan paused, tasted the spinach salad. "Mmm. Tasty," she exclaimed, then her expression darkened. "In the future, however, please don't bring my meals on this…" she pursed her lips and looked scornfully down at the wicker tray, "this piece of wood," she said with a dramatic shudder. "I'd like my meals delivered on a silver platter inside a covered dish."

Irma nodded gravely.

"I expect the exact same services extended to Mr. Brockington. Capisce?"

Milan enjoyed how the tables had turned on Irma. Just a few days ago, the woman was trying to take advantage of her, pretending to have her best interests at heart when all the while she was trying to pimp her. Now, through a twist of fate, she had to cater to Milan and act as her servant. It was just incredible the way Milan's life had improved.

"Will that be all, Milan?" Irma sounded appropriately chastised.

"Actually, no. I want the key to that trunk," Milan boldly informed her.

Irma shrank back in horror. "I can't give you the key. That's Mr. Brockington's nest egg. He's hiding that money from the IRS."

"I don't care who he's hiding it from. It's not as if he's ever going to get a chance to spend it." Milan exhaled and shook her head in frustration. "Oh, forget it, Irma. I don't even know why I'm bothering to discuss this with you. I'll speak directly to Noah. Thanks for lunch," Milan said dryly as Irma turned to leave. "Another thing! Stop by Noah's suite, tell the nurse that I said she can leave early. Now, go! Hurry, I can't bear the sight of you!" Grimacing, she fluttered her fingers to hasten Irma's departure.

Milan grinned. Bossing Irma was so much fun!

chapter fourteen

Dressed in a yellow cotton blouse, short tartan skirt replete with an oversized safety pin, lace-trimmed ankle socks, and loafers, Milan walked leisurely down the hallway toward Noah's bedroom. With her hair pulled up into a ponytail and adorned with a big frilly bow, she was in character and totally feeling the role of naughty schoolgirl.

As she approached the door, she heard his voice on the other side. "...the best years," Noah Brockington said to someone in an angry, rising tone. His voice sounded strong, not sickly at all and she could hear him clearly through the wood. Who was he talking to and *what* was he talking about? Curious, she stood outside the door to eavesdrop on the conversation.

"After all these years—It's just not fair...not fair at all," he whined. Then there was silence. No goodbye, farewell, or I'll talk to you later, just a melodic beep that indicated the call had ended. Hmm. Noah had just hung up on someone. She wondered who'd been on the other end of the phone. Greer? No, that didn't make a bit of sense. Greer was with her family on an all-expenses paid vacation, a gift from Noah. Why would he gripe and bemoan his fate in a conversation with Greer?

So, who was he talking to? It was perplexing because Noah hardly ever spoke on the telephone. In fact Milan couldn't recall ever hearing him communicate with anyone other than his household staff and that was done via the in-house intercom system.

She gazed down at her Monji rainbow watch, another feature of her adolescent costume. Not wanting him to know she'd heard a snippet of his personal conversation, she waited a full minute before knocking on the door.

"Come in," Noah Brockington called grumpily. Milan supposed he was still edgy from the mysterious phone conversation.

Slipping into the character of a timid young girl, Milan crossed the threshold to the bedroom suite, nervously twirling a bookbag. She stood, leaning on the side of one shoe, anxiously biting a fingernail, exactly the way she imagined a bashful little girl would do.

She noticed Noah's eyelids were puffy, the whites of his eyes reddish, as if he'd been crying. She thought he'd made peace with dying, but perhaps he'd started to feel regret. Gazing at him warily, she asked in a childlike voice, "Is everything okay? Should I come back later?"

Judging by the glint that suddenly lit his bleary eyes, Noah's mind was no longer on the troublesome phone call or his imminent demise. But Milan was curious about the cryptic call and intended to get to the bottom of it. She had absolutely no background information on Noah Brockington. She'd Googled his name, but nothing came up. Strange.

Greer's return could be the least of her worries. For all she knew, there could be a gaggle of greedy relations hovering in the background ready to pounce on Noah's millions the moment he croaked. She felt a stab of panic. Had he been talking to a relative? The thought of anonymous people breezing in and waltzing off with all his money made her nauseous.

And while Noah Brockington lay in his sick bed admiring her girlish attire with a growing bulge beneath the comforter, Milan was struck by the notion that she was the only person on the planet who truly deserved the dying man's fortune. It was, after all, she and only she who provided him with his dying wish: kinky pleasure. How many men lying on their deathbed had a young, attractive woman on call to play out their freakiest fantasies? No one that Milan could think of.

"Come here, little girl," he said in a raspy voice.

Milan shook her head and stiffened. "I'm not supposed to talk to strangers," she said, mimicking the voice and demeanor of a frightened little girl.

"Don't be afraid," he assured her. "I won't hurt you."

Shaking her head emphatically, Milan refused to budge.

"Come here, I've got something for you," Noah urged. When Milan still didn't move, he spoke in a cajoling tone. "I'll give you some candy—you like candy, don't you, little girl?"

"Uh huh," she said, still altering her voice, making it sound youthful and naive.

"Hard candy?" he asked in a low-pitched tone as he shamelessly stroked himself.

Milan nodded.

He lifted the bed cover and squinted beneath it. "There's lots of candy under here, my dear," he said and fixed his gaze on her. "Come and get some."

Dangling the bookbag, she took slow, hesitant steps toward the bed and then, as if too afraid to take another step, she stopped in the middle of the room.

Noah motioned for her to come closer, but Milan shook her head. She looked worriedly toward the bedroom door as if she were having second thoughts.

"Please come here. You can trust me; I won't hurt you. I'll give you a *big* piece of candy…" He paused in thought. "And two balls to play with. Imagine, my dear—two balls just for you."

Looking delighted by his promise, Milan brightened. In a matter of seconds, her expression changed from innocent to sultry as she provocatively bit the tip of her index finger and gave Noah Brockington a coquettish smile. She allowed the bookbag to slip from her hand. When it hit the floor, she naughtily kicked it aside.

Teasingly, she sucked the tip of her index finger. Then, removing the finger from her mouth, she tauntingly flicked open the top three buttons of the yellow cotton blouse. She'd always felt shortchanged when it came to her breasts. In high school, she'd felt mortally wounded by the slighting remarks the boys made regarding her double-A-cup status. Back then, lacking boobs was such a curse, such an abnormality, she'd felt…well, there was no kind way to put it. She'd felt deformed.

But not anymore. Her underdeveloped bustline was a turn-on to the man who held the keys to the castle—the man who could give her the lush life she was born to enjoy. She continued unbuttoning until the blouse fell open, showing off the little girls' training bra she knew would drive her rich lover wild.

Noah emitted a shameless groan. His breathing became ragged with lustful desire. From the breast pocket of his pajama top, he removed a monogrammed handkerchief and blew his nose. He stuffed the soiled cloth back into his pocket.

Eeew, Milan thought.

Impatiently, Noah patted the bed, urging Milan to join him. But she maintained her position in the center of the room.

Inch by inch, she raised the tartan skirt until a peek of white cotton panties came into view. Practically drooling, Noah leaned forward lecherously. Milan stood with her feet planted on the floor, her legs spread apart. She fondled her cotton-covered crotch, caressing it in an unhurried manner.

"Let me do that," Noah said in a hoarse voice. Reaching for her, he nearly hung off the side of the bed.

Milan ignored him. Using three fingers, she rubbed her crotch and then began rotating her slender hips. Sliding the fabric to the side, she revealed a hairless mons. She ran a finger between the lips of her silky moist slit.

The sight of Milan's schoolgirl-style striptease had Noah grunting and panting, his tongue lolling. He looked tortured, as if the routine was driving him insane. Pleased with the effect of her well-planned and perfectly exe-cuted performance, Milan advanced toward the bed. She sat down daintily on the bed beside him. "May I have some candy," she asked sweetly.

Noah's eyes gleamed excitedly. "Not yet, my dear. You'll have to find it. We're going to have a treasure hunt."

Milan's eyes grew wide. "I love treasure hunts," she cried out enthusi-astically. Twisting around, she pointed toward the heavy brocade drapes. "The candy's over there," she shouted.

"Cold," Noah said, shaking his head. "Very cold."

Milan frowned and furrowed her brow in concentration. "There," she said, now pointing toward the French Country bedside table.

"You're getting warm." He sounded pleased.

Concentrating even harder, Milan squeezed her eyes shut, both hands framing her face. Suddenly, her eyes popped open. A smile spread across her face. With narrowed eyes, she said, "I know exactly where it's hidden."

"Are you sure?"

"Positively."

"You must be absolutely certain because there are severe consequences if you're mistaken."

"What—what do you mean?" she stammered.

"Well," he said, tenting his fingers. "You'll have to be disciplined. If you give an incorrect answer, I'll have no choice but to paddle your little bottom." As he spoke, there was a tremendous swelling beneath the blanket.

It was a dead giveaway. "It's right here," she squealed, stretching out her arm and jabbing the hardened mound.

Noah emitted chortling laughter. "How do you know there's candy under there," he asked, taking a peek under the bed linen.

"I know I'm right and I'm going to prove it." Milan kicked off her shoes and began crawling toward the foot of the bed. The ruffled backside of her panties was exposed. Her intention was to taunt Noah with the embroidered words, *DADDY'S LITTLE GIRL.*

"Wait, my dear," Noah said, breathlessly. "You may find something that looks like candy, but how can you be certain unless you taste it?"

Hmm. He had a point and she was stymied for a moment. Fondling his sickly, but amazingly erect penis was one thing, but fellatio had not been part of the bargain. The old geezer had cunningly upped the ante. She tried to mentally calculate how much dick-sucking was worth. Ten grand? Twenty? Oh hell, if he expected her to dress up like a little girl and give him head as well, he'd have to really come out of pocket and make it worth her while.

She pondered the situation briefly and came to the sad conclusion that there really wasn't any amount of money that would entice her to put Noah Brockington's dick anywhere near her mouth. She couldn't do it; she didn't have the stomach for it. Going down on a sick older man would surely cause her to throw up. And hurling on her benefactor's crotch would most definitely unseal their deal.

Being quick on her feet—well, on her knees in this case—Milan blurted, "I made a mistake. The candy's in there!" She nudged her head toward the armoire. Though her threshold for pain was admittedly low, she figured being flogged by a weak and dying man would be similar to getting a spanking with a feather.

"You're sadly mistaken," he said with a glimmer in his eyes that was anything but sad. "And now you must pay the penalty for giving an incorrect answer."

"But—but, I'm certain…"

"You're wrong. Now, open the second drawer," he said, firmly, indicating the bedside table. Milan slid off the bed and flitted, unafraid, over to the table. Inside the second drawer, she found an oval leather paddle. She handed it to him and he appraised it adoringly. Noah Brockington was even kinkier than she'd realized.

"This paddle was especially designed for delivering a sound, over-the-knee spanking. Of course, my health has hampered my ability to take you over the knee, so you'll have to come close."

Shakily, Milan crept closer.

"Now, my dear, bend over and pull down your panties."

Continuing to go along with the charade, Milan wrung her hands fretfully and gave a shuddering gasp before finally bending over.

Instead of the mild stinging sensation she'd anticipated, the feel of leather against her derriere was pleasant, actually. She'd known there was no danger of Noah inflicting serious pain, but she'd hardly expected to become aroused by the light spanking.

Noah counted each mild blow and when he reached the number ten, he suddenly dropped the paddle and began to moan in ecstasy. Curious, Milan peered over her shoulder and felt thrilled to see Noah hunched over in the trembling throes of an orgasm.

She was overtaken by unexpected pleasure when he recuperated and began to cover her tush with worshipful kisses. Having her ass kissed in such reverence was oddly arousing, causing her small nipples to poke out against the training bra. Her clit responded also, hardening into a firm little bud. And her vagina, now creamy with desire, clenched and throbbed; it yearned to be invaded.

"I worship you, little girl," he uttered passionately, his face tightly pressed against her buttocks. A moment later, he began to sob, tears dampening her bare behind. Shocked, Milan pulled away, but Noah reached for her, wrapping his bony arms around her thighs. Clinging to her, he muttered words of worship and everlasting devotion.

The man truly had a thing for asses; his own as well as hers. So, being the opportunist that she was, Milan had no choice but to take full advantage of the weakness he'd shown.

"Noah," she whispered. "If you truly adore me, you'll make an honest woman of me." She paused, allowing the weight of her words to sink in.

"What do you mean, my dear?" he asked, still clinging to her.

She instantly launched into a sales pitch. "I know you're distraught and terrified of dying. I don't blame you. But you don't have to die alone. With me by your side as your wife, I promise to make every single day of your life pure paradise." She'd borrowed the last line from a Pure Paradise brochure, but had exchanged the word, *we* for *I*.

"My dear, are you proposing to me?" he asked, awed.

"I am, Noah," she said, sounding earnest as she shook free of his clingy grasp and turned toward him. She bent over the bed and gently wiped away his tears with her fingers. He reached for her again, this time desperately pressing his face against her thighs, as if he couldn't bear to be separated from her.

She couldn't enjoy his needy desperation. She felt awkward and undignified with her ruffled panties ridiculously wrapped around her ankles. It was difficult to try to strike a deal with one's pants down and while dressed in a silly costume. So she extracted herself from Noah's grasp, pulled up her panties, and straightened out the rest of her attire. She smoothed back her hair and continued to vigorously make her sales pitch.

"I know Elise did certain things for you, but were you as pleased with Elise as you are with me?"

"Not at all. Elise and I had a financial arrangement. With you I have so much more. An understanding. An emotional attachment," he croaked, sounding as if he were near tears again. "I doubt that I'd live much longer if you weren't brightening my life."

Approving of his response, Milan gave a tight, satisfied smile, but pressed on. "Have you ever experienced with *anyone* else the kind of forbidden pleasure you've shared with me?"

"Never," he said without hesitation.

"Noah, I want you to marry me."

"Marry? I—I can't, Milan. I'm a dying man. What sense would it make for you to be burdened with me?"

Noah Brockington was a very smart and sharp-witted man. For the life of her, Milan couldn't understand why he was pretending not to understand that it was compensation she was striving for, not a husband to share her life.

"When you said you worshipped me, were you speaking from your heart or merely playing with my emotions?"

"I'm completely sincere," he insisted. "I truly worship you; my only regret is that I didn't meet you when I was vibrant and healthy," he told her, sounding convincing.

Unimpressed, Milan looked away.

"My dear, I can give you all the benefits of a wife," he said pleadingly.

She stepped back, staring coldly at the hands that reached for her. "Oh, I see. You're willing to give me all the benefits of a wife. You think I should feel privileged to be your common-law wife," she said sarcastically.

"You're making my suggestion sound so...so crude."

"It is crude, Noah. You're unwilling to make our union sacred and legal. I'm insulted, Noah. I really am," she said, shaking her head bitterly. "What is it? Do you view me as some sort of sexual plaything, unworthy to be your spouse?" she spat angrily. Had she not realized that Noah Brockington derived tremendous freakish pleasure from kissing her ass, she may not have had the courage to challenge him.

Milan drifted off in thought. The man had shed tears of joy, he'd actually wept. So, counting on the fact that she was able to fulfill his countless sexual fantasies and that time was not on his side, Milan decided to call his bluff.

Turning her attention back to Noah, she said, "My feelings for you run too deeply to allow you to make a whore of me. Noah, I'm going to pack my bags." She sighed resolutely and without another word, turned her back to him.

"No!" he shouted, his voice stronger than ever before.

Striding toward the door, she stopped suddenly, twirled around, and said, "Hopefully, you'll find a more suitable companion. I'll be leaving your house tonight."

"Don't leave! My dear, I'll marry you; I'll do whatever you want."

Beaming, Milan rushed to Noah's bedside. He lay down and inched to the edge of the bed. His scrawny arms maneuvered Milan around until her butt was directly in his face. He lifted her skirt, hooked his fingers in the elastic waistband of her panties, and tugged them down.

"Sit, my dear," he offered in a throaty voice, inviting Milan to sit on his face.

And in that uncomfortable position, Milan expressed her urgent financial situation, disclosed her legal troubles, and came clean about her true identity. She also informed him that she preferred Ruth Henry. Greer had to go. Without hesitation, Noah Brockington agreed.

chapter fifteen

Getting paddled, having her ass worshipped, and face-sitting was exhausting. Well, she didn't actually sit on Noah's face. Afraid she'd crush the frail man's skull and end up with a murder charge if she placed all her body weight on his face, she'd altered her position and merely squatted over him. And all that squatting had put quite a strain on her quads. Now, she had sore muscles, a wedding to plan, and a million other things to attend to, including getting Noah's semen-covered crotch cleaned up.

Wearing flip-flops, Milan padded into the kitchen. She was naked beneath a terry cover-up. "I hope that nurse didn't leave yet," she told Irma.

Irma looked at her and blinked. "She left right after you told me to let her go home."

Milan sighed. "I was hoping I'd catch her. Oh well, I guess you'll have to do it."

Do what? Irma's widened eyes seemed to ask.

"Mr. Brockington needs attention. He had a little accident. Be a dear, and clean him up before you take his tray upstairs. I'll make sure you're compensated on pay day, okay?" Milan pinched off a grape from a fruit basket on the counter and popped it in her mouth.

As Irma well knew, it wasn't a request. Milan had added nursing assistant to her job description. Mumbling under her breath, Irma trudged upstairs. Milan headed off for the steam room, needing to soak her sore muscles.

Later, while soaking in the Jacuzzi, she called her sister, Sweetie.

"It's about time somebody heard from you," Sweetie gushed into the phone. "Me and Mommy were about to call the police and report you as a missing person. Oops! I guess mentioning the po-po ain't funny."

"Ha, ha, ha," Milan chuckled sarcastically. "Listen, I have some extremely good news..."

"What's that noise?"

"Noise? Oh," Milan blurted, suddenly enlightened. "You hear the bubbles from the Jacuzzi. I'm in the Jacuzzi, soaking," Milan said, giggling.

"Excuse me! Sounds like you got it goin' on out there in Radnor. You never got to relax in no Jacuzzi over at Pure Paradise. You mean to tell me those rich people in the suburbs are nice enough to let you chill in their Jacuzzi?"

"Uh huh," Milan uttered with pride. "Guess what?"

"What?"

"Are you ready for this?"

"I guess." Sweetie sounded doubtful.

"Drum roll, please." Milan paused. "I'm getting married," she shouted, squealing like a teenager.

"Something must be wrong with my phone. You're getting what?" Sweetie asked, dubiously.

"Married," Milan repeated, gleefully.

"Hold up! I thought you said you would never get married, but that's beside the point. You've been staying out in Radnor for how long? Five or six days, a week at the most? Who the hell did you find to marry that fast?"

"I'm engaged to marry—well, I don't have the ring yet. But I'm going to marry the very wealthy Mr. Noah Brockington," Milan said, enunciating clearly.

"You're planning on marrying the sick old man you're supposed to be taking care of?" Sweetie sounded horrified.

"Yes. And although he is sickly, he's actually not that old. He's in his forties or fifties—he's around Mommy's age. He gives the appearance of being elderly because he's in such poor health."

"Well, if he's so sickly, why the hell…" Sweetie fell silent as the realization hit her. "You ain't right, Milan. Girl, you know that ain't right at all. You gonna marry that poor man while he's lying on his deathbed just so you can pay off your debts?"

"I can do a lot more than pay off some debts with all the money he's going to leave me. Stop being so judgmental. I'm making his last days complete bliss. Noah Brockington has never been so happy in his life, so why shouldn't I reap some of the benefits? For all I know, he could be intending to leave his money to some ridiculous charity or to some distant relatives who don't mean him a bit of good."

Sweetie sucked her teeth. "Oh, and I guess you have his best interests at heart."

"I can't believe you're criticizing me instead of being happy for me."

"Why should I be happy over a wedding that's not based on love? Take me and Quantez, for example—"

Milan sighed.

"Me and Quantez don't have much," Sweetie went on. "But we love each other and we both love our kids. I would never trade what we have for all the—"

"Good for you and Quantez," Milan said, cutting her sister off. "I didn't call to listen to you pontificate over the joy of poverty and living happily ever after in ghetto heaven."

"Why are you so damn sarcastic and mean," Sweetie groused.

"Well, stop lecturing me and help me plan my wedding!"

"And where's it supposed to take place—at the poor man's deathbed?"

"No, he can get around with a walker. Sweetie, are you looking at the big picture, here? I'm going to be worth millions. I want a big, elaborate church wedding. I want my nuptials featured in *Philadelphia Magazine* and I want those pompous board members to eat crow when they find out that like the phoenix, I rose from the ashes—they couldn't keep me down."

"Aren't you worried that people might call you a gold digger?"

"People can call me whatever they want; I've been called worse. I'm taking advantage of a great opportunity, and that's called being smart."

"So, what's the deal—aren't you still hiding out from those board members?"

"Absolutely not. Noah's gathering his attorneys as we speak. Restitution will be paid and that unpleasant situation will be remedied before the close of the day."

"Lawd! You're nevah gonna change. Always trying to swindle people and make a fast buck."

"You sound just like Mom. I'd expect you to be happy for me. Look on the bright side—I'll never be broke again. And neither will you. You know I'm going to look out for you and your family. I'll take care of Mom, too."

"Well, since you're putting it like that, I guess I can get involved in this disgraceful wedding. Me and Quantez and the kids could use some extra money. How much are you planning on giving us?"

"More than you could imagine. In fact, I'll put you on my payroll immediately after the wedding. We'll work out your salary later."

"Salary? You expect me to work? What do I have to do?" Sweetie sounded frantic. Her voice went to higher pitch, as if the thought of employment was a terrifying consideration.

"Oh, I didn't tell you. After the wedding, I'm going to open my own day spa. My initial plan was to write a book, but I've changed my mind. As you well know, I was the brains behind Pure Paradise. The board didn't want to pay me what I was worth, so they canned me and made up those fraudulent charges. The nerve of them pretending that my expenses weren't all work related."

"Fraudulent? Milan, you were going crazy with that company credit card," Sweetie reminded. "You even bought that fifteen-hundred-dollar gold-plated vibrator with the company card. Now, how was that work related?"

"It relieved stress. Job-related stress," Milan exploded. "Compared to all the business I brought to Pure Paradise, all the money I made for that company, those credit card expenditures were just a drop in the bucket. Now, can we get back to the pressing issue of my wedding?"

"Yeah, but, uh…," Sweetie stammered. "I don't get it. Since you're working with all that money, why do you need *me* to help you plan the wedding?

What do I know about *elaborate* weddings? For the type of wedding you're talking about having, I think you need to hire one of those fancy wedding planners."

"Sweetie," Milan said with a long sigh. "I don't want a stranger handling the most important day of my life. I can do all the planning myself, but I need you to do..." She paused, thoughtfully. "I need you to do the grunt work."

"I don't like how that sounds. I'm the oldest sister, so don't think you're going to start bossing me around just because—"

"I only meant I'll do the major planning, but you'll have to tie up the loose ends, you know, pull it all together. Oh, and before I forget—I need you to give the news to Mom. Make sure you tell her I'm extremely busy and don't have time to listen to one of her lectures. Tell her, I'm marrying Noah Brockington with or without her blessing."

"Okay, it's your life. I'll make sure Mom gets your message. So...despite getting married and all, I guess you're still gonna have to invest in batteries for that gold-plated contraption of yours. I can't imagine a sick older man being worth a damn in the bedroom. Now take Quantez, for instance. Girl, he gives it so good, I couldn't even imagine—"

"Oh God! Whatever," Milan shouted in exasperation.

chapter sixteen

The buzz of the intercom woke her with a jolt. The button was on the other side of her bedroom, so she ignored it and placed a pillow over her head. She knew it was only Irma. It seemed the woman enjoyed a twisted sense of power when she awakened Milan at ungodly early hours just to inquire about her breakfast preference. Milan made a mental note to post a set of written rules in the kitchen. Rule number one would be: *Do not disturb Milan until after ten a.m.*

The buzzer sounded again. *The nerve of that woman!* Milan jumped out of bed and darted across the floor, then stabbed the intercom button. "What is it?" she asked, curtly.

"Good morning, my dear." Noah's raspy voice filled her bedroom. He'd never buzzed her before. She was startled and more than annoyed. The sound of his voice, magnified inside her private bedroom, felt like a terrible invasion of her privacy. They weren't even married yet and he was already taking liberties.

"Good morning, darling," Milan responded affectionately. In her mind's eye, however, she could see another set of rules that she'd post immediately after the wedding. She'd tack the code of behavior at eye level beside Noah's bedside table, with the number one rule typed in bold, large print!

"Would you be so kind as to sit with me this morning. There are financial matters that must be discussed."

"Of course. I'll be with you shortly." *Financial matters!* The words were music to her ears. She would have preferred to sweep into his suite wearing haute couture, but she realized she could persuade her future husband to strike a more generous bargain if she were wearing her naughty school-girl set.

When she arrived, Noah was sitting in the darkened room, hankie sticking out of his pajama top pocket, and the curtains were drawn as usual. He wore reading glasses and read by the light from the bedside lamp. Why didn't he just open the damn drapes? She really hated his suite of rooms. But not for long. In six months or less, the nuisance of a man would be dead and gone, and she'd have the stuffy old master bedroom suite completely renovated to suit her contemporary tastes.

Smiling, satisfied, she pulled up a chair and crossed her leg, bouncing it, expecting to entice him with her anklet socks.

Noah ignored her schoolgirl garb. He flipped through a stack of pages that looked as thick as a ream of paper. "My attorney, good fellow that he is, drafted a prenuptial agreement and dropped it off this morning at dawn. It's pretty standard, my dear," he said coolly. "With a few clauses, of course." Noah Brockington was clearly in a strictly business mode. "You may review the document at your leisure, but allow me to brief you on the highlights."

Milan nodded vaguely. She didn't feel comfortable when Noah was in control.

He pulled the hanky from the breast pocket of his pajama top and coughed into the white cotton. Irritated, Milan sucked in a breath. *Why don't you use freakin' tissues instead of those germy pieces of cloth?*

"I took care of your financial predicament; your former employer has been paid with a cashier's check. Nine thousand of the money you owed had already been deducted from your banking account."

Damn! She could have used that money. It seemed illegal for the bank to just extract her funds. *Oh well...*

"And for the record, no formal charges were ever made against you."

Relief washed over Milan. She smiled appreciatively. She even forgave Noah for pulling out his nasty handkerchief. In light of the fact that her name was cleared and she was no longer a hunted fugitive, Milan considered cutting her losses and taking the few thousands she had socked away and clearing out of the Brockington estate.

But her good common sense and driving need for material possessions kept her feet planted firmly in place. The worst was over. Noah Brockington's deranged mind couldn't possibly conceive an act more despicable than what they'd already done. She invested too much of herself to simply walk away. Yes, she was in for the long haul—or the short, depending how one viewed a life span of six months.

For Milan, six months seemed an incredibly long time to look at Noah's gaunt face. But then again, who knew? Perhaps he'd become violently ill midway, like in the next couple of months or so. So ill, in fact, perhaps he'd collapse into a coma and never ever bother her again.

However, the thought of a comatose Noah was just a fleeting fantasy. The sound of him clearing his throat was an irritating reminder that he was for the moment very much alive.

"My dear, you drifted off in thought. This matter is very important. It's imperative that you pay close attention."

She didn't have to take orders from him, she was free to leave, but on the other hand, she'd be a fool to walk away from his millions. So, she looked deeply into his eyes and gave him her undivided attention.

"As you know, I never married, and to my knowledge," he said with an annoying chuckle, "I have no heirs." Then he shook his head. "No heirs," he repeated, this time regretfully. "It's obscene for a man to have lived for forty-six years and not have a son to carry on his name."

Badly shaken, Milan swallowed, her mouth suddenly quite dry. She didn't like the direction of the conversation. Was Noah suggesting what she suspected he was suggesting? Surely the shriveled-up fool didn't have the gall to think he could generate healthy sperm in an adequate amount necessary to produce a child? And even if he could, which she seriously doubted, considering how sick he was, he had to be out of his mind if he thought she'd allow him to deposit said sperm inside her precious body.

Bearing a child had never entered her mind, and giving birth to a child sired by *him* was entirely out of the question. It was too revolting to even consider, so she stubbornly refused to allow her wandering mind to envision the vile and monstrous progeny of a dying man.

Noah yawned. "I've had too much activity," he said apologetically. "Look over the papers, my dear. We'll discuss our arrangement after lunch. I should be awake and feeling more chipper by then," he assured her with a loathsome wink. It took every bit of sheer will and concentration for her to refrain from barfing in his face.

Back in her bedroom, Milan angrily shed the silly schoolgirl outfit and slipped into a comfortable pair of low-slung jeans. She buzzed Irma and shouted into the intercom, "My room hasn't been tidied, my bed hasn't been made, and there's no sign of my breakfast. Is there a problem, Irma?"

Except for the sound of Irma's perpetual heavy breathing, there was silence. Irma apparently thought it best to count to ten before responding. "You usually don't wake up this early, so how was I supposed to know you were waiting for breakfast," she said, panting and sounding defensive.

"Well, now you know. After you're finished cooking, set the table. Oh! By the way, you sound as if you've just run a marathon, Irma. You really need to do something about your weight."

Irma ignored the insult. "You want to eat in the formal dining room? You're kidding."

"I kid you not, and stop questioning me. You're totally aware of my position in this household, so stop overstepping your boundaries."

There was more labored breathing. "How many should I set the table for?" Irma asked, wearily.

"Set it for one. And refer to me as Ms. Walden."

Silence.

"Did you hear me?"

"I heard you."

Milan really wanted to hear Irma call her Ms. Walden. Noah had just chipped away at her self-respect by catching her off guard and hitting her with a freakin' prenup. Before she looked over the prenuptial agreement— the legalese that threatened to rock her world—she needed a quick fix, an ego boost. She needed some respect, dammit.

"After you've finished your chores, I want you to run a few errands for me."

"Alrighty," Irma said good-naturedly, refusing to address Milan in the manner she'd requested.

After clicking Irma off the intercom, Milan scooped up the schoolgirl uniform and stuffed it in the back of the closet, inside a small, discreet alcove with a door, which she kept padlocked. Nosy Irma didn't need to know her secrets.

⚜

Milan sat at the dining table in the finely appointed room. The utensils were carefully positioned, plates, cups, saucers, and cloth napkins all in their proper place. The centerpiece, a vibrant bouquet of two-toned roses set in a glass bowl, was a dazzling treat to behold. Milan was impressed. Irma, full of surprises, apparently really knew her stuff. But not well enough to cater Milan's wedding, she thought haughtily.

For her wedding, only an award-winning catering service would do. She had an idea of the service she'd use, but wanted to check other options before she made a commitment. And thinking of making wedding plans put a knot in her stomach. Her mind flashed to the prenup that she was afraid to read, which was stacked neatly and locked inside the alcove.

"Oh, you startled me. Good morning, Ms. Walden," Ruth Henry, the nurse, greeted. *Ms. Walden!* Oooh, she loved the sound of it. Irma must have put a bug in the nurse's ear. Shrewd ol' Irma knew how to get on Milan's good side. Having the nurse address her properly was fine and dandy, but Milan still wanted to hear Irma say it.

Milan noticed the leather-bound volume in Ruth Henry's hand. The nurse, she'd recently noticed, spent more time in the library than she did in her patient's room, which was another matter Milan would have to address after she'd read the prenup and had gotten her bearings.

"I was on my way up to read to Mr. Brockington," the nurse said, holding up the book. "Do you think he'll enjoy Emily Bronte?"

She wanted to say, *For all I care, you can take that book and shove it.* But instead she smiled and said, "I'm sure he'll love it." The nurse nodded, her eyes even twinkled as she floated away clutching the book as if it were an elusive lover. What a nut! The woman was clearly a bibliophile. Milan wondered if there were support groups for the disorder.

After the meal Irma prepared, which was once again surprisingly elegant and upscale—an omelet cooked with herbs, tomatoes, spinach, and goat cheese; accompanied by a French baguette with strawberry preserves; fresh ground coffee; and yogurt parfait—Milan groaned when she pushed back her chair and thought of the unpleasant task of plowing through pages of legal jargon. But if she expected to continue enjoying sumptuous meals and being treated like a queen, it would behoove her to pull out the pesky document and start reading.

Hopefully, she'd been influenced by an overactive imagination. Surely Noah didn't expect her to become pregnant with his child. It was such a preposterous thought, Milan laughingly chided herself for being overly paranoid. Noah had been venting when he openly expressed regret over squandering his youth, but now he was eager to look ahead, grateful for the short time he had to spend with his young and lovely future wife.

Satisfied with her deductions, Milan smiled contentedly and rose from the table.

chapter seventeen

She quickly flipped through about twenty pages of whereas this and whereas that. Her heart lurched when she finally came upon Section Three—Property. Excitedly, she poured over the numerous pages. So, Noah had a home in the Pocono Mountains; beachfront property in Wildwood, New Jersey; and rental property scattered throughout the tri-state area of Philadelphia, New Jersey, and Delaware.

Section Four—Financial Disclosure revealed income of what appeared to be well over twenty-nine million. Perusing quickly, she skipped to Schedules A, B, C, and D. Excited, Milan skimmed the pages. She felt a hot rush and grabbed a handful of pages to fan herself and try to cool down. The column in Schedule F was headed with her name. It contained line after line of nothing but big fat zeros. She had zero assets. So what! She had intelligence, youth, and beauty. Those personal assets entitled her to boldly enter this union absolutely penniless.

Her eyes moved to Section Five—Children, a portion of the document that should have contained nothing more than a sentence or two. Too confused to focus on reading, Milan thumbed through ten or more pages. *Why so many pages? What the hell is this about?* Neither she nor Noah had any children, and thankfully, they never would, so why all the legal mumbo jumbo over kids? Reluctantly, she stopped skimming and forced herself to give the section a thorough going over. Milan sighed deeply, leaned forward, and began reading.

At first she thought her eyes were deceiving her, so she read the section four times. Summing it up, Milan concluded that Section Five stipulated that she had to give birth to Noah Brockington's male heir. If the first pregnancy did not result in the birth of a male child, she had to conceive twice more in an attempt to bear a Brockington male heir.

Reading quickly, her eyes zoomed across the page and unfortunately what she read was worse than anything she could have ever imagined. Attempts at reproduction, the document stated, would be conducted by a fertility specialist selected by Noah Brockington. Said fertility specialist would designate a cryogenic center to collect semen specimens and provide long-term sperm storage for future use in reproduction.

Milan stared at the page on top of the stack she held, her mouth hung open in disbelief and repulsion. *Oh my God, he's crazy. He's out of his freakin' mind! How can I bear children for a dead man?* It was a contemptible request. What rational woman would agree to such an obscene demand? For a man who was knocking at death's door, Noah Brockington was remarkably arrogant and self-assured.

Why, she wondered, would such a sickly and disgusting man even want to produce offspring? Could a man as unhealthy as he possess even *one* healthy gene? She doubted it, but even on the remote possibility that he did have a healthy sperm or two, Milan knew for a fact, she would not allow herself to be railroaded into having any contact whatsoever with Noah Brockington's vile and mutant gene pool.

Feeling flushed and queasy, she was unable to maintain a grasp of the pages. Listlessly, she watched them slip from her fingers, float down to the floor, and scatter around her feet.

Noah had delivered the marriage contract with an odd twist to his lips; she now realized his mouth had been set in a sneer. The crafty bastard knew she'd never marry him under such outrageous conditions. In her mind, she could still see his smirking image. Resenting even a mental picture of him, she shook her head, forcing his pompous expression from her mind.

But she couldn't shut out the thoughts or the imagery of their disgusting, perverted sex play. It had been all for naught, she sadly resolved. Then, in a burst of anger, she snatched up the papers, and stacked them firmly together, fully intending to storm angrily to Noah's room and throw the pile of absurd legalese smack in his haggard face.

But she couldn't move. She was so weary, bone tired, from years of striving so hard, yearning for and exhaustively chasing after a lifestyle that continually eluded her. It was so damn unfair. It was bad enough that she had to marry Noah for money he clearly no longer needed. Why'd he have to be so spiteful? And so power hungry? Why'd he have to involve *her* in his ludicrous scheme of spawning an entire brood of mutant children after his demise? Tears of frustration slid down Milan's cheeks. She dropped her head, buried her face in her hands, and sobbed.

After wiping away the final teardrop, she came to the firm decision that she'd put in too much time with Noah to give up a lifetime of luxury so easily. She spent an hour brainstorming ideas of how to break the prenuptial agreement. And finally, after reviewing the preposterous stipulation one more time, Milan broke into a sudden fit of laughter.

Why had she allowed herself to become so easily riled? There wasn't a court in the United States that would honor something so ridiculous. After Noah's death, with his fortune in her hands, she'd be able to hire a top-notch legal team who would argue that she signed the agreement under duress. Her brilliant attorneys would convince the court that the agreement was unconscionable and should be rendered unenforceable.

Feeling marginally better, Milan put pen to paper and signed her name on the designated line. She was still a bit irritated, however, since he hadn't said a word about increasing her daily allowance *before* the wedding, and being that he was terminally ill, what did he expect her to do money wise if he kicked the bucket earlier than expected?

The topic required immediate attention. It was time to pay her rich soon-to-be husband a visit. If she was going to match wits with Noah Brockington she was going to have to toughen up. No more ruffles, bows, or ponytails—not until he agreed to her terms. Intending to invoke authority and confidence, she peeled off the jeans and replaced the casual attire with a business suit.

Clad in navy blue Italian wool jacket and pants, she collected the papers, stuffed them in her briefcase, and closed the bedroom door behind her. Milan strode swiftly toward the master bedroom suite, prepared to sit down and play hardball with the man who stood between her and the lifestyle of the wealthy elite. She was certain the curve ball she planned to throw at Noah Brockington would solidify her position.

chapter eighteen

"**M**y dear," Noah addressed Milan from his bed. He looked thinner, as if he'd lost a few pounds since their encounter earlier that day. *Good!* She hoped his projected lifespan had been shortened by two months. She was certain she could pull together a fabulous wedding in just a month or two—with the help of a planner, of course. Yes, she definitely would need some professional help to get this wedding off and running with such limited time.

Milan pulled up a chair beside the bed. She pulled the document from her briefcase and placed it on the low table beside the bed. "Noah, I've read the prenuptial agreement." Looking at him intently, she placed her hand softly upon his withered veiny one. "It saddens me that our time together will be so short, but I want you to know that I'm honored that you want me to bear your child—your children if that's what you desire. I've signed the document; we can have it couriered over to your attorney today if you'd like."

"Your consideration astounds me. I must say, I didn't expect you to make such a hasty decision."

It's not like there's a hell of a lot of time to dawdle. "It was an easy decision," she said, smiling. She knew she'd missed her calling. She should have been an actress. Playing roles came so easily for her. "To have a part of you..." Milan touched her heart dramatically, closed her eyes dreamily and inhaled. "Your idea is brilliant; it would have never occurred to me that I could have a part of you with me long after you're gone."

Noah, despite his frailty, puffed up with pride. "Look at you! Dressed like a businesswoman." He motioned with his hand. "You look so beautiful… so severe. You're the exact replica of a chiding schoolmarm who'd dispense harsh punishment for the slightest infraction of a rule." As the words poured out of Noah's mouth, his eyes lit up with deviant desire.

No, no, no! No more stupid games. She wanted to scowl, stamp her feet, and slap him senseless, but she remained completely composed. "Noah, we must discuss my living expenses," she told him, calmly. "I'll need money to plan the wedding."

"How much do you need?" he asked eagerly. His dry lips were suddenly moistened—by drool, Milan suspected.

"At least one thousand a day," she said firmly.

Noah didn't blink. "Very well," he said hastily.

Milan was relieved that Noah agreed so readily. She wouldn't spend the cash, nor would she put it in the freakin' bank. Banks had the authority to put a freeze on one's funds and then spend the money as they saw fit. She'd put the money in a personal safe—let it stack up. A secret stash. The ordeal she'd suffered at the hands of her former employer taught her a valuable lesson: Expect the worst even in the best of times and always have access to emergency cash.

Breaking into her musings, Noah cleared his throat. "Mistress, I didn't complete my homework," he said, his voice taking on a boyishly high register.

Milan heaved a sigh, abruptly stood up, and marched to the corner where Noah's rolling walker was leaning folded against the wall. She yanked it open and pushed it roughly toward the bed. "Get up," she said through tightly closed teeth, "and get the money this instant."

Looking frightened, he scooted over and awkwardly transferred from the bed. He gripped the walker and trudged slowly to his dressing room with Milan impatiently at his side, urging him along.

Closet space took up one entire side of the room. Hunched over the walker, standing near a pillar that separated the dressing room from the bedroom, he pointed to one of the numerous closet doors. Milan flung the door open and to her surprise there was an old-fashioned footlocker cleverly concealed by racks of shoes. "As my wife-to-be, I grant you access to your daily allowance. You'll find the key in the fourth drawer inside the armoire."

Milan practically clicked her heels as she hurried into the closets, leaving Noah standing there in his pajamas, gripping the rolling walker. Anxiously, she opened the fourth drawer. The key was in plain view sitting atop a stack of crisp, neatly folded white monogrammed handkerchiefs. It was a wonderful sight, but she was sidetracked by the sight of the mound of handkerchiefs and couldn't fully enjoy the moment.

She snatched the key and rolled her eyes at the outdated square pieces of cloth, which Noah seemed to have an endless supply of to stifle coughs and to blow his perpetually runny nose.

How disgusting. Her thoughts shifted to the day of their nuptials. Suppose he had a bout of coughing or had to blow his nose while standing at the altar? Milan grimaced. It didn't matter, she'd have a box of tissues on hand because there was no way she was going to allow him to stick one of his damned monogrammed hankies in the breast pocket of his wedding tuxedo. She'd have to painstakingly oversee every aspect of his wedding apparel.

When she returned to the dressing room, Noah stood near the wall of closets, steadying himself with the walker. Milan suddenly had a notion that it would be cost efficient and a rather clever idea to bury her doomed soon-to-be spouse in his wedding-day attire. Oh, and she'd throw all those pesky hankies into the coffin with him. He might find the handkerchiefs useful in the afterlife. She let out a spiteful giggle.

Enjoying her wicked sense of humor as well as the feeling of the elusive key pressed against her palm, Milan tossed Noah a broad smile. By the time she inserted the key and turned the lock, Milan was giddy with excitement.

Inside the trunk was an obscene amount of money—stacks upon stacks of one-hundred-dollar bills. Gleeful and amazed, Milan pursed her lips and blew out a musical sound. Whistling was uncharacteristic and definitely beneath her—it was totally undignified—but the sight of all that money rendered her temporarily insane. And horny, she realized when her pussy began to twitch.

"How much is in there?" she asked, kneeling before the trunk as if it were a sacred altar. In awe, she stared at the money. Stabbed by the familiar pang of a lifetime of yearning, Milan felt close to tears. She wanted it. All of it! She wanted it so badly, the desire was palpable.

"Over a million, my dear," Noah responded. "Now, take what you need and lock the trunk." He looked around cautiously and then spoke in a hushed tone. "You can't trust the help these days, I'm sure you're aware."

Milan nodded absently and then greedily grabbed a tidy pile of the bills, which was secured with a purple paper band. She peeled off ten bills and slowly, reluctantly placed the rest of the stack back inside the trunk.

Hanging over his walker, Noah reached out and slammed down the top of the trunk. "Secure the lock," he ordered, wearing an impatient frown, "and return the key to its proper place," he added in a high-handed manner. His voice was steel.

Her heart sank. She was so disappointed, desolate. She'd wanted to bask in the glow of the money just a little longer. No, that wasn't entirely true. She desired more than just a visual. Actually, she wanted to sniff, caress, and fondle every single dollar. But Noah, ornery creep that he was, had put a lid on the money, instantly shutting off her feeling of euphoria. It was very mean of him to begrudge her such a small pleasure.

Determinedly, Milan kept a scowl from forming on her face and some-how managed to keep a calm demeanor. "Follow me," she said, as she stalked off from the dressing area.

The walker rattled and the wheels creaked in protest as Noah tried to keep up with Milan's pace. "My dear," he whined as he shuffled along. "You must slow down, I can't keep—"

"Follow me," she interrupted, using an implacable tone. "And stop your sniveling," she warned, giving him a stern look over her shoulder. He'd asked for a strict disciplinarian and she now fully intended to inflict severe punishment to such an impudent, ill-mannered pupil.

When Noah toddled into the bedroom, Milan slammed the door that led to the adjacent dressing room. She briskly headed to the bedside table and pulled open the drawer that stored the leather paddle.

Waving the paddle menacingly, her face contorted in an unforgiving scowl, Milan spoke through clenched teeth. "Get over here and drop your pants."

Noah smiled sheepishly.

"Do it," she yelled. "Now!"

Her voice, loud and shrill, took Noah by surprise. He gave a startled jump. Then, after collecting himself, he obediently shuffled toward Milan as quickly as the cumbersome rolling walker allowed. When he reached Milan, he gripped the side of the walker with one hand. With the other, he lowered his pajama bottom, awkwardly turned, and surrendered himself.

Paddling Noah had turned her on more than when he'd given her a light spanking. She probably could have had an orgasm if she'd spanked him as hard as she'd wanted to. But if she'd given in to her desire to give Noah the severe beatdown he deserved, she would have left some vicious bruises or broken a few bones. The type of bodily harm he had coming could have accidentally killed him. And then she'd be in a hell of a jam. On the lam, again. This time for murder. Being accused of murder and having to flee the country to escape a lethal injection was truly a gruesome thought.

Swiftly changing her thoughts back to a juicier subject, Milan came to the decision that she wanted sex. Badly. But most definitely not with Noah. He was sexually satisfied. The sound of his contented snoring seemed to echo through the halls, around the bend, seeping through the space beneath Milan's bedroom door.

Under normal circumstances, his snoring would have angered her to no end, but not today. She felt horny just thinking about the bright crimson shade his buttocks had turned after she'd paddled him. Judging by the way his body had tensed and the loud manner in which he moaned, he must have felt pretty heated, too. He was so hot and bothered, he cried out in passion, and then gushed out a tremendous load.

His bibliophilic nurse, pulled from the downstairs library where her head was undoubtedly buried in a book, was told by Milan to get upstairs and clean up the mess. It was high time for the woman to start earning her pay.

With her finances stable at least for the moment, Milan decided it was time to catch up on her membership dues and take care of her raging libido. No love toys, no self-administered finger tricks, and no pussy-sucking lips. The only thing that would pacify her sexual craving was a real-life, hard-pumping, thick-ass dick.

chapter nineteen

An hour later, under the pretext of having to run a few errands, Milan carefully treaded down a narrow cobblestone street in Philadelphia's Society Hill. The old residential street was actually an alley, and was conveniently hidden from public view. The real estate on this high-end alley, lined with Georgian-style homes, was ridiculously high.

Inside the darkened parking garage on Dock Street where she'd parked her car, she'd put on the bright blonde wig and slapped on a pair of dark glasses. Rushing to her destination, she hadn't bothered to button her coat. Now, dashing along, she caught a fleeting glimpse of her reflection in the window of one of the homes on the enchanting street. But the image she saw was horrifying and didn't coincide with the beautiful environment. Wearing huge dark sunglasses and the hideous synthetic wig, and with her shoulders hunched against the wind, she looked frightful—ghoulish.

Hastening her footsteps, Milan's heels clicked loudly as she forged ahead. The wind furiously whipped her open coat behind her as she hurried along, seeking immediate shelter from the bitter cold as well as warmth for her soul in the form of a quick sex fix.

At last she reached her destination, a gorgeous Colonial home situated at the end of the block. She pressed a buzzer, gave her code number, and instantly gained admittance.

Bringing her account up-to-date and scheduling a quick encounter using cash, instead of a credit card or a check, was not an easy transaction. The person Milan assumed to be the receptionist introduced herself simply as

Ilka. She gave no last name and no job title. She'd simply stated in an official manner, "I am Ilka. How can I help you?" Her tone did not imply an accommodating nature.

At any rate, Ilka was a fairly attractive but humorless woman in her mid-to-late forties, with her gray-streaked hair coiffed stylishly. She pushed back her chair and stood to gather and stack files, or perhaps the busy-work was just an opportunity to show off her expensive tailored suit, chunky jewelry with high-quality stones, not to mention a pair of green satin Manolo Blahniks with a rhinestone buckle and a four-inch heel. Her attire suggested that she was paid handsomely and held a prominent position in the secret sex club. But in accordance with the club's atmosphere of secrecy, Ilka's job title and true identity was apparently hush-hush. Milan totally envied the woman's affluence. She decided then and there that a thousand-dollar pair of Manolo Blahniks would be her very first purchase to celebrate her widow status. Hell, she'd run out and buy two pairs the moment Noah died.

Ilka located Milan's file and clicked her tongue in exasperation. "You shouldn't have come without an appointment. You're violating the privacy of other members and according to your records..." the woman paused, pursing her lips, "your membership has expired."

"I realize that," Milan said snippily. "When I realized I'd been remiss... uh, I'm in the midst of planning my wedding. You wouldn't believe how busy...," she stammered. "And, um, the membership fees just slipped my mind."

Ilka gave Milan a significant look. "Wedding? Will your spouse be applying for membership?"

Oh shit, why'd she mention *that?* Being married would totally complicate her current membership. "I'm not sure if I'll keep the membership after I'm married. Anyway, my wedding isn't until next year," she lied, hoping to redirect the conversation back to her current situation, which was critical. Ilka was adding to Milan's stress, which in turn increased her level of sexual need. Her pussy was aching. It needed the immediate attention of a swollen hard dick. Oh hell, at this point, she'd settle for anything hard inside her pussy or even pressed against her clit. She eyed the sharp corner of Ilka's desk and found herself inching up to it. She had to use all her inner resolve to restrain herself from throwing up a leg and fucking the shit out of the protruding piece of mahogany wood.

"I don't think we can resolve your issue today."

"I don't understand why you're making this out to be such a huge problem. I mean, it's not like I'm here trying to barter with colored beads," Milan said, her voice a frustrated high pitch. "I'm attempting to bring my account up-to-date," Milan said, flustered as she pulled away strands of synthetic hair that had attached to her glossed lips.

"As I've stated, our establishment does not accept cash. It's out of the question," Ilka insisted, using a formal tone. "Nor do we schedule spur-of-the-moment encounters," she said, waving her hand agitatedly.

Milan rifled through her purse and pulled out a wad of currency, expecting the arrogant woman to forget the stupid rules and become appropriately enthralled by the image of Benjamin Franklin gracing the folded bundle of bills.

Ilka pursed her lips disdainfully, recoiled, and staunchly refused to accept the cash.

Deeply humiliated, Milan's brown face felt flushed. If it were at all possible, her cheeks would take on the color of an embarrassed bright red. The level of humiliation she was experiencing was intense. Unacceptable. She'd really have to alter the state of her financial affairs and reopen her freakin' bank account ASAP.

"That's just not the way we do business here," Ilka repeated, throwing in a tsk to express her growing irritation. She gave Milan a wan smile. "Since you don't have a checking account, you'll have to purchase a cashier's check. You'll have to reapply and then we'll review your application."

"Are you serious?"

The beep of the desk console interrupted Ilka's response.

"Excuse me," she said and spoke into the phone using muted, confidential tones. And then to Milan's utter amazement, Ilka replaced the receiver and dazzled her with a smile. "Something's come up that might suit your needs. A very important client is en route, he's bringing along a couple of friends…" Ilka paused.

"What sort of friends? A married couple?"

"I didn't ask the marital status of his friends. He's paying for a group sex encounter," Ilka stated crisply. "Interested or not? I have to make arrangements for my client." Ilka had already started browsing though files.

"Can you give me some details?" Milan asked pleadingly.

"What difference does it make? Here at Tryst, we provide an upscale environment for sexually addicted people…"

Milan looked dumbfounded. Did Ilka just call her out of her name? Sexually addicted people! Weren't they the types of people who had random sex several times a day? Surely, Ilka wasn't referring to her; she just liked to get her freak on every now and then.

"Listen, I'm offering you an invitation as a guest for today. Are you interested? My time is limited," she said, opening a folder with a flourish. "Hmm," she said, as she perused the confidential information. "This one looks good." Ilka reached for the phone.

Milan glanced around uncertainly, then blurted, "I'm in!"

Obviously pleased, Ilka slid open a desk drawer and offered Milan a silver case, which Milan knew contained a silver key. Milan was a bronze key member and found that she was rather excited to hold the silver case.

Then Ilka touched her forehead in a "silly me" manner, and retrieved another case—this one gold. "I'm so distracted. Our client is a gold key member." Ilka exchanged cases and pointed to the stairway. "Make yourself comfortable. Our guests shouldn't be long."

❦

The room was much larger, much more impressive than the bronze key rooms she'd previously been assigned. But too overwrought from having to rack her brain over the ridiculous prenuptial agreement she'd been forced to sign, physically exhausted from whipping Noah's ass during the schoolmarm session, and emotionally drained from dealing with the insufferable and unbending Ilka, Milan really couldn't appreciate the plush interior of the gold key room.

She had just enough strength to get out of her clothes and recline on the inviting king-size bed. She needed a moment to relax and prepare for a mammoth orgasm. Maybe two, if she was lucky. She exhaled in delightful anticipation. A trio would soon surround the bed and get busy, touching, sucking, and licking her, searching for her erogenous zones. Who knew? With a party of three she very well may have huge multiple orgasms.

Voices were heard outside the door. Her lips stretched into a smile. Party time!

She turned enthusiastically onto her stomach, buried her face in the pillow. A flurry of pre-orgasmic excitement pulsed between her legs as she imagined the fulfillment of being pleasured by a group of two men and a woman. A lot of fucking and sucking was about to take place. She snaked a hand beneath her tummy to calm her pussy down.

The feeling of sexual excitement swiftly turned to dread and then escalated to full-blown terror when the door opened, emitting a chorus of entirely male voices. Voices slurred by alcohol.

What the fuck? What happened to the wife? Curious, her head shot up, but was shoved back down. She let out a frightened yelp, but the sound was muffled by the pillow.

"I heard you like it rough," said one of the voices.

Rough! Are you crazy? Ilka knew she didn't go for the rough stuff. It was clearly stated on her profile that she engaged only in encounters with couples who enjoyed giving pleasure. Not pain! This was a terrible mistake. She tried to lift her head again to explain that a mistake had been made, but he slammed her down again. Her wig was crooked; she could feel it turn askew. Pinned down by powerful hands, she thrashed about and struggled.

"How do you know, ever tried it?" asked another.

"Not yet, but I'm gonna find out."

Suddenly, her legs were roughly pulled apart. "First dibs," blurted yet another voice, deeper and gruffer than the other two.

"Stop!" she screamed, but the sound was muffled by the pillow. She flailed her arms, scratched at the headboard, kicked out her feet.

"Isn't this great?" asked one of the men in a voice filled with pride. "She's a real fighter; I bet that black cunt is hot and ready."

Milan was jostled about and then flipped over onto her back. She tried to fight, but it was hard to do any real harm to three men. During the tussle, her shades were knocked lopsided; reflexively, she adjusted them before resuming the fight. *This isn't happening; it can't be happening. I did not offer this club an enormous amount of money to end up getting gangbanged by a group of drunks.*

A pair of hands grabbed at her breasts. "Not much up here," complained the man.

"Small boobs means she's got a tight little snatch," the gruff-voiced man advised wisely.

Milan mentally sorted out words of protest. She kept her eyes closed, preferring not to see their faces in case there was still the remote chance that she could reason with them and turn this appalling situation to her advantage.

Perhaps the encounter-gone-wrong could be salvaged if she could impress upon the brutes that she hadn't agreed to a rape scene. She'd felt assured of multiple orgasms when she thought she had agreed to an encounter with two men and a woman. Now, being manhandled by a gang of ruffians, she doubted if her terrified pussy could tweak out even one small orgasm.

If she could get her wits about her, if she didn't have to swat away so many pairs of hands, she'd do her best to convince them that they could all have a good time if they'd stopped acting like animals for just one freakin' minute. She'd be more than willing to fuck the three of them, if they'd accept her terms. She had specific sexual conditions, otherwise she simply couldn't cum.

But when Milan parted her lips to speak, the words were halted by a huge hand forcibly pressed against her mouth. Panicked, she scratched the hand and savagely bit into flesh.

In an instant, there was a sound similar to a bomb exploding inside her head. After a second or two, she realized a fist had connected with her skull. "Fuckin' bitch," the bitten man yelled, his words laced with undisguised hatred.

She didn't lose consciousness, but she wished she had. Her eyes were wide open now. Thoughts reeled as she took in the surreal scene. The encounter was totally out of hand. A deeply tanned short man with strong, beefy arms flopped down on the bed next to her. In one movement, he forcefully yanked Milan on top of him. Wielding his dick like a knife, he repeatedly stabbed her vulva, even her anus as he sought her vaginal opening.

Inhaling deeply and blowing out alcohol-coated breath, the short burly man entered her viciously, pushing upward, his hairy tummy smacking against hers.

Her pussy was trying to recover from the shock of being raped when one of the burly man's buddies sidled up to Milan and mounted her from behind.

Double penetration—pussy and ass violation. It was all too much; she'd seen enough; she had to close her eyes. When she felt someone turning her head to the side, her eyes popped open in alarm. Could this scene get any worse? A chubby guy with ivory-colored skin, very blue eyes stood over her, naked. He was a baby-faced, doughy type and he swayed to and fro in a macabre dance. As he grinned and gyrated, Dough-boy's dick swung perilously close to Milan's face. He taunted her with his appendage as if it were a delectable treat. His pubic hairs grazed her nose, his stiffening dick brushed against her lips. And when it became sufficiently hard, he stuffed it inside her mouth.

"Oh, shit. Yeah, baby," shouted the man beneath her as he gave several hard thrusts.

Mercifully, he'd come to the orgy prepared with a tube of lubricant, which he'd generously slathered on her anus. Otherwise, Milan would have passed out…gone into shock…or died. Behind her, the butt man cupped her breasts as he plunged into her ass, bellowing, "Hell, yeah, this is some good ass."

"Hey, baby," the chubby guy said, steadying himself with the heel of his hand pressed against Milan's forehead as he thrust in and out of her mouth. "Want me to pull out before I cum? You want me to give you a pearl necklace?" he wanted to know, mischief dancing in his eyes, as if dribbling cum on her chest would be as gratifying as receiving a set of actual pearls.

Milan thought about biting off the head of his dick, but reconsidered when she envisioned Ilka helping her gold key members dispose of Milan's mangled, lifeless body. Milan was, after all, a mere bronze key holder, a lesser member who'd defaulted on payments. Yes, she was totally disposable, she sadly acknowledged.

The drunken party of three was finally satiated. "You were great, kid," the burly man said, patting Milan's shoulder.

"Did you have a good time?" Dough-boy asked, sounding as if he sincerely hoped Milan had enjoyed being raped.

"Yeah, let Ilka know the next time you wanna party with us," said the third member.

Laughing and joking with each other, the three men left Milan inside the posh room with her blonde wig askew, sunglasses tangled in the bed linen, a pounding headache, and cum oozing from three different orifices.

The only saving grace was that the three molesters were all quick shooters. And they all had pencil-thin dicks, even the chubby guy.

❧

She wanted to bathe, rinse her mouth out with at least a gallon of Scope, take a handful of painkillers, and put this appalling disaster out of her mind forever.

Completely disheveled and burning with shame, Milan hurried through the vast lobby, wishing there were some discreet exit that would allow her to avoid Ilka. She hated that she'd been so hot and horny that she'd accepted an encounter with no questions asked.

Ilka sat in plain view behind her desk. As Milan approached, she lowered her head, brows knitted in concentration as she busily leafed through paperwork. The woman didn't so much as arch an eyebrow in acknowledgment of Milan's presence. The person responsible for her suffering had the gall to refuse eye contact, as if Milan were an irritant, a nuisance, something akin to an insect.

Humiliation instantly turned to burning anger. Milan's echoed steps screeched against the tiled floor as she came to a halt and stared daggers at Ilka. She'd intended for her glowering gaze to sufficiently express her indignation and her displeasure, but then she heard Ilka cluck her tongue in disdain, as if she'd expected Milan to make a last-ditch effort to plead her case and to once again attempt to reactivate her membership using vulgar dollars instead of the required credit card. Milan cleared her throat to get Ilka's attention.

Ilka looked up; annoyance crinkled the corner of her eyes. She sat up straight as if her swivel chair were a throne, squared her shoulders in a regal manner, pursed her lips, turned up her nose, and looked at Milan with the disgust of a royal figure subjected to the aggravation of a peasant begging for alms.

Overcome by a surge of rage, Milan quickstepped over to the desk, reached back, and slapped Ilka across the cheek so hard, the woman spun around in her chair several times. When the chair finally stopped spinning, Ilka huffed and gasped and sputtered angrily. "You've assaulted me," she shouted with her hand gingerly covering her wounded cheek. "I'm taking immediate legal action against you."

"Be my guest. Go ahead and sue me," Milan scoffed. "I'll have this sex den exposed so fast, you'll be the top story on today's five o'clock news."

Ilka opened her mouth to speak.

"Say another word. Don't make me get ghetto on your ass." Milan lunged toward Ilka with a raised fist. Ilka flinched and held up her hand defensively. But Milan restrained herself from hitting Ilka again. Instead, she pacified her violent urge by sweeping all the papers off the desk and then wheeled around and strutted toward the door.

Sweetie was right. You can take the girl outta the projects…

Outside in the cold fresh air, Milan beamed. She wished Sweetie could have witnessed her performance; she would have been so proud.

She discarded the wig in a public trash bin as she rushed to the parking lot. Inside her car, she inspected her appearance. She looked and felt terrible. She didn't want to go home just yet. Having to deal with Noah's urges at a time like this would push her to homicide. Milan paused at a red light and wondered how she could possibly make herself feel better.

She thought for a few moments and then it hit her. A big sparkly diamond ring would surely boost her diminished self-esteem. She made an illegal left turn at the intersection of Seventh and Market Streets, steering her car toward America's oldest diamond district, Philadelphia's historical Jeweler's Row on Sansom Street.

After admiring nearly a dozen glitzy possibilities, she selected a pricey four-carat, princess-cut diamond ring that the jeweler swore was flawless.

chapter twenty

L ater that night Milan bestowed the pleasure of her company upon Noah Brockington, allowing her fetishist future husband unlimited access to her derriere. Lying horizontally, she curled into a fetal position with her buttocks pressed against his face.

Of course, Noah had no idea of Milan's painful ordeal at Tryst, nor did he realize that his ass fetish was finally being put to good use. His cool, moist tongue served as a salve on her ravaged anus. Milan moaned softly as Noah licked the wounds that had been inflicted during the terrible act of sodomy earlier that day.

"We need to set a date," Milan murmured, seizing the opportunity to have her way while Noah was in a sexually euphoric state. "I went to a jeweler and selected an engagement ring. It's going to take about two weeks to pick it up, but I have to make a down payment tomorrow." Milan paused and waited for Noah to respond.

"Of course. How much do you need?" he asked breathily. His words, carried by a rush of air, tickled her ass as he spoke.

"Thirteen thousand," Milan said calmly. "I have to pay the balance—an additional twenty thousand—when I pick up the ring."

"Very well," he said without emotion and quickly resumed the anal play.

The flick of his tongue was no longer soothing. Noah had been at it for well over a half hour and the sensation had become annoying. No, it was worse than that. It was revolting. Milan grimaced in disgust. What had she ever done to deserve this torture? A woman with her exceptional qualities should not have to lie in bed with a sickly pervert for material gain. It was regretful that she hadn't been born into a family with money. "It's so unfair," she avowed softly, shaking her head.

To tolerate Noah's slimy loathsome tongue, Milan began to visualize her magnificent engagement ring. She mentally caressed the platinum setting and then found herself breathing hard, moaning, winding her hips, and pressing her behind against Noah's eager parted lips.

❧

At ten o'clock the next morning, ticked off that she had to suffer through a spur-of-the-moment "little girl" session with Noah before he grudgingly handed over the down payment for her engagement ring, Milan sped out of the driveway and careened down the private road that would connect her with the world beyond the Brockington estate.

Intending to impress anyone she came into contact with, Milan wheeled Noah's vintage car. A three-page to-do list was folded neatly inside her Coach hobo bag. She began her journey at a suburban branch of Wachovia Bank where she purchased the thirteen-thousand-dollar cashier's check, crossed that errand off her list, and then zipped toward the expressway that would take her to the diamond district.

As she drove along the streets of downtown Philadelphia, the rage she'd felt when Noah had insisted she dress up was still with her, encouraging her to recklessly aim for potholes instead of swerving around them as she would have if she'd driven her own car.

Inside the jewelry shop, she was disturbed to learn she'd have to wait four weeks for her engagement ring. "I can't wait four weeks. I need the ring back in three weeks. Or sooner. Is that possible?" Feeling wealthy and superior, Milan waved the cashier's check in the face of the gleaming-eyed diamond merchant but clasped it tightly between her fingers as she waited for his reply.

"Of course," he answered, eyes shifting dishonestly.

Milan puckered her lips in thought. "I want that in writing," she said firmly. She finally released the check when the salesman affixed his signature to the bottom of a receipt that promised delivery of the ring in three weeks.

Back inside Noah's ugly yet prestigious vehicle, Milan crossed the engagement ring off her list and steered the automobile out of Philly and back to the Main Line where she had an appointment at the area's premiere bridal salon.

But the fitting for Milan's wedding dress was a total disaster. The seamstress, named Teresa, could not zip Milan into the size eight dress she'd selected. "This can be easily altered with more fabric or we can order a size ten," Teresa assured Milan.

"I don't want it altered and I don't wear a size ten," Milan said testily as she stepped out of the heavily beaded gown.

"Hon, if you want this dress ready in four weeks, you're not going to have time to lose the weight," Teresa said wearily.

"I'll be back for another fitting next week," Milan told the woman, pointing her finger for emphasis.

Irma was to blame. Milan was convinced the vengeful and jealous-hearted woman had deviously fattened her up by spiking her meals with wheat germ or some hidden high-calorie additive that had increased her weight and forced her into the next dress size. Milan sped away from the bridal salon, and slowed the car and parked when she spotted a high-end Main Line fitness center.

She needed a personal trainer, dammit, and she didn't have time to comb the earth in search of one. Certain that a certified and qualified personal trainer awaited her inside the ritzy fitness center, Milan pushed open the door.

"I'm looking for a trainer," she stated when she reached the reception desk.

The receptionist, a young woman who looked no more than nineteen or twenty, twenty-one tops, regarded Milan with mild distaste. "We're not giving out guest passes today; you'll have to pay the fee. It's seventy dollars." The young woman's snooty tone implied that she viewed Milan as someone unable to pay.

The nerve! It didn't matter that she was dressed in tasteful, expensive attire. Obviously, the silly little receptionist couldn't see past Milan's complexion, but that was her problem. Milan didn't have the time nor was she inclined to wage war with an insignificant, unskilled worker. "As I said…" Milan sighed. "I'm looking for a trainer. The cost is irrelevant," she added, haughtily.

The receptionist sighed also. "There's only one trainer available at the moment." She aimed a finger in the direction of a huddle of athletic-looking men, but did not specifically point out the personal trainer.

"Oh yeah, he's gonna charge you separate from the guest fee." She raked her fingers through thick lustrous red hair, turned up her nose, and looked away from Milan and squinted at the computer screen on the reception desk.

The receptionist's cool detachment aggravated Milan. The girl was overly confident and way too pretty to be a typical college student who worked as a receptionist to hustle up extra cash for books and pocket money. This arrogant girl had to be a local, a privileged Main Liner. Her vibrant red hair and porcelain skin indicated wealth, position, and power. Milan eyed the receptionist's attire. She was graceful and slim, a size three, Milan surmised, dressed casually in jeans. But not an ordinary pair of Gap jeans. She was wearing a four-hundred-dollar pair of True Religion jeans, something no struggling college student could ever afford working as a receptionist.

Yes, this girl came from money. Her daddy probably owned a fitness franchise. Milan, who yearned to be the owner of a string of day spas, felt instant resentment toward the receptionist, who'd most likely inherit the chain without so much as lifting a finger or even cracking a polite smile for a potential client.

When seconds seemed to stretch into minutes and the young woman still hadn't beckoned the trainer, Milan glanced at her watch and then at the receptionist. "Which guy is the trainer?" she asked, annoyance coating her tone.

"That one—Todd," the girl replied, annoyed that Milan had bothered her. Again, she absently pointed to the gathered group of muscular men.

"Well, would you do your job and get Todd over here so I can make an appointment?"

The girl drew back, offended. "My *job*! Oh God, I don't *work* here." Her slim body twitched involuntarily, her eyes rolled toward the ceiling several times. "My dad owns this place. And numerous others. I'm just helping out for the day," she exclaimed. She was so insulted that she'd been mistaken for hired help, her white skin became pink with indignation.

Daddy's little girl, Milan thought with heightened resentment.

"Todd!" the girl bellowed, her red-painted lips stretched to capacity.

A well-developed white guy wearing a tank top with the club's signature logo snapped his head toward the huffy fit-club heiress and then made a beeline to the reception desk.

Milan was pissed at how fast the trainer had jumped when the bratty receptionist snapped her fingers. No one jumped when Milan snapped her fingers, she solemnly acknowledged. Even Irma moved at her own slow pace whenever Milan barked an order. Milan looked forward to the day when she too had the power to make people jump at her command.

"What's up, Casey?" the trainer asked.

"She's looking for a personal trainer," huffed Casey. She remained pink-faced; her sour expression screamed that she detested being told what to do.

In an instant, Milan decided that she hated Noah more than she'd ever hated anyone on the planet. She despised him more than she despised Dr. Kayla Pauley and the Pure Paradise board of directors. It was Noah's fault that she—now a denizen of the Main Line herself—was being slighted and discriminated against and treated like a hood rat who had shown up uninvited to a society ball dressed in an outfit with a giant logo emblazoned on every article of ghetto wear, her teeth bejeweled with diamond chips and gold plates. She had nothing in common with the stereotypical urbanite. She was classy, sophisticated, and dressed tastefully. How dare a spoiled little brat treat her like common trash?

Had Noah honored her with a proper engagement announcement and an introduction to society, she would not have been snubbed by a freakin' barely legal Main Liner.

To hell with that size eight wedding dress, Milan suddenly decided. The wedding was off! She'd marry the pompous, tight-fisted pervert while he lay in his sickbed, propped up by his freakin' pillows. Hopefully, he'd drop dead immediately after the bedside ceremony.

The hell with all the tedious preparations necessary to make their wedding day perfect. The small fortune she'd planned to fork over on a stupid bridal gown, ceremony, and reception would be better spent pampering herself with high-fashion clothing, dozens of pairs of four-hundred-dollar designer jeans, tons of jewelry, and a solo honeymoon to Hedonism III in Jamaica to get her freak on the way she liked it.

"She wants a trainer?" Todd repeated, looking uneasily from Milan to Casey. Then he gave an anxious backward glance at the two muscle men he'd been talking to. "Today?" Todd asked, worriedly.

"That's what she said," Casey answered, glancing absently at her slender hands and neatly trimmed, unpolished nails.

"I'm booked up today," Todd said, holding up the palms of his hands regretfully. He gave Casey an apologetic look for having to turn away a paying client. Then, wearing a hopeful expression, he added, "Gerard may have an—"

"Oh well, I guess we can't accommodate you," Casey interjected. She wore a look of triumph. Her complexion, Milan noted, was no longer pinkish, and had returned to its former melanin-deficient Nordic shade. "Sorry," Casey said, singing the word and not sounding sorry at all. "Guess you'll have to take your business elsewhere."

Milan no longer desired a personal trainer or anything else the snooty fitness center had to offer. A litany of insults gathered at the tip of her tongue. Prepared to hurl the passel of contemptuous words at the unpleasant, smug young girl, Milan's eyes gleamed with malice as her lips parted.

But the words caught in her throat. Her pulse fluttered, and then raced, and she felt faint—unable to speak or function. Caught in a bout of sudden paralysis, Milan watched helplessly as a strikingly beautiful man with a shaved head strode past the high-tech treadmills, rowing machines, climbers, and steppers. His perfect body appeared to have been handcrafted from clay. His complexion, smooth and flawless, looked edible, like dark caramel.

He stopped and spoke briefly to the two waiting exercise devotees. One of the men promptly pointed in Milan's direction. Her heart thundered inside her chest. Like a trapped bird, she helplessly observed him. Her eyes, the only body part that functioned properly, beheld him in worshipful adoration as he glided toward her in sexy slow motion.

"Oh, here's Gerard, now," Todd said eagerly when the buff hottie approached. "She's looking for a trainer," he said. Gerard wore a muscle shirt identical to Todd's with the fitness center's logo in the center.

Milan sucked in her breath. Gerard's physical attractiveness put her on edge, and caused her body to become rigid. Insisting that her nervous system cooperate completely, Milan willed her lips to form into a smile. "How are you? My name is Milan," she said, using a professional voice. Then, she threw in a self-assured chuckle to cover her nervousness and said, "I'm desperately looking for a personal trainer."

"I'm your man," Gerard said, his low-toned voice oozing sensuality. There was a lilting hint of something foreign in his tone. Was it British? French? She couldn't place it. Whatever—he sounded exotic and sexy as hell.

Undeniably lust-struck, Milan experienced a strange sensation. She wanted to feel his ripped body, run her hungry hands over his broad shoulders, his well-defined forearms, his muscular back, and up and down the isolated muscles on his abdominals. Through the fabric of his cotton tank top, a rock-hard eight-pack was discernible. Her eyes wandered down to his developed quads and calves. She shuddered.

Though she rarely gave head—had never wanted to—her tongue craved the flavor of his hidden muscle. Expecting his dick to taste as good as he looked, Milan looked forward to the deliciousness of some hard dark caramel candy. Given a chance, she'd suck on it until he pleaded for her to stop.

For the first time in her life, Milan felt the overwhelming urge to kiss, taste, and touch. Never had she felt the urge to sexually please another person as strongly as she felt at this moment.

Casey gawked as Milan brazenly devoured Gerard with her eyes. Intending to put a stop to any possible hanky panky between the two, the young woman blurted, "Gerard, I forgot to mention it, but you have an appointment at noon."

Gerard pondered briefly, his thick brow crinkled. "At noon? Which client? I never book anyone at noon."

"Uh," Casey hesitated. "It was one of your regulars. The name's in the computer. I'll check it out in a minute."

No way was Milan going to let a snotty kid get the best of her.

She promptly pulled out a notepad and jotted down her cell phone number. "Listen, give me a call and let me know when you can squeeze me in." She gazed at Gerard with seductive eyes and threw him a flirty smile.

He accepted her number and returned the smile. The sexy spread of his lips had Milan wanting to spread her legs. Right there in the gym. On top of one of the weight benches.

Gerard wasn't ordinary handsome. He was centerfold material. No, he was more than that. His facial features and cut body exceeded male model status, his look was cinema worthy. He was sexier and better looking than Taye Diggs, Adewale Akinnuoye-Agbaje, and Denzel Washington combined. Milan wondered why Gerard was wasting his time training obnoxious Main Liners when he could be in Hollywood making megabucks.

Casey mumbled something under her breath as she eyeballed the piece of paper Milan had given Gerard. Her face turned pink again. Pinker than before, Milan noted with enormous satisfaction. And the way Casey glared at Gerard made Milan wonder if he was fucking the boss's daughter.

Probably, Milan decided. Gerard had the rich and commanding presence of an African prince. She couldn't blame the girl for wanting to keep the handsome hunk all to herself. It wouldn't have surprised Milan one bit if Casey threw a tantrum, snatched the paper from Gerard's hand, and ripped it to shreds.

But Casey never got the chance. Gerard folded the paper and stuck it in the side pocket of his loose-fitting shorts.

Mission accomplished! The way Gerard smiled at her, one would have thought she'd put pen to paper and divulged her carnal desire: *Wet pussy looking for hard dick!* But she hadn't. Her cell number was the only thing she'd written down. It was obvious to Milan that Gerard wanted her as badly as she wanted him. She was deliriously happy.

Beaming, Milan pranced toward the exit sign.

chapter twenty-one

Back home, Milan daydreamed about Gerard as she munched on a salad she'd prepared herself. She didn't trust Irma messing around with her food anymore. Clearly the woman would have to go. But getting rid of Irma, she realized, was something she'd have to discuss with Noah. Convincing him that Irma was sneakily trying to ruin her figure might not be an easy endeavor.

After eating, she glided to Noah's room to break the news of their down-sized nuptials.

"Excuse us, please," she said, politely dismissing Ruth Henry, who was reading to Noah from one of his boring leather-bound books. The nurse had the nerve to cut her eye at Noah as if she expected him to protest. Milan felt her temper mounting. "Excuse us!" She used a stronger tone, which prompted the nurse to close the book and jump to her feet. The woman was doing more freakin' reading than nursing, but then again, there wasn't much else for her to do since caring for Noah only required restorative walking and dispensing his medication.

Ruth Henry scurried away and Milan settled into the chair the nurse had vacated. Leaning forward, hands clasped in front of her, she looked Noah in the eye.

"Yes?" Noah's eyes gleamed with sexual expectation as if Milan had interrupted his reading time because she was overcome with a sudden and urgent need to get into something freaky.

She hated the way his filthy mind stayed in the gutter. Pretending not to have noticed his lecherous look, Milan smiled pleasantly. "I've been doing some thinking," she said, unclasping her hands and gently stroking his scrawny wrist.

Noah tilted his head; the gleaming eyes became dull and narrowed with suspicion. "How much money are you trying to extort from me now?"

Milan gave a soft burst of laughter and patted Noah's hand. "I didn't come to your room to ask for more money."

"Oh, no?" He had that raunchy look again, which she again chose to ignore.

"Not at all," Milan said, smoothing the hair on the back of his hand. "Darling, I've been selfish," she whispered with a contrite head shake. "I truly value our time together. Only the good Lord knows how much time we have left." Her words trailed off as she gave a dramatic sigh of regret. "So, instead of wasting time with a big circus of a wedding, I've decided to streamline our marriage plans." She gazed at Noah.

"Fluff my pillow, would you, my dear?" he asked, though they both knew she'd just been given an order.

Milan readjusted the pillows, but it took a large amount of self-restraint to not take one of the pillows and smother the slimy bastard to death.

"Go on," Noah said when Milan resumed her seat.

"I want to have our wedding ceremony here at home. There's no reason for you to leave your room. The minister can marry us right here." She paused and gave a hand gesture. "I was thinking we could have a bedside ceremony when the ring is ready in about three weeks."

"Bedside ceremony?" Noah asked, thoughtfully stroking his chin. "Splendid idea," he remarked a moment later.

Ugh! She hated the way he spoke. *"Splendid idea!" He's so freakin' full of it.*

Still, despite Noah's annoying patterns of speech, Milan was delighted that he had so readily agreed. Completely satisfied with the bedroom encounter, Milan stood. She gave Noah a quick peck on the cheek and turned to leave.

He cleared his throat. "My dear?" The way the words were formed in a question caused Milan to involuntarily bristle.

She swiveled around to face him. "Yes, darling?" she asked pleasantly, though she wanted to pimp smack him for delaying her departure. She had a date with her golden dick—a mechanical quickie to tide her over until Gerard gave her the real thing.

"I know it's been quite a while…" Noah wore an awkward expression. "If it's not too much trouble, I'd appreciate a soothing."

A soothing! Oh no! She'd thought those days were over. She'd rather plunge her finger into a pot of boiling water than stick it up Noah's sagging ass. Thoughts zoomed inside her head as she tried to think of a way to get out of the distasteful act.

"Use the pineapple massage oil," Noah told her. The finality in his tone informed her that he intended to have his way. With amazing agility, Noah flipped over. Lying on his stomach, he closed his eyes and waited.

Furious, Milan yanked the doors of the armoire open. That book-reading nurse had better get prepared to add anal massaging to her job description because this would be the last freakin' time Milan touched Noah's nasty ass.

⚜

Milan found Ruth Henry kicked back in the library, engrossed in a book. She sprang the news of the soothing as gently as she could.

"There's nothing clinical about anal penetration. It's improper," Ruth Henry sputtered, objecting to the revision of her nursing duties. "I refuse."

"Suit yourself," Milan said with a shrug. She held out her hand, gesturing for the nurse to hand over the leather volume she'd been reading. Ruth Henry reluctantly relinquished the book. "I doubt that your next assignment will be this easy," Milan said with a sneer. "Where else will you be allowed to idly wile away your work day lounging inside your patient's extensive personal library?"

Ruth Henry looked away, worried. Finally, she met Milan's gaze. "How often do I have to administer this, uh, soothing?"

"I'd like you to give Mr. Brockington a ten-minute daily back rub—once a day after he's had lunch—after which you can give his soothing."

Reflexively, the nurse flinched. Her eyes darted about the room, looking at everything except Milan as she considered the immoral proposition. "I'll have to wear surgical gloves," she finally said. "I insist," she blurted before Milan had spoken a word.

Milan shrugged. "Whatever." She handed over the book and Ruth Henry clutched the tome as if it were a long lost-lover. *What a nutcase!* "Oh, one more thing. Make sure you thoroughly clean Mr. Brockington after he ejaculates," Milan said calmly, as though asking the woman to make sure she changed Noah's soup-splattered bed clothes after every meal. The nurse drew back, balking at the idea.

The sudden buzz of her vibrating cell phone made Milan's heart flutter. She dismissed the idiot nurse from her mind and breezed out of the room.

"Hello," she whispered into the phone.

"Hey, it's Gerard." His voice, rich, deep, and exotic, penetrated her ear.

"Hi." She sounded demure. Girlish.

"Can we meet?"

"Of course," she said without hesitation. If he'd told her to jump, she would have asked eagerly, "How high?" It was the most incredible feeling, this sudden desire to please.

"Cool. Where would you like to train? Your place, mine, or at the gym?"

"Your place."

"I charge one hundred and seventy an hour, but I have to be up front with you. I expect you to commit to training at least three times a week. Can you make that commitment?"

"Yes, of course."

"You'll sign a contract?"

"No problem."

Gerard was direct; he got straight to the point. Milan liked that. She liked the idea of a man taking charge. He gave her his address. "Be prepared to work hard," he warned her. "See you at seven."

Milan, dressed in red-and-gray designer sweats, arrived at Gerard's house at seven o'clock sharp. She rang the bell. Waited. No answer. She pressed the bell three more times. Still no answer. She checked her watch. It was only three minutes after seven, but a gusty wind sent her running to the warmth of her car. Assuming Gerard had gotten tied up in traffic, she decided to give him a little more time.

Fifteen minutes later, her cell rang. "Listen, I got tied up with one of my clients. I'm in traffic now, about a half-hour away. We can reschedule if you want to…" Gerard paused, "or you can wait." He sounded as if he were testing her.

"I'll wait." Milan couldn't believe she'd uttered those words. But there was no denying it, she wanted to see Gerard too badly to balk about the delay. She'd work out a little—lift some light weights if he insisted—but she preferred to cut to the chase. She wanted to throw up her legs and let Gerard pump some iron into her hot hole.

Forty-five minutes later, Gerard rolled up in a shiny black Land Rover. He noticed Milan and honked the horn in greeting. Milan turned off the ignition and excitedly scrambled out of her car. She wore a broad grin to assure Gerard that she honestly didn't mind having to wait. Why she felt the need to be so damn accommodating was a mystery. She, a paying client made to wait, was smiling in gratitude that her trainer had finally arrived almost an hour late.

Gerard lived alone in a sizeable, well-maintained, and nicely furnished single home in the Overbrook section of Philly. He wasn't a Beverly Hills fitness trainer to the stars, so she couldn't help wondering how he was able to afford the expensive truck and his impressive home. Perhaps he'd inherited the property, Milan surmised as Gerard led her down to the basement, which served as a fully equipped gym.

"I'll take your coat," he said as he pulled off his own soft leather one. He hung both coats on a rack in a corner and pointed to a chair that was placed next to a desk. "Have a seat." Milan sat. Gerard pulled open a drawer and retrieved a one-page contract. "You can look this over."

Milan presumed the contract was standard—something downloaded from the internet. She pretended to peruse it, but couldn't keep her wandering eyes on the page. Filled with desire, she watched Gerard as he paced across the tiled floor. His high, tight ass aroused her. When he stooped to pick up a blue plastic mat, Milan fantasized about squeezing his ass while his hard sweaty body pounded against her soft willing flesh. Damn, she needed some dick!

Gerard took the contract after she affixed her signature. "I'll give you a copy at our next session. Is that okay?"

Mesmerized by his masculine good looks, she could only nod as he placed the mat on the floor.

"Lift your top, let me see your abs," he said in a matter-of-fact tone.

Self-consciously, Milan unzipped the stylish gray jacket and then raised the red cotton top. Though she didn't have a potbelly or anything, she was a bit ashamed of her lack of muscle tone.

Gerard patted Milan's tummy and frowned. "This area needs some work. Okay, let's get started. Hit the mat."

Milan didn't want to hit the mat, she wanted to hit the bed and tangle up the sheets. But she sweetly obliged, giving Gerard twenty painful leg lifts and twenty agonizing crunches. She couldn't hold her smile in place when he ordered her to do twenty bicycle maneuvers.

When she reached the last three torturous movements, she collapsed and said pleadingly, "I can't do anymore." Her face was contorted in an awful scowl; she knew she was not a pretty sight. And she was sweating profusely. Perspiration soaked her scalp and trailed down her forehead, drenching her hair and ruining her makeup.

"Three more!" Gerard insisted in the booming voice of a drill sergeant.

Emotionally, she found his commanding personality a complete turn-on, but physically Milan could not take anymore. "Listen," she said, breathlessly. "I'm really out of shape; I don't think I can do any more." She repositioned herself and grimaced as she struggled to rise to her feet. Her stomach muscles were cramping, they hurt like hell. "Why don't I just pay for the session," she offered, adding another facial contortion to express the depths of her pain.

Feet spread apart, arms folded across his broad chest, Gerard peered at Milan, a frown etched into the corners of his mouth. "You insult me."

"How?" she asked, clearly astonished.

"I didn't rush through traffic to watch you plod through a few exercises,"

Gerard spoke angrily. His eyes blazed, he seemed barely able to suppress his rage. "I didn't agree to train you so you could waste my time," he scolded. "I take fitness very seriously. I thought you were ready to make a lifestyle change, but I was obviously wrong." Gerard stepped around the desk, grabbed the contract, and ripped it half. "Keep your money." He turned around. "I'll get your coat and walk you to the door."

"No!" The word burst from her lips without warning. The intensity of Gerard's anger was insane. There was a strong possibility that she was insane also. But it didn't matter, her pussy was on fire and she was willing to do whatever it took to get back into her trainer's good graces. "I want to commit. Really," she declared, nodding. Ignoring her throbbing stomach muscles, she dropped down on the mat. "I'll do it. I'll give you the last three." Bending at the waist, she pulled her limbs into place and twisted her torso, alternately touching elbow to knee. "One, two, three," she shouted as she performed each repetition.

Holding her coat, Gerard stood over her, regarding her with renewed interest. Milan saw approval in his eyes and smiled. "Ten more," he said softly. There was a hint of tenderness in his tone, which seemed to promise a lengthy, thick, and long-lasting dick.

Motivated by the unspoken promise, Milan grunted and groaned through ten more excruciating exercises. At the completion, Gerard reached for Milan's hand. Gently, he pulled her to her knees and then released her hand.

Why didn't he want her to stand? Confused, she lifted her chin, her eyes searched his face.

"Milan, do you understand the nature of our relationship?" Gerard's voice was silk.

She didn't understand, but was afraid to admit it. Not wanting him to shove her coat into her arms and show her to the door, she nodded vigorously. Though the kneeling position made her feel utterly ridiculous, she sensed that Gerard would disapprove if she stood. So she remained on her knees, her face at crotch level. Gerard took a step forward. He pressed the back of her head, burying her face into his crotch.

She clung to him. Feeling his dick twitch and spring to life was bliss. At first she nuzzled his crotch, inhaling deeply, drawing in and memorizing his scent. Hesitantly, her lips touched the nylon fabric. She felt an urgent need to ravage him with her tongue. Hungrily, she began to lick his fabric-covered crotch, impatient for him to pull his pants down and stuff his penis into her mouth, choke her, fill her aching stomach with his healing ejaculation.

For the first time in her life, Milan felt uninhibited. Free. Free to give, free to be weak, free to totally submit. She was ready and willing to do anything and everything to please her trainer. Ah, so that was the nature of their relationship. She looked up at him. Enlightenment shone on her face.

"I'm proud of you, Milan," Gerard said, smoothing her damp hair while Milan resumed licking his fabric-covered dick. "I'm going to prepare a new contract. Is that okay with you?"

"Yes," she murmured. Her urges were unbearable; she craved his taste. Acting purely on impulse, she reached out. Slipping her urgent fingers beneath his waistband, she gave a slight tug at the elastic.

But Gerard took a step back, causing her hands to slide away. He pulled her up to her feet and offered Milan her coat. "I'll call you when the new contract is ready, and then I'll put you on my schedule," he said, his tone dismissive.

A few minutes later, Milan stood outside in the cold, still sexually frustrated and with aching abdominal muscles. What had just happened? Hadn't she done everything he'd asked? Why wasn't she upstairs in Gerard's bedroom, stripped naked, fucking him until her pussy was raw?

Hoping Gerard would have a change of heart, Milan sat for a few moments inside her car. Then an attention-grabbing yellow Hummer pulled up and parked behind Milan. An Asian woman wearing a full-length chinchilla got out of the flashy vehicle, dashed past Milan's car, and hurried up the steps to Gerard's home.

Milan watched through the frosted windshield as Gerard opened the front door. He and the woman embraced briefly in the entryway and then went inside. A sharp pang of envy knifed into the pit of her stomach as Milan drove off.

The Asian woman was probably a client of long standing, she told herself as she headed back to Noah's home in Radnor. It was just a polite, meaningless hug.

Determined to feel better, Milan resolved that her next encounter with Gerard would be a two-hour session. She'd work her butt off. And most important, she'd make sure she was his last client of the day.

chapter twenty-two

With agonizingly slow movements and cradling her stomach as if she'd recently undergone a caesarian section, Milan took faltering steps into the kitchen. The simple act of opening the refrigerator door caused her to wince in pain.

"What's wrong with you?" Irma asked, eyeballing Milan as she poured a cup of coffee.

"What's wrong with me is none of your business, actually," Milan snapped. "I don't want coffee but you can make yourself useful and get me a glass."

Irma speedily retrieved a floral-etched crystal tumbler from the cabinet and gave it to Milan.

"By the way," Milan said, narrowing her eyes coldly. "I want you to know that I'm onto your scheme."

Irma jerked in shock. "What scheme?"

Milan poured orange juice into the tumbler. "I've gained weight, thanks to you."

Irma's jaw dropped.

"That's right. I blame you for this agonizing pain. My body's sore from doing a zillion abdominal exercises, trying to get rid of this excess weight."

Irma looked Milan up and down. "I don't see any extra weight. But even so, what do I have to do with it?"

"You're spiking my food...possibly my morning coffee as well."

"That's ridiculous."

"You're trying to make me as plump and undesirable as you." Milan paused and waited for Irma to react.

Irma accepted the insult without batting an eye. "What could I put in your food that would make you gain weight? I give you the food you ask for and I cook it the way you want it. If you want it steamed, that's what I do. When you tell me to bake your fish and chicken and whatnot, that's exactly how I fix it. If you're gaining, it must be from the extra snacking you do up in your bedroom or when you're outside of the house," Irma said saucily.

"I don't snack." Milan snorted with disgust. "You've been putting something in my food, Irma. I don't know what, but I will not eat another morsel cooked by you."

"That's fine with me!" Irma responded and clucked her tongue.

"You're not indispensable, you know. Anyone can make Noah's soup! I'm going to speak to him this instant. I'm going to tell him that I can no longer tolerate your impudence. He's going to have to terminate you, or he can find himself another wife." Milan chugged down the orange juice.

"I wouldn't bother Mr. Brockington right now, if I were you."

"Who are you to tell me when I should bother *my* fiancé?" Milan put a hand on her hip.

Irma waddled over to Milan and spoke softly. "He was on the phone when I took up his breakfast."

"So what? He was probably speaking with his attorney."

"Well…I don't think so. He was crying…" Irma paused to let her words sink in. "Blowing his nose and bawling something awful."

"What did you overhear?" Milan asked, suddenly curious.

"He told the person on the other end of the phone that nobody loved him; that there wasn't a single soul on this earth who truly cared about him."

Milan couldn't deny that Noah's words were true, but she needed to convince him that *she* cared. She'd have to start behaving in a loving manner. She couldn't risk him changing his mind about their marriage. With her heart set on having Gerard—buying huge blocks of his time to keep him to herself—having access to Noah's money was more important than ever.

"No, it doesn't seem like he'd speak in such an intimate manner with his lawyer," Milan confided to Irma, momentarily regarding the woman as friend instead of foe. "Who do you think he was talking to?"

Irma scrunched up her face as she thought. "To be honest with you, I think he was talking to Greer," she said, twisting her lips in disgust.

"Greer! Why would he be talking to Greer? She's fired!"

"She is? I thought Greer was on vacation."

"No, I called the agency and had Greer replaced. I asked Ms. Henry to take care of Noah permanently."

"Does Mr. Brockington know? He was really attached to Greer, you know," Irma said, sounding apprehensive.

"No, he doesn't know. He doesn't need to know," Milan softly scolded. "As long as Ms. Henry is performing her nursing duties satisfactorily, Noah won't complain."

The slice of seven-grain bread and the hard boiled egg she'd planned to have with the orange juice no longer interested her. Draining the juice, she handed Irma the empty tumbler. "Where's Miss Henry?"

Irma gave Milan a look. "Where do you think? She's in the library; where else would she be?"

Slowed by her aching muscles, Milan maneuvered past Irma and then managed to whirl out of the kitchen. It was time for the nurse to stop her incessant reading and start earning her keep. Having his perverted yearnings satisfied was a surefire way of keeping Noah's mind off Greer.

Milan stormed into the spacious library. Sure enough, Nurse Henry was lounging, smiling, with her head buried in something by Shakespeare. Milan rolled her eyes to the ceiling. "It's time for Mr. Brockington's soothing." Milan spoke sternly. Her voice echoed inside the quiet room, startling Ruth Henry.

The book slipped from the nurse's hands and plopped into her lap. She picked the book up, saved her page with her own personalized bookmark, and frowned down at her watch. "I thought you said to give Mr. Brockington a back rub and…do that other thing after lunch."

"Change of plans. I don't know how to put it in medical terminology, but I need you to take care of him whenever it's necessary."

"You want me to do it PRN?"

"I guess," Milan said absently. "What's PRN?"

"In nurse's lingo, PRN," Ruth Henry informed her, "is the abbreviation for 'as required.'"

Milan narrowed her eyes coldly. "That's exactly what I want you to do. Soothe him as required. And it's required right now," she said bluntly and then watched Ruth's expression flicker from anger to acceptance. Resignedly, Ruth closed the book. The nurse had never asked for extra compensation or any type of bonus. Apparently, the fear of being ejected from the library motivated the woman to agree to provide anal probing—PRN. *Now, that's sick!* Milan thought, shaking her head disgustedly.

Ruth Henry caressed the book and then placed it in an empty space on one of the many shelves. Straightening her shoulders, she left the library to administer to her patient.

Milan's thoughts turned back to Greer. Her lips turned up in a spiteful grin. That greedy heifer would have to peddle her pills elsewhere. Greer could try every trick in the book, but she would never get back into the Brockington estate. Not with Milan standing guard.

❧

Milan used a pleasant-sounding, professional voice for the first three messages she left on Gerard's voice mail. There was an annoyed lilt in her tone by the sixth message. She marked the tenth message urgent. And by the fifteenth, she pleaded with Gerard, begged him to please return her call. But hours elapsed without a word from him. Clutching her cell phone, she finally fell asleep.

Early the next morning she was jolted awake when the phone vibrated against her hand. "Hello?"

"It's Gerard."

Milan's heart leaped into her throat. "Good morning," she murmured and excitedly sat up straight. Just hearing his deep sexy voice made her want to forgive his delay in returning her calls. But being a business professional, Milan couldn't stop herself from bringing up the subject. "I left a million messages yesterday," she said in a mildly chastising tone.

"Yeah, you were on some kind of rant."

"I wasn't on a rant. Well…not by choice. I'm surprised you're not more professional. Being self-employed…um…you know, I thought it would be in your best interest to return calls in a timelier manner."

"Milan," Gerard said with the patience of a tolerant parent, then his tone toughened. "You only needed to leave one message. I caught your drift, you didn't have to say the same thing over and over. When you filled my mail box to capacity, you prevented my other clients from being able to get in touch. That's bad business."

"I'm sorry. I was just so anxious to get started. I didn't mean—"

"Your behavior yesterday was a little over the top. I called to tell you that I've changed my mind about accepting you as a client. You're too headstrong a person; my instincts tell me that I can't train you. You're obstinate. Much too willful to submit to rigorous training."

Panic seized Milan. Wanting to get in better shape was just a ruse. She didn't need to fit into a wedding gown but she had to keep up the charade to be near Gerard and hopefully get in bed with him. She'd never had a boyfriend, never wanted one, and had most definitely never experienced the rush of first love. Was she experiencing love for the first time? Undoubtedly, she'd felt a severe physical attraction to Gerard at first sight. But was that really love? How could she know when she had no comparative experiences? Milan had always been strictly about self.

Her rational mind told her she was being obsessive, the way she'd been about her career. Perhaps she was replacing her lost occupation with Gerard, fixating on him to fill a void. Whatever the case, she needed this man. To her utter shame and bewilderment, she needed this beautiful stranger from out of the blue as desperately as she needed to breathe. Losing him was not an option. She'd say, do, and be whatever he desired. Nothing was more important than getting back in his good graces.

"I'm not willful," Milan protested. "I was excited about getting started. I apologize for my behavior. I promise it won't happen again."

There was silence on the other end of the line. Milan literally crossed her fingers as she waited for Gerard to make a decision.

"I'm going to put you on the schedule…"

Milan breathed a sigh of relief and then smiled broadly.

"But you're on probation," Gerard added. "I'll fit you into a half-hour slot for now. During that half-hour, I'll go over my rules and regulations. If you cooperate fully, I'll give you a full hour."

A half-hour? What could she accomplish in that measly amount of time? But she didn't dare complain, she simply said, "Thank you."

"I'll see you in an hour," Gerard told her and then terminated the call.

Confused, Milan stared at the tiny phone in her hand. He'd hung up without giving her any instructions. Should she be prepared to pay for the session? She didn't want to offend him with a monetary offer if he wasn't willing to accept payment yet. As she pondered the payment aspect of their relationship, the phone buzzed in her hand. He'd read her mind! She and Gerard had to be soul mates or something. Delighted, she flipped it open. "Hi," she gushed happily.

"You sure sound cheerful," Sweetie said, suspiciously. "What's up? Did that old man croak or something?"

"Damn. You have such horrible timing. I was expecting a call from someone else."

"My bad. Excuse me for intruding," Sweetie said sarcastically. "Dang. Can't even be nice to you."

"I'm sorry, Sweetie, my mind is on something else right now."

"Something other than your lavish wedding? Now, that's a surprise. Anyway, I had some free time and was just calling to find out if you needed me to do anything, but never mind. I'll just continue to do what you always accuse me of doing—put up my feet, yak on the phone, and watch TV."

Milan sighed. "The wedding is off."

Sweetie gasped. "You're kidding. What happened? Ol' Dude caught on to your schemin,' gold-diggin' ass?"

"You're so crude. In response to your question, Noah didn't catch on to anything. We're still getting married. But I've decided that due to his declining health, a big extravaganza wouldn't be in his best interests."

"Hmm. You're talkin' to your big sis. And I know you like the back of my hand. What's the real reason you're calling off the big shindig? Is Ol' Dude refusing to pay or did you decide to spend all that money on something else?"

"Sweetie, go play sleuth with someone else. I told you the reason. Now, I have to go. I have somewhere to be in less than an hour."

"Hold up. What about all that cake you promised? I held up my end of the bargain—you still gon' break me and Quantez off?"

"Yes, Sweetie, you and Quantez will benefit when I marry Noah," Milan said, shaking her head in exasperation. "Look, I have to go; I'll talk to you later."

There wasn't enough time to look her best. In less than fifteen minutes, Milan threw together a barely presentable look, dashed past Noah's bedroom, and raced down the stairs and out the front door.

chapter twenty-three

Milan rang Gerard's doorbell several times but he didn't answer. The sight of his truck parked in front of his house was comforting. At least he was home, not miles away stuck in traffic. It wasn't as cold as the day before and she didn't mind waiting outside, so she went back to her car and sat. Patiently, she applied mascara and lip gloss and fussed with her hair. Forty minutes later, Gerard opened the front door. Any lingering doubt that she was prepared to do anything he demanded quickly faded the moment she saw his face. He was the picture of masculine perfection. She immediately felt a sense of overwhelming gratitude at being given a second chance.

On some level, she realized that her feelings for Gerard went beyond a passing interest. She had willingly crossed a threshold and embraced a new lifestyle. It was such a contradiction of her personality for strong-willed and feisty Milan Walden to allow Gerard to subdue her. But there was no denying that obeying Gerard and submitting to his will aroused her, making her pussy throb with expectancy.

The visual she'd held in her mind for the past few days did not do Gerard justice. In person, she was reminded that he was unnaturally handsome, without flaw. Gerard wore sweats and flaunted his biceps in a sleeveless T-shirt. His feet, exposed in a pair of black Armani flip-flops, were smooth and manicured. His shaved head was shaped perfectly. Milan felt warmed by his magnificent presence.

Instead of going down to the basement, Gerard motioned for Milan to take a seat in the living room. It was toasty and warm inside, but he didn't offer to take her coat. Though she wore cashmere-lined leather gloves and had a wool scarf draped loosely around her neck, she didn't dare remove any article of outerwear or even unbutton her coat without Gerard's explicit permission.

He sat in a chair that faced her and folded his hands. "I asked you if you understood the nature of our relationship. You told me that you did. I don't happen to believe that you do."

She didn't protest. She was silent, waiting for Gerard to continue.

"I can sculpt an ordinary body into a work of art."

Milan felt let down, but she didn't show her disappointment. She didn't really care about a sculpted body. She only cared about being with Gerard.

Gerard looked at her intently. "I get the impression you're not committed to improving your body."

Milan's face flushed. *Damn, I'm busted.*

"And that's too bad," he said, shaking his head. "To me, you're a piece of clay that could be shaped and molded into the perfect woman—my perfect mate."

Perfect mate! Now, he had Milan's undivided attention. Her eyes, filled with adoration, focused on Gerard's face.

"I'm glad I tore up the contract you signed," he said, nodding his head as if ripping up Milan's contract was the best idea he'd had in quite a while.

Milan's heart dropped. "I thought you were preparing a new contract?"

"I didn't get around to it. Glad I didn't waste your time or mine."

Unable to bear being dismissed again, she stared at him in dismay. Then she started talking fast. "I'll be honest with you—I was at the gym looking for a trainer, then for no reason that I can explain, I just changed my mind." Milan conveniently withheld all information concerning her pending nuptials. "When I saw you…" Abruptly, her words halted. She dropped her gaze and focused on her hands, which were folded in her lap. "I felt an immediate and profound attraction," she admitted. "Gerard," she said softly, "I've never experienced the kinds of thoughts that I have about you."

"What kind of thoughts?" he asked.

She forced herself to look at him. "Sexual thoughts. I think about you and me—us—constantly. My fantasies are so bizarre…" Milan paused, shaking her head. "I'm starting to wonder about my sanity. The freakish thoughts that run through my mind wouldn't be considered normal."

Milan's admission did not prompt Gerard's eyes to grow large and lustful; he didn't give her a sly smile or throw her down to the floor to ravish her body; instead, he asked with an impassive expression, "What do you imagine, Milan?"

She silently scanned her mind for an answer that would tantalize Gerard and keep him interested. "I don't care about myself," she blurted, shocked by her admission. Since when didn't she care about herself? Was that a true statement? With no time to analyze her own sick psyche, Milan forged ahead. Uncensored and unrestricted words spilled from her lips. "I want to fulfill all your sexual desires."

"Where exactly is this going?" He checked his watch impatiently. "Could you be more specific?" he said, obviously unimpressed.

Her stomach tightened. Gerard's lack of enthusiasm made her nervous. Fearing he'd soon become annoyed and send her home, she spoke quickly, "I see myself being controlled by you. Being forced to do any freaky thing you want me to do."

"Milan," he said, with laughter. "I'm not that guy. You have me all wrong. What makes you think I'd enjoy *forcing* you to do anything?" He gave her an indulgent look. "Take the other day for example. Did I force you to get down on your knees? Did I give you any indication that I was trying to do anything other than help you improve your body?"

Yes! You certainly did give me the impression that you wanted me down on my knees! Milan wanted to protest loudly, but instead, she said in a voice thin with worry, "No, you didn't force me to do anything."

"Then why'd you drop down and try to give me head?" he asked calmly.

She had to force her mouth to stay shut. What kind of game was Gerard playing? He'd pressed her face into his crotch, taunting her with the possibility of giving him head and then he'd pulled her to her feet. Squirming miserably, she felt she had no choice but to go along with Gerard's game. "I couldn't help myself," she said with a shrug. "If you would have allowed it, I would have done a lot more," Milan confessed.

Gerard nodded in thought. "I want you to know…," he said, briefly pausing to make eye contact, "I enjoyed our moment."

Elated by his admission, she wanted to flash a cheesy grin, but she restrained herself, kept her face straight and continued to conduct herself in a serious manner.

"You made me feel good by willingly expressing your feelings with me. I don't want to force you into anything. Dominating you by force would not be pleasing," Gerard said. "Understand?"

She wasn't sure if she understood, but nodded anyway. "I'm sorry," she said, sounding contrite. "Words can't adequately express what I'm feeling. These emotions are so new. I'm confused."

"I need you to articulate your feelings. I want to have a clearer understanding."

Why was he making her squirm? How much clearer could she be? Didn't he get it? She wanted him to take control. To own her. Milan swallowed nervously. "When I'm near you, close to you like this, I get a rush. It's more than sexual. The need to touch you is so powerful...when you deny me, when you won't let me see you, it makes me cry." Her voice caught. Pouring her heart out was embarrassing. Yet at the same time, she was intensely aroused by the extreme humiliation. "Gerard, would you please give me another chance?" she asked, humbling herself further. Though it was mind-boggling, she was unable to stop herself from begging. She was asking for another opportunity to touch him. To suck his dick. There was little doubt that she'd lost her mind. But she didn't care. In this moment, the only thing that mattered was coming up with creative ways to serve him.

"Let me show you how devoted I can be," Milan told him.

Standing with his arms folded, Gerard's eyes challenged her. "Show me," he said in a low tone.

Still fully clad in her coat and scarf, she slid off the sofa and sank to the floor and groveled at his feet. Her lips brushed the top of his bare foot, hesitantly at first, and then with much ardor. Filled with waves of unbridled passion, she urgently kissed each foot. She licked the sides of his feet, her tongue slipping in and out, caressing the space between his toes.

Accepting her desire to worship him, Gerard bent and patted the top of Milan's head.

Had she not been jolted by the peal of the doorbell, Milan would have bathed his feet with her tongue. Gerard looked at the door and glanced down at Milan. "Don't answer it. Please!" she begged him. Her parted lips were eager to journey upward from his feet.

But he slowly withdrew his foot. Milan moaned. It was a soft strangled sound. Again, the feelings of humiliation and rejection were oddly stimulating. Milan was past the point of ordinary arousal. Her panties were drenched, and painful daggers of desire shot straight into her pussy, making her clench up and emit soft cries of acute yearning.

"I'm expecting one of my advanced students. I didn't take your coat because I knew you wouldn't be staying very long. I'm sorry, you're going to have to leave, Milan."

Milan wanted to cry from disappointment.

Gerard reached for her hand and helped pull her up. Though he was kicking her out, the tenderness in his eyes made it a little less painful.

"When can I see you again?" she wondered aloud.

"In a few days. I'll call you." Before opening the door, his eyes swept over her. "In the future, don't wear any makeup or fancy clothing or hairstyles. I want to see you in your natural state. I want to see who you really are."

He opened the door, welcoming in the same Asian woman Milan had seen the other day. The woman was breathtaking. She didn't wear much makeup, just eyeliner to accentuate her slanted dark eyes. She was a natural beauty—the kind of woman Milan instantly despised. This time she wore an expensive-looking, white, waist-length, down-filled jacket with a fur-trimmed hood that shouted money. Her clingy workout wear showed off a to-die-for body. As if being a ravishing beauty with a great body weren't enough, the woman had the nerve to be rich.

"Milan, this is Ming. Ming, Milan," Gerard said, introducing the two women.

Besieged with envy, Milan forced a smile. "Nice to meet you."

"And you." Ming extended her hand. The gesture seemed condescending. Though the day would come when Milan would be rich too, until Noah's money was transferred over to her, she was still just ordinary.

The amounts of money Noah doled out were too inconsistent to make a difference in her current financial status. Since they'd agreed to wed, he no longer paid for her sexual favors. The money she'd managed to squirrel away would have to tide her over until her dying fiancé finally gave up the ghost.

In the meantime, the promise of his entire estate was supposed to be a comfort, like having money in the bank that you couldn't touch for eons. Feeling terribly impoverished, Milan gave Ming a quick, self-conscious, glove-covered handshake. She noticed a big gleaming diamond ring and a platinum wedding band on Ming's other hand. She was married. Good!

"I'll call you," Gerard repeated, opening the door wider.

Kicked out into the cold and feeling dazed, Milan took unsteady steps to her car.

chapter twenty-four

Milan stood motionless, shocked at finding Noah sitting in the dining room. He sipped his disgusting soup while Irma flitted around him, her chubby body moving with amazing swiftness as she reattached the Velcro-strap of his awful terry-cloth bib that had come undone. She reached over to smooth out the front of the bib, her doting gestures making it clear that her loyalty lay with Noah Brockington. The cook was sucking up so flagrantly, it wouldn't have surprised Milan if the woman had the sudden notion to hand-feed her wealthy employer.

Milan detected a healthy color in Noah's cheeks, which she found displeasing. Gazing at him suspiciously, she also noticed with much annoyance that he seemed to have put on some weight. What was Irma putting in his soup? Probably the same weight-enhancing substance that she'd used to lace Milan's nutritious meals. Did this burst of sudden well-being have anything to do with Noah's desire to produce healthy sperm? Milan winced at the thought.

Noah lifted a spoonful of the chunky milk-colored concoction to his mouth. Irma hovered nearby, her lips puckered as if prepared to blow and cool off the chowder with her own breath.

"Noah, what are you doing downstairs?" Milan said tersely. "There's a draft down here. Where's the nurse?" She shot an accusatory look at Irma. "We need to get him back in bed. He's much too ill to—"

"It was his idea," Irma said, sounding defensive. "After he got that phone call, he perked up and wanted to come downstairs."

"What phone call?" Milan asked Irma. She hoped Greer hadn't telephoned and put ideas in Noah's head.

"Don't chastise Irma," Noah interjected. "As she said, it was my idea. And by the way...where have you been, my dear?" He took a loud sip of soup. "Your comings and goings are becoming rather frequent. Do you have a secret lover, my dear?" Noah asked with a taunting glint in his eyes.

Noah's question, a ringing accusation, put the room on pause. Irma stopped fussing over him; she folded her arms, squared her shoulders and waited for Milan's comeback.

Milan was momentarily stumped. But not for long. Fast on her feet, she rapidly assembled believable explanations. "I've been looking for a nutritionist and a trainer. I need to be in the best shape of my life to carry and deliver a healthy baby." She cut an eye at Irma. "Oh, you didn't know, did you? Noah and I are going to be parents." Milan faked a big smile.

"Umph," Irma grunted, obviously displeased.

"I found a personal trainer. But I'm still interviewing nutritionists," Milan said and then turned her attention to Irma. "No offense to your lack of good nutritional information and low-level culinary skills, but during my research I discovered that certain fruits and vegetables were discovered to have extremely high levels of pesticides—even after they've been washed." She paused, noticing both Noah and Irma hanging on to her words. "I'm switching to an all-organic diet and it would be wise for Noah to consider doing the same."

Milan returned her attention to Noah. "A good nutritionist could create a more appealing and much healthier meal plan than Irma can come up with. And, darling, a healthy diet promotes abundant and healthy sperm," Milan informed her fiancé with a broad smile. Noah looked impressed and Milan sighed in relief. She had to give herself a "thata-girl" pat on the back. Milan always came out of any corner she was backed into, swinging wildly.

"I do feel a bit of a draft," Noah finally concurred with a shiver.

"What were you thinking, Irma? How could you allow him to sit downstairs without a sweater?" Milan chastised. "Come on, darling, let's get you back upstairs." Milan made the motions of helping her fiancé out of his seat, and then hissed at Irma, "Get that nurse in here!" Irma scurried away.

Moments later, Ruth Henry rushed into the dining room. "I'm sorry, Ms. Walden. I wouldn't have left him if Irma hadn't told me it was all right." Intending to exercise her newfound clout, Milan whipped around to verbally reprimand Irma, but the worthless cook was conveniently out of Milan's eyesight. Milan could hear her rattling pans in the kitchen. Milan sucked her teeth in exasperation.

As the nurse escorted Noah up the wide staircase, he turned and looked over his shoulder at his fiancée. "My dear, if it's not too much trouble, would you pay me a visit?"

Off the hook of having to soothe her patient, Ruth Henry smiled adoringly as if Noah had just said the cutest thing. "I'll help him out of his pajama bottoms," the nurse offered, her voice lowered to a confidential whisper.

Milan rolled her eyes. She felt like backhanding Noah. If he knew what was good for him, he'd drop dead soon after they tied the knot. Lingering around too long might not be a wise decision because she couldn't promise that elder abuse was beneath her.

She didn't know what Noah wanted, however, anal play was out of the question. She'd passed that assignment onto the nurse. Dressed in little girls' attire, she joined him in his bedroom.

"What a pleasant surprise. It's been ages since I last saw you. Have you been busy with your studies, little girl?" he addressed Milan.

"Yes," she replied in a childlike voice, despising herself for having to play along. But competing with that rich Asian bitch was going to be expensive. If she was going to outshine the heifer, she needed Noah's money more than ever.

Noah sat up straighter and narrowed his eyes suspiciously. "Have you been keeping up with your studies?"

With her mind on Gerard, Milan didn't know what Noah had just asked her. Genuinely perplexed, she shrugged her shoulders.

"And what kind of response is that?" Noah asked sternly. "Give me a straight answer."

"I don't know."

"No!"

She ventured a guess. "Um...No."

"And what has taken precedence over your studies? Boys?"

Before Milan could come up with an answer, Noah pointed to the nightstand. "Get the paddle. You've been a very naughty little girl."

Up until that point, Milan had been distracted. But now, facing a paddling, she was suddenly alert and unafraid.

Quite willingly, she retrieved the leather paddle and gave it to Noah. Obediently, she lifted her skirt, bent over, and exposed her bottom. Noah struck her, but of course, he was much too weak to cause her any pain, and his light flogging distracted her; relieved her from having to interact with him. With her back to him, she didn't even have to look at him. She was able to let her imagination run wild. *"Gerard,"* she whispered with each soft blow, pretending that it was her trainer who lovingly whipped her ass.

chapter twenty-five

Milan expected to be ecstatic when Gerard finally summoned her, but she was far from thrilled. In fact, she was profoundly disappointed when, instead of inviting her to his home, Gerard told her to meet him at the gym in Ardmore, the same gym where they'd met. She'd been looking forward to some uninterrupted private time with him, not grunting and sweating amidst a large group of anonymous people. And she positively did not relish the idea of another encounter with that little snob, Casey. Hopefully the spoiled-brat receptionist was back at school or on a ski trip in Aspen or wherever little rich bitches spent their time.

No such luck. Perched behind the desk was none other than the utterly detestable redhead. *Doesn't she ever go to school?* Milan wondered in agitation.

"I'm supposed to meet Gerard here," Milan said. She hated having to address the bone-thin brat.

"Name?" Casey asked, curtly.

Milan frowned. "Milan Walden."

Casey perused a large black appointment book. "He wants you to wait for him in the consultation room," Casey said, her lips pursed with animosity as she pointed at an open door across the room.

Milan's scowl deepened. She would have loved to get ghetto on Casey. Keeping her hostility in check and her head held high, Milan turned away.

"Excuse me," Casey said in a snooty voice.

Sighing, Milan spun around. "Yes, what is it?"

"The consultation isn't free, ya know." She sounded snippy. "It's two hundred dollars. You're assigned to two consultants. That'll be four hundred dollars."

"Two consultants?"

Casey gave her a sideways glance. "Is that a problem? I can cancel, ya know."

"No, no. I wasn't expecting two consultants." Hell, she wasn't expecting a consultation at all. Hadn't he already done a full body scan in his basement gym? But if Gerard felt she needed a second consultation, she had no choice but to go along with his request.

"Cash, check, or credit card?"

Milan paid in cash. Looking for Gerard and the mysterious second consultant, Milan scanned the room as she moved with lead feet toward the consultation room.

The wait inside the sparsely furnished room seemed endless. Milan apparently spent more time waiting for Gerard than actually being in his presence.

At last the door opened. To Milan's astonishment, Gerard entered with Ming. "How's it going, Milan?" Gerard asked. Ming, carrying a clipboard, was decked out in stunning pink activewear. Why the hell did Gerard bring his disarmingly pretty student along?

Responding to her look of bafflement, Gerard explained, "Ming recently received her personal training certification. She'll shadow me for a few weeks and then spread her wings," Gerard said, nodding at Ming proudly.

Milan felt deflated, like she'd been punched in the face, kicked in the stomach, and stabbed in the back all at the same time. What was going on here? According to her bejeweled left hand, Ming was married. But were Gerard and Ming having an affair? She needed to know. "Are you and Ming, um…?"

"Partners?" Gerard filled in.

Milan nodded dumbly.

"No, not yet. Ming is married to the guy who owns this place." Gerard and Ming laughed. Excluded from the inside joke, Milan gave a tight smile. "But in the near future, she's going to be opening her own personal training center with a team of experienced and highly qualified trainers, and we'll be working together as partners. She'll bring the capital, I'll bring my extensive expertise," Gerard responded while Ming silently beamed.

"You're married to the owner? The receptionist, uh, the redhead is your daughter?"

"Casey's my prize possession. She's my stepdaughter," Ming said crisply.

Before Milan could process the information, Gerard murmured to Ming. "Okay, we'll start the assessment."

"I need you to undress," Ming told Milan.

Milan shot her a searing gaze, then turned a softer look toward Gerard. "Is this necessary? You already told me which areas of my body needed work."

Gerard's face darkened. Remembering how seriously he took fitness, she was sorry she'd opened her mouth. "But I guess there's no harm in a second look." She chuckled, feeling like a complete fool as she came out of her coat. With Gerard and Ming staring at her, she felt clumsy and awkward as she stripped down to her bra and panties. Ming's presence in the consultation room humiliated Milan in a way that did not bring on any sexual urges.

"I want you to mark the areas on her body that need work." Gerard handed Ming a black marker pen and took the clipboard from her hand. Milan wanted to recoil but determinedly stood tall.

With her brow furrowed, Ming studied Milan as if she were an inanimate object. She placed Xs on both Milan's shoulders and then searched Gerard's face. He nodded his approval. She put a big X on the center of Milan's chest. Stepping back to inspect Milan from a different perspective, she came forward, her expression intense as she vigorously marked Milan's stomach, hips, and thighs. Milan could have cried from mortification.

"Turn around," Ming said sharply. To prove to Gerard that she was serious about fitness, Milan obeyed the Asian bitch's stern order. She flinched at the feeling of the cold marker tip as Ming drew Xs up and down the length of her back. Milan prayed Gerard had not given Ming an indelible marker.

"Pull down your panties, I want to take a look at your gluteus maximus—the largest muscle in your body."

Milan's face grew hot with embarrassment. She cut her eyes at Gerard.

"She has to assess your body, Milan. Do as she says."

Cringing, Milan pulled down her panties.

"Clench your glutes," Ming demanded.

Milan quickly obeyed, tightening her butt muscles.

"She doesn't have much of a butt," Ming remarked with a tsk. "Unclench," she ordered. Again, Milan did as she was told. "It's small but saggy," Ming told Gerard, disgust coating her words. She marked each butt cheek with long angry strokes.

"All right, cover your butt," Ming said snippily. She gave a soft but disrespectful smack to Milan's ass. With a flurry of Xs, she finished off the back of Milan's thighs and legs. "Put your clothes on," Ming barked.

While Gerard and Ming observed her, Milan got dressed. Hurriedly, she stuck her legs into her sweats, pulled her top over her head. Had Milan been light complexioned like Sweetie, her face would be a bright red. Mercifully, her dark complexion hid her burning shame.

"Great job, Ming," Gerard told the Asian woman.

"Thank you," Ming sang the two words as she snapped the cap on the marker pen.

"Milan," Gerard said, "congratulations, you're in." He gave her a big smile. "You've proven yourself. I'll train you in my home gym. As I told you, my fee is one hundred and seventy per session. You'll need at least three sessions a week. We don't need a contract, do we?"

"No, I won't miss a session," Milan said eagerly.

"Cool. I'll see you tomorrow at noon."

She'd endured Ming's cold pen and stinging criticism. And now she'd finally have Gerard all to herself. For Milan, tomorrow couldn't come fast enough.

❧

With dollar signs in her eyes Milan paid Noah a late-night visit. She skipped into his bedroom suite dressed in a frilly yellow polka-dot dress with white ruffled anklets.

Having to pay Gerard a little over five hundred a week would deplete her savings in no time. Noah was going to have to supplement her income. Discussing money with Noah had become quite awkward, but she sincerely hoped they could work out a payment arrangement.

Noah didn't so much as blink or nod in approval when she approached dressed in the fantasy costume. She hated it when he didn't respond appropriately to the effort she put into fulfilling his perverted desires. The man had such gall.

"I noticed a great deal of dust while dining downstairs this afternoon. It appears the house isn't being properly cared for. Perhaps doing housework as well as preparing meals is overwhelming for poor Irma," Noah stated when Milan entered his room. She hadn't planned on discussing the appearance of his home and she couldn't have cared less about Irma's work load.

"You're absolutely right. I'll look into a cleaning service tomorrow," Milan said, quickly.

"Good idea. Now, when is your ring being delivered? You should contact the jeweler and tell him to put a rush on the order."

Milan regarded Noah with a look of bafflement. Since when was he interested in anything that concerned the wedding other than trying to entangle her into an absurd legal commitment to bear his child?

Responding to her perplexed expression, Noah said, "I had a telephone call today."

Milan's ears perked up. She was relieved that he'd finally decided to shed some light on his clandestine phone calls.

"I invited my dearest friends, a chap named Hayden McIntyre and his wife, Emma, to our wedding. They're prominent people, very influential, and Hayden has agreed to be my best man. Knowing that my time is limited..." Noah Brockington sighed, closed his eyes, and wrung his hands as if he now dreaded the imminent death he'd claimed to have made peace with. "Hayden was rather taken aback when I told him we hadn't set a definite date." Noah waited for Milan to respond. She didn't. She was too stunned to speak. Noah had friends! That dear friends had materialized out of the blue and were attending their private ceremony was a bit unsettling, to say the least.

"With your numerous absences," Noah went on, "I wasn't sure when we'd be able to discuss our wedding plans, so I took the liberty of setting a date. I've selected the third Saturday of next month. Hayden and Emma will be flying in from London the night before the wedding."

Three weeks! "Yes, um, I suppose, that date will work," she replied, her speech faltering. How dare he set a date without her consent! The time frame was absurd. And who the hell were these dear friends of his? He'd never mentioned them before. *Hmm.* On second thought, as long as they weren't money-grubbing relatives who intended to cut into her inheritance, Milan decided not to concern herself about the British couple.

She hadn't come to Noah's bedroom to discuss their wedding. She'd come to seduce him, to wheedle him out of a couple thousand to pay for extended playtime with Gerard. With money on her mind, Milan took a seat on the side of Noah's bed and stroked his arm. "I'll get in touch with the jeweler, but I want you to promise me you'll save your strength and let me worry over the ceremony. It's customary for the groom to be spared all the pre-wedding drama." Milan hopped off the bed and twirled around. "Do you like my pretty dress?" she asked in a girlish voice.

"It's adorable," Noah said absently. He pulled out a yellow legal pad and a pen from beneath his massive heap of pillows. "I suppose we'll need a matching set of wedding bands," he said, jotting down a list of wedding essentials. "Have the jeweler pay us a visit. I'll need to be sized, and of course I'll want to take part in the selection. I want something with a vintage look."

Milan couldn't believe her ears. Why should Noah care about his wedding ring—a ring that she intended to slip off his finger and sell on eBay the moment he was pronounced dead?

"If the engagement ring you've chosen doesn't match our vintage bands, I'm afraid we'll have to make another selection for you, my dear."

Noah's sudden show of interest in the wedding was more than annoying, it was despicable. Wasn't his insistence that she bear his mutant spawn more than enough involvement? Now it appeared that in order to show off for his dear friends, he intended to overstep his boundaries and completely take over the planning of the wedding. Weird! But what could she expect from a nutcase like Noah?

Then Milan felt a flash of appreciation. Despite having to wear rings of Noah's choosing, a speedy wedding meant she'd have her hands on Noah's money a lot sooner than the projected date. Of course, she'd have to wait for him to croak to get the whole enchilada, but in the meantime she'd be entitled to a wife's spending rights.

It appeared that trying to keep up with Ming would be a costly enterprise. Milan had wanted to puke when Gerard announced that he would be spending an enormous amount of time with Ming after they opened their training center. *Their training center!* Envy burned her cheeks. Considering that she aspired to open her own day spa, she felt she'd handled the dreadful news extremely well. It would have been an incredible coup for Milan to have Gerard as *her* business partner. His expertise would be a great benefit to her and additionally, he'd be delicious eye candy for her clientele.

Ming had her husband's money at her disposal, enough money to lure Gerard into a partnership. But once Milan received her inheritance from Noah's estate, she'd finagle him away from Ming's training center. In the meantime, she thought with a great sigh, she'd have to haggle over every dollar she extracted from her tightwad fiancé.

"Darling," Milan said, dragging out the word and using a whiny tone. "Let's discuss the wedding tomorrow. I want to have some fun tonight." Slowly and seductively, she lifted the frilly yellow dress.

Noah reluctantly stopped writing and pulled his eyes away from the writing pad. "Not tonight," he said tersely. "I'm busy attending to matters that should have been handled weeks ago." He returned his attention to his notes. "Have you contacted a florist?" he asked without looking up.

"Not yet," Milan muttered, her eyes cast down to her patent leather Mary Jane shoes. *Damn!* Her chances of getting some quick loot out of Noah looked rather dismal.

"There's no kind way to say this, Milan." He cleared his throat. "Your apathetic approach to planning our wedding hints that there's a propensity toward laziness and possibly a lower IQ than I'd thought. That type of genetic flaw could have a profound effect on the intelligence of our off-spring. Perhaps I should rethink—"

"Rethink what? Our wedding?"

"No, I try to be a man of my word. I'll go through with the wedding, but I may have to rethink parenting a child with you. DNA evidence has proven that—"

"I completely understand. If you don't want me to bear your child, it's fine with me," Milan interjected, greatly relieved that Noah didn't think she was intelligent enough to bear his children. She was brilliant and she knew it; it didn't matter what Noah thought as long as he gave her his money.

According to a recent study, Milan had learned, it was concluded that men over forty were predisposed to father autistic children. Noah had a hell of a nerve being worried about her genetic contribution to the intelligence of their child when he needed to be concerned about the damage his old ass would wreak upon innocent offspring.

"My dear, instead of assisting me, you're standing there looking lost in thought. If you don't mind, I would appreciate some private time to try to pull together a respectable wedding."

"Of course, darling," Milan said sadly. Then, while she still had Noah's attention, she made a last-ditch effort to encourage his cooperation. Darting her eyes toward the drawer where the leather paddle was contained and back to Noah's face, Milan said, "I guess I've been a very naughty girl."

"Indeed you have. And what happens to naughty girls?" he asked, his eyes suddenly bright with mischief.

"Naughty girls get spanked," she said, attempting to sound contrite while giving the impression of being a bundle of nerves as she dramatically gnawed at her bottom lip.

"No! Naughty girls are sent to their own room. Good night, Milan," Noah said sharply and returned to his note taking.

Milan was stunned. It was bad enough that she'd have to dip into her savings to pay Gerard, but being kicked out of Noah's room was an embarrassing disgrace.

chapter twenty-six

The next morning, Milan slipped past Noah's suite while he and Irma huddled together. She figured they were creating a wedding menu because she heard him remark, "Roasted Chinook salmon with white truffles is very impressive."

Milan deduced that Noah was dictating what he wanted to serve his prestigious friends.

So…Irma was finally being made to earn her pay. Milan figured Irma was probably freaking out over Noah's lofty menu. With experience comparable to that of a short order cook, the self-proclaimed caterer had to be sweating bullets. She hoped Noah's affluent friends enjoyed fried wing dings and soup because without an explicit recipe and preparation instructions, Irma was pretty much useless. She doubted the woman had ever heard of a truffle. *Lots of luck, Irma,* Milan thought with a smirk as she crept down the stairs and out the door.

"Welcome," Gerard said when he opened his front door. The single word—so unexpected yet so appreciated—resonated as if it echoed. With a smile in her heart and an overpowering desire to please, Milan stepped inside. As usual, Gerard looked magnificent. His smooth and silky dark skin always appeared to have a glow.

She noticed right away that Gerard's feet were bare. Even his feet had that luminous glow. Was he testing her? Would it be in good taste to immediately drop to her knees and kiss them in gratitude or should she wait for him to order her to do so? Milan wished she knew the rules of training. However, not knowing was intriguing and kept her on point. She hoped his bare feet were a sign that he intended to train her upstairs.

"Among other muscles, Ming marked your deltoids. They're easy to develop, so we'll start with your shoulders, using light weights," Gerard informed her, the welcome gone from his exotic voice.

Just hearing the Asian drill sergeant's name put a bad taste in Milan's mouth. "Follow me," Gerard said brusquely and headed toward the basement stairs. He stopped and slipped on his flip-flops, which were situated in a corner at the top of the stairs.

Milan was perplexed. Why had his mood gone sour? She didn't want to go down in the basement and work out—she wanted to stay upstairs and kiss his feet, suck his dick, and if there was a God, perhaps she'd get fucked.

In the downstairs gym, Gerard pointed to the coat rack. "Hang up your coat." He sat behind his desk as Milan crossed the shiny tile floor to do as she was told. She hung up her coat and dutifully waited for further instruction.

"You can pay the fee now, Milan."

With cash in hand, she rushed over to Gerard. He counted it and put the money in a cash box and locked it. He stood and walked over to gleaming rows of stainless steel dumbbells. After studying them, he selected a pair of ten-pound dumbbells and passed them to Milan. "We'll start with the military press. Your knuckles should face the ceiling as you raise the weights to your shoulders," he said, demonstrating the movement.

Forty-five minutes later Milan, drenched in sweat, completed the grueling training session. Her shoulders ached from performing a series of exercises that included the military press, side lateral raise, front lateral raise, upright row, bent over row, and twenty agonizing push-ups.

After performing the last push-up, she lay flat on her stomach, too exhausted to budge. "Great job," Gerard told her. "Milan, is there something you want to ask me?" His tone took on a tenderness that Milan hadn't heard before.

Not wanting to waste an opportunity, Milan rose to her knees and whispered, "Yes, there is something I want to ask you." She took a deep breath. "Can I give you oral sex?"

Gerard shook his head solemnly. "No, I can't let you do that." He turned his back. "Not yet," he said, walking away. He stopped, facing her as he leaned against the desk.

Milan, a few feet away from him, remained in position—on her knees. "Why not?" she asked, her voice cracking with emotion. "I did the exercises; I didn't complain."

"You're not ready. I want to take you through the stages slowly. Submission is a total lifestyle change."

Submission. Ah! He'd finally spoken the word. And the sound of it was at once exhilarating and humiliating, causing Milan's pussy to emanate intense heat. She wouldn't have been surprised if the heat burned a hole in the crotch of her pants, allowing smoky pussy fumes to filter through.

"Gerard, please tell me what to do?" she pleaded.

"Do you have any experience being submissive?" he inquired.

"No," she responded, shaking her head. "Not really. I role played with this older man, let him spank me with a paddle, but I was just pretending to be submissive. With you...when I'm with you, I'm really powerless. I want you to take total control of me."

"Why do you want to relinquish your authority to me?"

"I don't know. I've never experienced what I'm feeling now. It's as if I'd be willing to subject myself to any humiliation—even physical abuse—just to be with you. If you knew the personality I show the outside world, you'd know that this humble person you've come to know is totally out of character for me." She looked off in thought. "It's so bizarre and far-fetched, but when I'm with you, I feel this liberating sense of excitement knowing that behind closed doors the mask I wear is stripped away and I can expose myself—and show how vulnerable I am."

"I'm not surprised that others consider you a confident and strong-willed person. Because you are."

Milan shook her head. "No, deep inside, I'm very weak and self-conscious. My mother and my sister are the only people who know that I keep

up a false front. And it's such a burden to pretend to be someone I'm not."
Confessing had a purging effect. Milan felt emotional, close to crying.

"I believe it takes a very strong person to be able to submit completely,
to place yourself under the power of another. I've had lots of relationships
with women who expressed the desire to become submissive," Gerard
confessed. "I am dominant by nature and perhaps women sense it and are
aroused by it. Practically every woman who has hired me as a trainer
eventually wants me to train her on a personal level."

Milan felt an instant letdown. Intense envy enveloped her. Was Ming
one of the submissive women he spoke of? Milan didn't want to be a part
of a harem. She wanted Gerard all to herself. Hadn't he previously confided that he was looking for a mate?

As if reading her mind, Gerard said, "But it didn't always work out. I've
discovered that sporadic erotic power exchanges with a variety of women
have left me unfulfilled. Those women—my initiates or apprentices, if
you will—for one reason or another always fail to give me what I really
want. I'm looking for a twenty-four-seven life partner, not an occasional
playmate. I want complete ownership. A marriage of sorts."

Marriage? Milan gulped. Should she tell him about her pending nuptials?
The urge to be honest with Gerard was overwhelming. Maybe it would
be best to quietly call off the wedding to Noah and run off into the sunset
with Gerard. *No!* She shook her head as she quickly changed her mind. It
would be foolish to drop Noah when he only had a few months to live.
His money would ensure that she and Gerard could begin their life
together financially independent. Also, having Noah's millions would be
a surefire way to get that pesky Ming out of the picture. For good.

"Are you looking for a twenty-four-seven situation?"

Deciding that she'd just have to wing it and juggle the relationships
with Noah and Gerard, Milan nodded eagerly. Still on her knees, she
looked up and gazed into his eyes. "Yes, I'd love to." It was absolutely
unbelievable that this devastatingly gorgeous man wanted to be with her
twenty-four hours a day? Milan was flattered. Honored, actually. And
beside herself with joy.

Gerard looked down at Milan. "It could take months before I decide you've been properly trained and ready for a long-term commitment. In addition to achieving a perfect body, you'll have to learn how I want to be served, not how you wish to serve me."

Milan looked puzzled.

Gerard enlightened her. "You asked if I would allow you to perform oral sex. Once you've learned the art of surrendering, you'll know when it's appropriate to ask to service me. You'll be sensitive to what pleases and displeases me and know when it's appropriate to service me with your mouth or any other part of your body."

His words stimulated her. She was intrigued by the mystery that surrounded her new lifestyle and warmed by the idea that the time would come when she'd know exactly how to give Gerard pleasure.

"Going through a series of physical exercises is not proof of your devotion," he told her. "I won't agree to formally own you until your behavior reflects an enthusiastic desire to put my needs before your own. So let's start off with some ground rules. You are never to address me by name. Address me as sir."

Though Milan didn't dare ask his actual age, she guessed he was in his early thirties. She considered him an authority figure, so calling him sir didn't seem absurd at all. In fact, it seemed completely appropriate. Milan nodded in agreement. When Gerard gave her a hard stare, she realized her error. "I mean...yes, sir," she quickly corrected.

"The moment you step foot inside this house I expect you to bow your head and greet me formally. I'll want you on your knees occasionally, but being on your knees too often will damage their appearance and that won't please me. There will be some limits to the degree of servitude you display when we're out in public, but if and when you're collared—"

"Sir?" Milan questioned, not quite understanding the meaning of being collared.

"Never interrupt me. If you want to speak, ask permission. Is that clear?"

"Yes, sir," she said, looking at the floor, embarrassed that she had to be admonished so soon. "May I have permission to speak, sir?"

"Go ahead."

"I've heard of people involved in S&M wearing collars. Is that what you're referring to?" She felt equal amounts of fear and excitement. Did Gerard plan to lead her around with a leash attached to a collar? It was not the type of scene she would have ever pictured herself involved in, but for some reason the idea of wearing a collar was so bizarre, so kinky, she winced in sexual agony. Bending at the waist, she cupped her crotch and pressed her fingers against her clitoris.

"Why are you touching yourself?"

"I can't help it; I'm horny."

"Remove your hand. You need to exercise self control."

Reluctantly, she pulled her hand away. Being deprived of the calming effect of her fingers pressing against her clit was torture, a kind of torture that stirred her to an even higher level of arousal. Clenching her thighs together, she forced herself to endure the smoldering flames that licked at her vaginal walls.

"Look at me," Gerard commanded her. Her head snapped up. "Come," he said.

Milan did not stand. Instinctively, she went to him, crawling on her hands and knees like a bitch in heat.

When Milan reached the area where Gerard stood, he slipped off his sandal and began to caress her lips and her face with the ball of his foot. "You like crawling to me, don't you?" he asked, looking down at her.

"Yes, sir. I do," she replied between the kisses that she tenderly placed on each of his toes.

He pulled his foot away and slipped it back inside the sandal. "But I distinctly told you that I didn't want you to damage the appearance of your knees." He sighed. "I'm disappointed, Milan. Deeply disappointed."

Panic seized her. "I'm sorry; I forgot…sir."

"It's time for you leave, Milan. Go home and think about our session. I'll call you in a few days."

"Please, sir. Don't make me leave. I'm so very sorry. It was a lapse in judgment; I swear it won't happen again."

"Milan," Gerard said, using a patient tone. "I don't enjoy dispensing corporal punishment. It shouldn't be necessary this soon." He solemnly walked around the desk and sat in the swivel chair. "Obviously, the only way you're going to learn is through discipline. I want you to get undressed. Hurry! Take off your clothes."

"Everything?" she asked worriedly. She was sweaty from the workout and didn't want to offend him with body odor.

"Yes, get naked and lie on top of the desk," he ordered her as he cleared away papers and other clutter from the surface of the desk.

Milan twisted her torso to pull the spandex top over her head. Burning with shame, she stripped down to bra and panties. Gerard sat in the swivel chair and coolly observed her as she nervously shed her undergarments.

chapter twenty-seven

Butt naked and quivering in fear, Milan hoisted herself atop the desk. The wood felt cold beneath her exposed buttocks. "Should I lie on my stomach?" she asked, assuming she was going to get a spanking. "No. I want you on your back."

Milan did as she was told. No longer concerned about emitting an unpleasant odor, she would have spread her legs in a hot second if he wanted her to. She hoped fucking her forcibly was Gerard's idea of punishment. But she knew that was only wishful thinking. Gerard would not give her the thing she craved most, not this early in their relationship.

"Close your eyes," he said in a stern whisper.

She closed her eyes. She heard a desk drawer sliding open. Her eyelids fluttered in nervous expectation. What was he taking out of the drawer? A dildo? She preferred getting a flesh and blood dick, but wasn't opposed to being penetrated by a sex toy.

Then again, maybe he had a paddle hidden in the desk. If he intended to spank her, why had he instructed her to lie on her back? Waves of anticipation mingled with strong sexual desire caused her nipples to stiffen. Her entire body ached with desire.

Without warning, her nipples exploded in pain. She gasped and shrieked in horror. Something horribly tight had been clamped on them. Reflexively, her eyelids flew open. "Keep your eyes closed," Gerard commanded. Instantly, Milan squeezed her tear-moistened eyes shut, but not before Gerard placed a blindfold over them. Being deprived of sight was scary. And stimulating.

Something cold—a metallic necklace-like object—dangled between her breasts. She shivered and shook so badly, the necklace began to clink, creating a faint rustling sound. Through the haze of pain, Milan began to understand what was happening. Gerard had fastened pincers to her nipples. She'd seen the torturous devices in sex stores, in catalogs, on websites, but she had never imagined being tormented with the creepy-looking twin clamps that were connected by a metal link chain.

"Is your pussy wet, Milan?" Gerard asked seductively.

"Yes," she murmured.

"Wrong answer," he said and began to roughly twist the pincers, turning them back and forth until Milan uttered an agonized whine. Amazingly, her clit swelled in response to the intensified nipple pain. She clenched her fist and bit on her lip to stifle a moan as her pussy began to tighten with yearning hunger. Never in her life had she experienced a sensation that hurt so good.

"Is your pussy still wet?"

"No!" she quickly shouted, not wanting the pain to escalate.

"I'll have to check. Dishonesty is unacceptable, so I hope you're not lying. Scoot down to the edge of the desk," he ordered. "Put your feet up and open your legs."

Terrified and aroused at the same time, she slowly wriggled toward Gerard. As if she were getting a gynecological exam, she lay with her butt at the edge of the desk, her thighs spread wide, her pussy exposed.

Tenderly, Gerard separated her pussy lips as if they were the petals of a rare and delicate flower. Milan moaned softly. Having such a sensitive area touched by Gerard's magnificent hands was sheer bliss. It took every ounce of restraint not to hump his fingers and plead for any type of penetration—a fingertip, a knuckle, the side of his hand. As if annoyed by her uncontrolled moan, Gerard roughly pulled her labia apart, stretching her pussy lips and forcing her hole fully open. He inserted a finger and Milan shuddered. Her vaginal muscles clenched around his long finger, and her hips began to move.

He rotated his finger. "Does it feel good?" Gerard asked, inspecting her pussy.

She stopped moving. Unsure of how to answer, she muttered an incoherent guttural sound. With his face only inches away from her pussy, Milan was losing her mind hoping beyond hope that his lips and tongue would soon connect with her tingling pussy.

"What did you say? I didn't understand your response." Gerard's breath taunted her, tickled her pussy, made her pant and hump without shame.

"Yes, it feels good, sir," she admitted.

He withdrew his finger. "You lied to me."

"What?" she asked, her mind in turmoil.

"Your pussy is wet," he said accusingly and then wiped his sticky finger across one and then the other of her clamped tender nipples. The creak of the desk drawer opening put a chill down Milan's spine. What object of torture would Gerard use on her now? Could she endure more pain?

Her rambling thoughts were interrupted by the sensation of something cold and hard being stuffed into her vagina. It didn't have the shape or feel of a dildo. Whatever it was, part of it protruded from her vagina. It was something totally unfamiliar.

Milan jerked as if she'd been given an electrical shock at the unmistakable sound and smell of a match being struck. *Oh my God, what did he plant in my pussy—a stick of dynamite?*

"Do you trust me, Milan?" Gerard's voice held a hypnotic quality that eased her confused mind, and seemed capable of putting her in an erotic trance.

She believed that whatever was in her pussy was going to hurt her. Badly. But it wouldn't kill or permanently maim her. "Yes, I trust you sir," she responded, her voice filled with devotion.

The heat from the lighted match warmed her open thighs as Gerard taunted her with the small flame. Then the warmth traveled to her vagina. She inhaled sharply. "Do you still trust me?"

"Yes, sir," she said with an uncertain tremble in her voice.

"Don't move," he warned and lit another match. She wanted to jump off the desk and run, but she obeyed him and lay perfectly still. Without burning her flesh, Gerard deftly singed the pubic hairs that surrounded her labia. The crackle and smell of burning hair was horrifying, but she endured the punishment without flinching.

When he finished searing her pubic hair, he lit yet another match. Had her bravery incited him to take the fire play to another level? Maybe she should have whimpered and moaned. "Sir?" Her voice cracked. "I'm afraid, sir."

"As I feared, you don't trust me. Okay, Milan...I'll stop." He pulled the object out of her vagina.

Still blindfolded, Milan had no idea what he'd removed from her pussy, but she knew she wanted him to replace it. Not because it felt good, it didn't. The object felt foreign, cold, and uncomfortable. But being with him, even under the most extremely painful circumstances, was better than being away from him.

"I'm sorry, sir. I was scared for just a moment. But I do trust you. Honestly. I do."

He took in her words, but didn't speak. Then, he eased the object back inside her and lit a match. Milan heard a sizzling sound. Tiny sparks flickered against her inner thighs. In an instant, she realized that a candle had been inserted inside her vagina. She also became aware that the candle was lit. The knowledge that hot melted wax would soon spill on her exposed labia made her eyes pool with tears that dampened the blindfold.

An apprehensive moan issued from her lips. Gerard rose from his seated position and stood over her. His towering presence filled her with excitement and fear.

His full lips touched her aching clamped nipple. He kissed the distended, inflamed tit, soothed it with the tip of his tongue. Milan shivered in delight. Gerard nibbled at the swollen nipple before shocking her by biting deeply into the irritated flesh. At that exact moment, hot wax dribbled down between her legs, scorching her thighs and pussy lips.

Milan yelled. The sound was a mixture of passion and pain.

Her pussy made a squishy sound when he extracted the thick candle. Her labia, stiff and heavy from the dried candle wax, were stuck together. Gerard used his fingers to pry them apart; the pain was indescribable.

Milan grimaced from unqualified pain while Gerard peeled the dried wax from her enflamed pussy lips. "I don't like hurting you, Milan," he told her in a somber tone. "I hope I won't have to punish you like this anytime soon."

"You won't, sir. I promise."

"Don't you think you owe me an apology?"

Milan bobbed her head up and down enthusiastically. "I'm sorry for making you hurt me, sir." Unable to control her emotions, she began to sob. "Forgive me. Please."

"I forgive you," he said and then removed the blindfold.

She blinked as her vision adjusted to the bright room. Milan remained in position as Gerard returned to his seat. He softly touched her open slit. "Your vagina is beet red. Is it still sore?"

It hurt like hell but she didn't know whether to lie or tell him the truth. She opted for the truth. "It hurts very badly, sir, but I deserved it," she said. "I appreciate the extra training time you gave me," she added, pouring on the praise.

Milan noticed that Gerard's pattern of breathing changed slightly. He must have liked her responses. Without preamble, he dipped his middle finger into her open slit. With his moistened finger, he gently massaged her reddened labia, circling the tender lips until they glistened with her sticky wetness.

"Oh," she murmured.

"Does your sore pussy feel better?"

"Much better," she replied breathily.

He stuck his finger in deeper, rotating it as he extracted more thick, syrupy juice. Milan couldn't help herself. She pushed down on his middle digit, humping it like it was the penis she yearned for. Gerard's hand went suddenly still and then he eased his finger out of Milan's hot hole. *Oh no! What did I do?* Her heart raced with fear. She couldn't endure any more pain.

"Are you trying to steal an orgasm? Are you trying to cum without permission?" His tone suggested more punishment was imminent. "Your thieving cunt is undeserving of my finger."

"Yes," she confessed. "I was trying to cum without your permission. My pussy's a disgusting thief. A kleptomaniac. I try, but I can't control it." Again, she heard Gerard's breathing quicken. Her self-deprecating words obviously pleased him. She smiled to herself, delighted that she was slowly learning the way to his heart.

"I'm touched by your honesty but I can't put my finger inside a conniving cunt."

"I understand," she said sadly.

"Stay in position, but don't touch yourself," Gerard warned her and left her alone in the basement, lying naked atop his desk.

Needing desperately to be fucked with something, Milan moaned in frustration, but she obeyed Gerard and kept her hands to herself. A few minutes later, Gerard returned. He presented a large unripe banana. She longed to have his finger back inside her, but resolved to make the best out of the situation.

Sitting at his desk, Gerard took his time peeling the banana. When he'd pulled the banana skin halfway down, he inserted the rigid fruit into her throbbing vagina. Milan's starved pussy tried to gobble the fruit up. The soft moist banana skin soothed her injured vaginal lips and teased the sensitive hood of her clit while the phallic-shaped meat of the fruit provided unmeasured pleasure.

Slowly, Gerard eased the banana in and out, then increased the speed. In less than five minutes, Milan tensed, and her eyes became glazed. She made gurgling sounds as if choking from passion as the familiar tingling surged through her body. The building climax had a dizzying effect; blood rushed to her head. Her body shook and her pelvis rotated at a frenzied pace as she strained to reach an orgasm. Finally, her knees locked together and Milan writhed in mad ecstasy as she climaxed. Her juices gushed and flooded out over the banana, making it soggy and limp.

※

On the way home, Milan drove with her thighs separated. Her pussy hurt. So did her tits. She drew a deep, satisfying breath. The physical discomfort was a warm reminder that Gerard had taken the time out of his busy day to properly train her. Being humiliated was kinky and had aroused her. But being disciplined with nipple clamps and hot wax had taken her to new heights of ecstasy. Just thinking about what Gerard had done to her created an excitement that was evident by the creamy moistness that formed between her open legs. Mere humiliation and verbal abuse, though sexually stimulating, would never get her off the way the erotic merging of pain with pleasure had.

She pondered her new sexual identity. Could a person suddenly exhibit submission traits or had she always needed a firm hand to guide her? Gerard had said he didn't like to use corporal punishment, but he'd revealed another part of her subconscious desires that she hadn't known existed. With growing realization that she'd stepped way outside the parameters of what was considered normal, Milan knew that she would eagerly follow Gerard's lead down every dark corridor that lurked inside his mind.

chapter twenty-eight

Ruth Henry flitted past Milan wearing a smug smile. Milan figured the bookworm nurse was gloating because she'd managed to fill her voracious reading appetite without disturbance while Milan was out of the house.

"Did you give Mr. Brockington his soothing?" Milan barked as she pulled off her coat.

"Actually, no," the nurse said casually. "We were waiting for you to get home before I start the procedure."

Milan scowled. "What are you talking about? What procedure?"

Ruth Henry's face flushed with excitement. "I think Mr. Brockington should explain. He asked me to send you to his suite the moment you got home."

Milan sucked her teeth. She was getting quite sick of being summoned to Noah's room. She wanted to go straight to her own bedroom, have Irma bring her a meal, and spend the remainder of the day fantasizing about Gerard. But if she expected to stay in Noah's good graces, it would behoove her to go upstairs and see what he wanted.

Wearing a navy dressing gown and sitting up straight in the lush velvet chair, Noah Brockington looked amazingly healthy. It was a frightening sight. Had that smirking nurse been slipping him some new wonder drug? Milan wanted to ask him outright if he still expected to expire on schedule as promised. She'd been crossing off the weeks and according to her calculations, he had less than four months to live.

"I believe I owe you an apology, my dear," Noah said.

"Uh, you don't owe me an apology," Milan stammered. "I know you want to make sure your friends are impressed at our wedding."

"My dear, you misunderstand," Noah said with a chuckle. "I want to apologize for suggesting that you see a specialist."

Still confused, Milan squinted and nodded dumbly.

"As you know, I don't trust doctors and it would be the height of hypocrisy to insist that you put up with the poking and prodding of a physician when I wouldn't allow it myself."

Taken aback by Noah's sudden change of heart, Milan was momentarily speechless. Then, relieved that Noah had come to his senses, she smiled— a big cheesy grin. She'd never intended to go through with the pregnancy, she didn't even like entertaining the thought of having to bear his child. He'd finally come to the realization that someone as jacked-up as he would unquestionably produce a horribly deformed and monstrous baby.

"So, after putting our heads together, Ruth and I concluded—"

Ruth! When did he start calling his nurse by her first name? And what in God's name had the two creeps concluded? Milan braced herself for the distasteful information.

"We thought it best if you underwent at-home insemination. We considered freezing my ejaculation after she provides her daily soothing, but Ruth says fresh semen is more effective."

I'm throwing up in my mouth! Milan's hand reflexively covered her lips. Dry heaving, her body spastically jerked forward.

Noah ignored Milan's theatrical reaction. "Ruth's quite competent and will oversee the procedure. Considering my short life expectancy, I decided to give myself the gift of life before I pass on," Noah said with a chuckle.

She'd always known Noah was insane, but the degree of his insanity had gone undetected. It was time to get the hell out of his house. Milan knew she should be in her room quickly packing, but morbid curiosity kept her rooted in place. "The gift of life?" she asked meekly.

"Yes, instead of having you inseminated after I've gone on to the great unknown, I've decided to get started right away. I'll feel as though my time on earth has been worthwhile if you conceive my heir while I'm still alive."

Milan shook her head. "That's not stipulated in the contract, Noah. You can't suddenly—"

"My dear," he said in a tolerant tone, "I've added an addendum to the contract. It's in the top desk drawer." He waved a hand in the direction of the desk she'd never seen him utilize.

Walking as if in a trance, Milan went to the desk and retrieved the addendum. As she hastily eyed the legalese, Noah babbled excitedly. "Now, in order to determine when you're ovulating, Ruth will need a urine specimen and the exact date of your last menstrual cycle. But for back-up insurance, just in case you get the dates mixed up, I don't want to miss an opportunity. So we'll be getting started today."

Today! Milan gaped at Noah and then her shocked eyes went back to the first page of the addendum. It appeared that Noah was willing to pay ten thousand dollars for the first insemination, five thousand for each successive treatment, and an additional seventy thousand dollars when she successfully conceived. He promised to alter his will, granting her a five-hundred-thousand-dollar bonus after she gave birth to a healthy child.

With her jaw dropped and hysteria mounting, Milan was too freaked out to even string together a slew of expletives that would adequately express her rage and horror. She flipped to the last page that suggested that the original contract, which entitled her to most of Noah's estate, would be broken if she didn't agree to the new stipulation. Damn, she should have consulted an attorney before signing the original contract.

Noah gripped his walker and lifted himself out of the chair. "I'll want you to sign the contract right away," he said. Milan felt helpless to refuse the offer. In a trancelike state, she signed her name.

"Put the document back in the desk drawer. I'll have a copy for you in a few days," he said. Giddy with excitement, Noah gave Milan a smile and a flirtatious wink, but as far as Milan was concerned his smile looked like a mocking smirk and the wink resembled an unappealing facial tic.

As if all that wasn't bad enough, he then did something completely outlandish and totally out of character. Holding tight to the handles of his walker, he leered at Milan. As if he were a male exotic dancer, he gyrated and then did a double groin thrust for emphasis. "Tell Ruth to come at once. Tell her I'm feeling rather perky and would appreciate a soothing."

A look of disgust crossed Milan's face. She whirled around, hurrying away to pass the distasteful news on to the nurse.

Noah cleared his throat. "My dear—"

She stopped. She held her breath but didn't turn around. She didn't dare. Who knew how many other depraved tidbits were stockpiled in his arsenal, ready to be hurled in her direction?

"After you've delivered my message, please wait in your bedroom. I'll buzz you when Ruth is ready to begin the procedure."

She'd considered him too sickly and confused to take his vile and indecent proposal seriously. She thought it would be easy to outsmart a dying man. But she'd underestimated Noah. Now Milan was sick, sick to her stomach because she'd been too lazy to wade through the legal jargon of the original contract and too cheap to use her savings to consult an attorney. It was pure idiocy not to have an attorney go over the document word for word. Now it was too late. She was in over her head. Noah had her backed into a corner and she was too weary and unprepared to come out swinging.

Angered by the looming defeat, Milan flung herself on the bed. She lay flat on her back, listening to her heart pound. How long would it be before Noah's hoarse voice crackled over the intercom? She cast an anxious glance at the Waterford crystal clock on her nightstand. Like a time bomb, each tick of the dainty clock infused Milan with terror. How long would it take for Noah and the nurse to get their freak on? Not long, she conceded sadly. Noah was a quick-shooter; it would be only a matter of minutes before she was summoned.

Had she known the situation would take such a terrible turn, she would have kept Greer around. The greedy traveling nurse would never agree to Noah's scheme. Why would someone plotting on their own fair share of his estate willingly assist him in his quest to produce an heir? Hell, for the right price, Greer probably would have helped Milan scam Noah. But Ruth Henry couldn't be bought. The nutty nurse considered herself a straight arrow and wouldn't dream of duping her employer.

What am I going to do? Agonizing over her predicament and racking her brain to come up with a resolution to the problem, Milan sat on the edge of the bed and rubbed the back of her neck.

Figuring it was time to cut her losses and hightail it out of Noah's home, Milan didn't make a sound. Mentally packing her bags, her eyes bounced around the large room, trying to estimate how quickly she could gather her belongings and get out the front door without having to look at Noah's shriveled-up face.

Two raps on her bedroom door startled her so badly, she let out a yelp. "My dear, is everything all right?"

Incredibly, Noah was on the other side of her bedroom door. Astonished that he'd actually hobbled down the long corridor, Milan stared at the door in mute horror for several moments. The man was unbelievably determined.

With nowhere to run or hide, she unlocked and opened the door. Bent over his walker, Noah wore a warm expression. "You were taken off guard, my dear," he said kindly. "I hope this monetary offer will reduce your apprehension." Holding her with a steely gaze, he offered the cash.

"It's all there. Ten thousand dollars. Take it," he encouraged, his eyes narrowing, challenging her.

Reluctantly, she glanced at the money. Seduced by the sight of the bulky wad of cold hard cash, she gave a soft sigh of discomfort.

Sensing that he needed to close the deal quickly, Noah pressed the wad against her balled fist. "Come, my dear. Ruth needs to get you prepped."

Prepped! What the hell does that involve? While momentarily distracted by the puzzling thought, her fist unclenched. Seizing the opportunity, Noah slipped the bundle of cash inside her slightly cupped hand. "There's much more where that came from," he said, his voice quiet and compelling. The feel and smell of the money overpowered her, rendering her helpless to refuse.

With amazing agility, Noah hurriedly made his way down the lengthy corridor. The rolling walker creaked in protest at the increased speed. It was a travesty. She didn't feel at all like herself. She felt like a player in a dark comedy as she followed the squealing sound of the sick man's walker. Assuring herself that she was of sound mind and that she was making the right decision, she thought of Gerard. If she was going to pull Gerard out of Ming's business venture, she'd need all the capital she could get her hands on.

Other than having to endure a terrible bout of nausea, there was nothing else to worry about. She was on the pill and Noah was sterile. He had to be. His worthless sperm deposit could not possibly be a threat to her. However, the thought of having his repulsive sperm deposited inside her body was truly repulsive and made her flesh crawl. But if she were to ever get rid of Ming and live with Gerard full time, she'd need lots of money. Having Noah's money was essential. *I can bear this. I must bear this,* she told herself as she rounded the corner and headed toward the master bedroom suite.

chapter twenty-nine

nside the suite, Ruth Henry had set up a makeshift examining room. Milan bristled at the sight of the sheet-draped metal table and a smaller table with a measuring cup covered with Saran Wrap and carefully laid out medical instruments on top. Milan nearly passed out when she noticed that intermingled with the gleaming medical apparatus was, of all things, a plastic turkey baster.

The nurse wore a white coat, and a stethoscope hung jauntily around her shoulders. After assisting Noah back to bed where he was provided an unobstructed view of the proceedings, she picked up a clipboard and turned to Milan. "Have a seat. I need to ask you some questions and then I'll take your vital signs," she told Milan crisply. Her voice was filled with a self-important tone Milan hadn't heard before.

Somewhat dazed, Milan slumped into the velvet chair. Ruth asked her a series of questions: the date of her last period, if she'd ever had an abortion, was she taking birth control. The nurse listened to Milan's heartbeat and then stuck a thermometer in her mouth. "Okay," she told Milan a few moments later. "I have to check your blood pressure." The nurse wrapped the cuff of the digital machine around Milan's arm and pressed the start button.

"All right, let's get you prepped. Go get undressed," she said, pointing to Noah's private bathroom. She handed Milan a paper gown. "Leave it open in the front," she instructed. Next she gave Milan a small plastic cup. "I'll need a urine sample." Milan hoped the lab that tested her urine didn't detect traces of the contraceptive pills in the urine sample.

Obviously the nurse had been briefed by Noah prior to today. She'd ordered the materials from a medical supply company. It couldn't have been by chance that the woman was so well prepared and fully equipped with the tools of the trade.

The session with Gerard had left her pussy in such bad shape, urinating was extremely painful. While sitting on the toilet, Milan nervously ran her fingers against the hard, singed ends of her pubic hair and against her irritated labia and clit. There was no way to conceal the damage Gerard had done to her feminine parts. Besides, she feared the procedure Ruth was about to perform was far worse than she feared exposing the condition of her pussy. When Milan emerged from the bathroom, her uncooperative legs would not move toward the examining table.

"Don't be nervous, my dear," Noah called excitedly from his bed. Depraved as he was, Milan would bet her savings that the pervert had a hard-on beneath the covers.

Ruth went into the bathroom carrying a basin filled with soapy water. "You need to lie on the table with your knees bent and spread wide apart, so that I can see your vulva clearly."

Feeling like a battered warrior, Milan didn't ask any questions, she just did as she was told. Ruth returned, snapped on a pair of surgical gloves. She let out a gasp and gawked at Milan's burned pubic hairs and bruised genitalia.

"Can you please get started?" Milan snapped. Her pussy, she knew, looked like it had been to hell and back, but Ruth didn't deserve an explanation.

Shaking her head and grimacing, Ruth sponged the badly singed forest of hair. She rooted though the tools on the table and a razor materialized in her hands. "For sanitary purposes, I'm going to shave, uh, your pubic hairs," Ruth said, sounding uncomfortable.

Knowing that protesting would be pointless, Milan nodded. She stiffened in fear as Ruth brought the menacing blade close to her vagina. But it turned out Ruth was an expert. After four or five skillful strokes, Milan's pussy was sheared clean.

The nurse removed the plastic wrap from the measuring cup that served as a semen container. She stirred the nasty contents with the turkey baster and positioned herself between Milan's trembling legs.

Ten thousand now and five thousand a day, she repeated over and over as if the words were a religious mantra.

"I'm going to slowly glide the syringe into the vagina. I have to get close to the cervix to coat the outside and deposit as much sperm as possible," Ruth said, her head slightly turned as she ignored Milan and spoke to Noah.

"Good, good. Make sure you get it all in, don't waste one drop of that freshly ejaculated sample," Noah responded, his breathing heavy and lustful.

The nurse returned her attention to Milan. "Before I inject the semen, I need you to have an orgasm."

"What? This is starting to sound really freaky. Shouldn't this procedure be, uh, more clinical?"

"It is clinical. But you need to have a powerful orgasm," Ruth remarked. "Having an orgasm helps the cervix suck up sperm. It helps get more sperm up there, and may increase the sperm's travel speed."

Milan felt fury surging through her. Lifting her head, she yelled, "Are you crazy? How can I have an orgasm under these circumstances?"

"Well, what works for you? I have a vibrator on hand. Can you get a big climax from clitoral stimulation?"

"Use your finger, nurse," Noah ordered from his bed. "She'll have an orgasm quicker if you use manual stimulation."

Ruth squeezed the bulb at the end of the baster, filling the tube with Noah's vile seed. Milan closed her eyes. She couldn't bear to watch as she was degraded and defiled. Without permission, the nurse boldly massaged the hood of Milan's clitoris, rubbing it rhythmically with a latex-covered finger. The nurse increased the tempo and Milan's body unwittingly responded to the stimulation. When the veins in her forehead began to protrude and her breathing escaped in small pants, the nurse slowly inserted the semen-filled turkey baster.

The next day Milan underwent a second treatment and was paid five thousand dollars. She douched repeatedly before journeying to Philly for her training session with Gerard.

"My pet," Gerard greeted her with a smile. His honeyed baritone voice caressed her ears and had the effect of a fast-acting narcotic, filling her with instant euphoria.

"Good afternoon, sir," she replied and nodded in deference to her trainer. Her heart soared. She quickly pushed the violation of being injected with Noah's slimy sperm from her mind. Here with Gerard she could forget all her problems. Here she could be her true self. This was close to heaven. If she could be granted one wish it would be that Gerard would forgo the exercises and allow her to worship him without restraint. But her yearnings would never be considered. She was not there to experience erotic satisfaction.

"It's a great privilege to serve you. I'm here to fulfill your every desire," Milan said breathily and then dropped her eyes submissively. She'd done her homework. Through research on the internet and even in Noah's expansive library, she was learning the fundamental rules of the S&M lifestyle. Gerard looked impressed. He closed the door behind her and nudged his chin toward the floor, gesturing for her to bow down. He didn't grant her permission to remove her coat, so she dropped to her knees draped in full-length leather.

Gerard had just finished a workout. She could tell by the way his dark skin gleamed from perspiration, and she could smell his musky masculine scent. It turned her on. She wanted to bury her face in his groin, inhale his scent, but she had to follow the routine. He was barefoot, an indication that she should honor him by kissing his feet.

Adoringly, she kissed each toe and licked his feet. Gerard's fingers snaked into her hair. Grabbing a handful, he pulled Milan upward until her face met his crotch. With his hand holding her head firmly in place, she inhaled deeply, as if he emitted oxygen of which she'd been long deprived. Perhaps today she'd be allowed to fondle his dick. Maybe he'd let her stroke his dick until he came in her hand. With her head filled with delicious fantasies, she moaned as she took in his scent.

"Today, I'm going to give you a total body workout," he told her abruptly, his words catapulting her out of her private heaven. She was so overcome with disappointment she could have cried.

"Stand," he commanded. Milan stood up immediately. "Go downstairs and hang up your coat. Take off everything except your socks and sneakers. We're going to do circuit training for an hour but before we start, I want you to warm up on the treadmill. It's set for thirty minutes, and I'll see you afterward."

After Gerard went upstairs, Milan heard voices. *He's watching TV.* She gave a satisfied smile. She'd earned his trust. He knew that she would follow his orders without his scrutiny while he kicked back and watched TV. Having his trust warmed her. She beamed as she quickly undressed.

Surrounded by mirrors, Milan understood that Gerard wanted her to view her slackened body from every angle. Her self-consciousness about her body image would be an incentive to work harder. Alone and naked, she considered her reflection. The dark skin of her hairless pussy startled her; she'd forgotten that Ruth had shaved it clean. Her inner lips, no longer hidden by a thicket of public hair, jutted outward. No longer red and sickly looking as they'd been after being doused with melted wax, her pussy lips had regained their dark hue and healthy puffiness.

She could feel her nipples hardening at the thought of the sweet torture Gerard had inflicted upon her. She gazed at her image, then got on the treadmill. Exercising face-to-face with her reflection, she watched as her hand moved involuntarily, grazing her small breasts. Her fingers caressed and then pinched the swollen nipples. Her pussy twitched at the memory of the nipple clamps. More than anything, Milan wanted to explore her dark damp tunnel, but there was no time for self-indulgence. Gerard expected her to work out on the treadmill for a half hour.

At the precise second that the timer went off, she heard Gerard's footsteps on the stairs. When she saw his beautiful image in the mirror she gave him a proud smile.

"Good job, Milan. Now, I want you to…" His speech halted. A look of surprise registered on his face. Then a scowl of disapproval hardened his features. "Who told you to shave?" he asked sharply. He then pointed angrily in the vicinity of her vagina and abruptly paced toward his desk.

Milan hung her head in shame. She couldn't tell Gerard the truth. She suspected he'd make her leave—banish her from his life forever if he knew of her relationship with another man. "No one told me to shave, sir," she said and swallowed nervously. "I took it upon myself. I thought it would please you."

Gerard didn't comment. He seethed quietly, his silence speaking volumes, letting her know that a severe reprimand was forthcoming. Overtaken by fear, Milan held her breath. A quiver moved through her body as she awaited the fate that would be a duet of pleasure and pain.

Soft footsteps were heard coming down the stairs. "Ah, Ming," Gerald whispered fondly. Milan gasped, realizing that the voices she'd heard earlier hadn't come from the TV at all. Ming had been in the house all along; she'd heard them conversing.

Ming came into view, looking flustered. Her coat—the beautiful full-length chinchilla Milan had seen her wearing weeks ago—was draped over her arm.

"I thought we were going to spend some time together, but obviously you have other plans," Ming said, shooting a hateful glance at Milan. Trying to hide her nakedness, Milan reflexively covered her private parts with both hands. "I'll leave you with your new playmate," Ming said sarcastically. "I'll see you tomorrow. Sayonara, baby." Ming whirled around.

"Wait. What are you talking about?" With an expression of bafflement, Gerard looked around. "I don't see anyone else. There's no one here except you and me."

Ming brightened suddenly and gave Gerard a wicked but knowing look. Milan was completely mystified and couldn't take the look of bewilderment off her face.

"Now, go upstairs and hang up your coat," Gerard said warmly.

"I don't feel like carrying this to the upstairs closet. I'm too tired," Ming whined. She held out the heavy coat for Gerard to take. "Here darling, do something with this."

"Leave it down here. Hang it on the coat rack," Gerard told her.

Ming looked around dramatically. "Where?" she asked and shrugged her shoulders. "There's no room on the coat rack."

The conversation between Ming and Gerard was so bizarre, Milan momentarily forgot her embarrassment over her nudity. She twisted her neck to check out the coat rack, which held only her leather coat. Totally baffled, she gazed at Gerard and Ming. It was bad enough that Ming was in the house, but they were speaking in code and Milan felt like an uninvited guest.

"You're a creative woman. Milan's limbs are compliant, why not fashion yourself a coat rack?" Gerard suggested.

Though Gerard referred to her, he didn't give Milan so much as a glance. She had no clue what he was talking about but sensed that trouble was brewing.

Briskly, Ming crossed the room. "Take off those socks and sneakers. You look like a fool."

Milan quickly wedged off her sneakers and kicked them aside. "Take off the socks and get those cheesy sneakers out of my sight," Ming barked.

Cheesy! The sneakers cost ninety dollars, an acceptable price for a pair of sneakers. But Ming was wearing Gucci bamboo sneakers, so Milan supposed her own footwear paled in comparison.

"Take your Nikes over there." Gerard pointed to the vicinity of the desk. "Put them under the desk, Milan," he told her in an amused tone.

No sooner had Milan tucked her disdainful sneakers under the desk than Ming stormed over to her and yanked her by the arm. Dragging a perplexed Milan to the nearest corner, Ming gazed over at the coat rack as she manipulated Milan's arms, roughly bending each arm at the elbow.

With her arms held out at her sides, hands pointed upward, Milan's limbs were positioned to resemble the prongs of the coat rack on the other side of the room.

chapter thirty

Ming stepped back and observed her work as Milan, confused and humiliated, stood naked in the ridiculous position. She paced back and forth in front of Milan. "You've been reduced to an item of furniture; you're nothing more than a coat rack," Ming spat. "A very sturdy coat rack," she added with bitterness. "So don't you dare move. And if you allow my chinchilla to touch the floor, there will be severe consequences." She dropped the weighty fur coat on Milan's right hand.

The coat was incredibly heavy, and hot. But to get back in Gerard's good graces Milan had to function as a sturdy coat rack.

Satisfied, Ming pranced over to Gerard. She wrapped her arms around his neck. "I was fuming mad when you left me alone upstairs so you could be with…" She turned and glared in Milan's direction. "So you could be with that dirty trash with those big feet."

Dirty trash! Big feet! At that moment, Milan was ready to drop Ming's coat and whip her ass like she would have when her sister made her fight the kids who taunted and teased her back in the projects. But Sweetie wasn't here and Milan was without power. She'd lose Gerard if she defied his command. *Big feet, stinky stink, Milan.* She was sadly reminded of the terrible taunting she endured during her childhood. And she was as helpless as she'd been before Sweetie had taught her how to fight.

It was as if her life had gone full circle and once again she had to endure the jeers and taunts that exist in the life of a despised person. Admittedly, she was despicable. She supposed she'd always been aware of her wretchedness but had succeeded in fooling the public. She'd successfully convinced her classmates and later her coworkers that she was superior. She'd even convinced herself. For a while. But now she had to face the glaring truth.

Dr. Kayla Pauley and the board at Pure Paradise had finally come to realize her deficiencies. That's why they got rid of her, sending her right back to oblivion where she belonged.

Gerard had instantly seen through her façade. And she was grateful to him for allowing her the freedom cast aside pretenses. For as long as he allowed her, she would grovel at his feet, thankful to him for taking the time to teach her the many aspects of submission.

Gerard was an awesome trainer. Being relegated to the position of an inanimate object was humiliating and thrilling at the same time. It was also quite painful. She'd only been in position for a few minutes and already the muscles in the arm that held Ming's chinchilla throbbed. But knowing Gerard was testing her limits, she persevered, suffering through the pain.

"You always know how to please me," Ming cooed. It was the first time Milan had heard the vicious woman use a soft tone. Then Ming wrapped both arms around Gerard's neck. "Why won't you let me leave my husband so we can be together?"

"Ming," Gerard said, removing her hands from his neck. "A relationship between two dominants won't work. We can always play together, but a twenty-four-seven relationship between us wouldn't last. You know that. I've been honest with you; I've told you what I'm hoping to achieve with Milan. I want to own her for life and that's a very serious undertaking."

"Milan!" Ming screeched. "Why do you want to own her? Ugh. She's so unattractive. And she has those big clumsy feet. In China, her feet would have been bound at birth."

Milan cringed at Ming's insults. But other than grimacing slightly, there was nothing else she could do.

"Listen, forget her. You can be with me as an equal partner. If I divorce my husband, I'll get half his money. This house and the SUV I bought you are nothing compared to the fabulous life you can have with me. I could buy us a bigger mansion than the one my husband and I own. And

I'd be willing to share my beautiful submissive girls with you. They could serve us both around the clock. So why do you need *her*?" Ming asked, her pretty face contorted in disgust.

"I've already told you, I don't want a full-time relationship with another dominant. You'll have to enjoy the time we spend together when we open the training center," Gerard said firmly.

The training center! Milan was suddenly enlightened. Ming and Gerard didn't plan to open a fitness center, they planned to open a facility where they would train submissive people. It was a brilliant idea, but she hated the idea of Ming being near Gerard for many hours of the day.

Milan resolved that she'd have to use her submissiveness—her unrelenting loyalty and devotion—to win Gerard's love. Somehow, she'd figure out a way to get Ming out of his life, forever.

"Does that unattractive scum know?" Ming nudged her head in Milan's direction. Her malicious words brought Milan out of her delicious revenge fantasy. "Did you tell her that it will take years of servitude before she can earn the privilege of having her fuck hole filled with your dick?" Ming shot Milan a smug look and then returned her focus to Gerard. "How long do you think she'll grovel, bow, and scrape when she finds out that I'm the only woman deserving the pleasure of riding your beautiful, immense, black dick?"

Gerard chuckled. "You just had to ruin the surprise. I'm sure my little pet suspected that she would have to jump through numerous hoops to get it, but she had no idea of your position."

"For your information, little mutt," Ming turned her slanted eyes on Milan, "*this* belongs to me." Ming caressed Gerard's groin. The gesture sent a flurry of arrows through Milan's jealous heart. "Come, darling, let's give the big-foot slut a spicy demonstration."

Stripped naked and forced to stand stock still while holding up Ming's coat was humiliating enough, but she felt a powerful surge of shame when Ming and Gerard approached, inspecting her closely. "What happened to her cat?" Ming asked sarcastically, referring to Milan's shaved pussy. Ming bent slightly to scrutinize Milan's vagina. "What an ugly cat. It's covered with disgusting bumps. That's not a professional wax job; looks like she used a razor on her snatch." Ming turned up her nose. "Ugh. How primitive."

Ming's insults stung, yet, oddly, Milan felt a bead of moisture ooze out of her pussy lips. Ming saw the lust that bubbled out of Milan's vagina. "Look! Her bald snatch is drooling." Ming scraped her finger between Milan's pussy lips and held it out, showing Gerard the incriminating sap. "Her cat's creamy. This bitch is hot for you," she informed Gerard as she buried her finger inside Milan's syrupy pussy again and extracted more evidence.

Using her finger like a dagger, Ming finger-fucked Milan, daring her to move a muscle or even grunt or moan. For Milan, the stimulation was unbearable, erotic torture. She wanted to hump Ming's viciously probing finger, she yearned to spread her legs so her pussy could feel the jabbing pain more deeply but, denied the right to make a sound or move a muscle, Milan instead bit down on her lip until she tasted blood.

Gerard inched closer to better observe Milan taking the pussy stabbing. Milan's eyes darted to Gerard's crotch. The bulging outline that began to form in the front of his sweatpants filled her with hope. But that hope was quickly dashed.

Ming smeared Milan's juices over Gerard's crotch. "See how his penis grows big for me?" Ming slipped her hand inside Gerard's sweatpants and gripped the enormous dick that Milan had yet to see in the flesh. Then Ming grabbed Milan's free hand and lowered it to the crotch of her own jeans. "Feel what the touch of his big machine does to me," Ming uttered breathlessly. Milan could feel the Asian woman's spicy nectar seeping through the thick fabric of her jeans.

Gerard swept Ming up in his arms and carried her toward the stairs. Ming wrapped her arms around him and began uttering love cries and soft cooing sounds. Gerard stopped his stride. "Ah, Ming," he said, his voice filled with warmth and adoration for Ming. Then he leaned down and placed a love bite on Ming's neck.

Milan felt helpless and unworthy. Like scum.

Overcome with passion, Ming began kicking out her tiny feet. "Put me down, I don't want to go upstairs. Do me in front of your slut bitch."

"You want Milan to watch?" Gerard murmured, his accented voice a low rumble of sexiness.

"No, she can listen to the sounds of our passion. She is not allowed to view the penis that belongs to me! Let her suffer the torture of desiring something she can never have."

He eased Ming down. She began peeling off her clothes, revealing a magnificently toned body, the kind of body Gerard wanted Milan to possess. Proudly flaunting her nudity, Ming strutted over to the area where the exercise mats were stacked. "We can fuck back here. On the floor."

Gerard nodded, looking pleased by Ming's bright idea.

Milan watched helplessly as her trainer strode past her. She couldn't see him but could hear the rustle of his clothing being shed. She wanted to scream, *Don't do this to me. Please. Help me. Don't leave me with a damp, empty pussy.* But she knew her cries would go unheeded. Nothing she said would stop Gerard from filling Ming with his wonderfulness.

She'd forgotten about the pain in her arm, but the disappointment of being left with an unattended throbbing pussy made her begin to focus on her stiff neck and cramped muscles.

She hated Ming. She wanted to fling the fur coat down to the floor. But she didn't. She couldn't. She had to bear any humiliation Gerard dispensed if she expected to become his property. Milan understood that holding up her adversary's prized possession allowed her to experience the degree of humiliation necessary to explore the depths of her submissive nature.

Stripped of her identity, she remained in the degrading position of a human coat rack while Ming and Gerard fucked behind her back. She closed her eyes and tried to blink back the tears that wet her lashes as she was forced to listen to Ming cry out in pleasure, speaking at first in English and then switching to a love language that sounded like Chinese.

chapter thirty-one

"The jeweler was here," Irma told Milan. "You weren't here so Mr. Brockington asked me to guess your ring size. I told him my guess was that you wore a size six."

Milan shrugged. She wore a size five and a half, but didn't feel like quibbling over the size of a ring she'd be wearing for only a short time.

"Mr. Brockington wants to have an engagement celebration. He's waiting for you in his room." There was a warning tone to Irma's voice.

After the atrocious punishment she'd experienced at the hands of Ming, Milan was too physically and emotionally drained to care about the liberty Noah had taken in selecting her ring and involving her in an impromptu engagement celebration. Who would be the guests? she wondered, but she really didn't care. All she cared about was getting Noah's money, and being wealthy enough to match the gifts Ming showered on Gerard.

After the bitch had relieved Milan from coat rack duty, she'd had the audacity to order Milan to clean Gerard's cum from her Asian pussy. She got the bright idea to transform Milan into a human bidet, but thankfully Gerard had come to her rescue, telling Ming that functioning as a coat rack was sufficient punishment for Milan. Milan was *his* possession, he continued, and *he'd* determine when she began training in pussy licking.

Then he patted Milan on the head, telling her she'd been a good pet.

"I shouldn't have to wash myself when she's perfectly capable of using her tongue to clean my pussy," Ming had said and grabbed Milan's arm.

"No, she's tolerated enough of your abuse." Gerard pulled Milan away from Ming. Milan flushed at the memory. Never had she felt so loved, so protected. Furious that Gerard had stood up for Milan, Ming began cursing. Her angry words came out in a hot flurry, a hateful mixture of English and Chinese.

When Milan was finally alone with Gerard, he treated her with a tenderness he hadn't shown before. "Do your arms still hurt, my pet?"

"No," she lied.

"Don't lie to me. If you lie, I'll have to discipline you." He spoke so softly. His accent was so damn seductive, Milan was tempted to lie again. To get his undivided attention, she was willing to tolerate another punishment. But fearing he'd call Ming back and enforce the pussy licking, Milan quickly told the truth. "Yes, my arms hurt, sir." Milan hoped she'd never be forced to taste Ming's pussy. She wasn't a lesbian. Sure, she'd allowed married women to eat her pussy at the sex club, Tryst, but she'd never given *them* any head. She prayed Gerard would use her mouth for his benefit only. In the meantime, to avoid his wrath, she'd be sure to walk a very straight line and obey his every command.

Gerard reached out and rubbed her shoulders and forearms. Then he kissed her forehead and told her it was time for her to leave. Milan would have stayed with him forever if he wanted her to but, satisfied with his show of tenderness, she gathered herself and left.

❧

With Irma present as the only invited guest, it turned out that the engagement party wasn't much of a celebration at all. Milan and Irma gathered at Noah's bedside and when he presented the ring she thought she'd faint from fury. The ring was a hideous silver relic with a cloudy diamond.

"Do you like your ring, my dear?" Noah asked after placing the ugly thing on her finger.

Refusing to pretend to be impressed, she grimaced at the ring. "How many carats?"

Noah chuckled indulgently. "It's not the size that matters. It's the clarity, my dear. Why, that one carat is absolutely flawless. Hold it up to the light."

Without enthusiasm, Milan held her hand toward the chandelier and glanced up. "You see," Noah said excitedly. "It's absolutely flawless."

The cheap bastard had bought her an ugly one-carat engagement ring. But amazingly, it didn't matter. Nothing mattered except pleasing Gerard. And because Noah's nurse had insisted on shaving her pubic hair, she had failed to please her trainer today.

Milan didn't know whom she hated more—Noah, Ruth, or Ming. While she pondered the hatred she felt for each individual, Noah rattled on about the clarity of her revolting engagement ring.

Noah would die soon, she told herself, and then Ruth would go away. Ming, however, would remain a stubborn thorn in her side. Thus it was Ming, Milan decided whom she hated the most.

Irma poured champagne into three crystal flutes that were set on a silver tray. To get the engaged couple's attention, Irma cleared her throat and tapped delicately on her glass. "I'd like to propose a toast. Congratulations to you two lovebirds, Milan," Irma said dully.

"I'm honored to be the guest at this important celebration." Irma's words rang false as if she were reading from a script, but Noah didn't seem to notice. He looked appropriately touched, smiling and beaming at each insincere word that fell from Irma's lips.

"I hope this marriage lasts for years to come and produces a house filled with children."

"I'll drink to that," Noah said, taking a sip of champagne.

A house filled with children! Milan almost choked. How did Irma know about the childbearing clause in her prenup? Was the cook in on the scheme? Did she also have a hand in the plot to burden Milan with a dead man's kids? To calm her frazzled nerves, Milan turned the flute to her lips. Guzzling down the champagne, she added Irma's name to her hate list.

Thank God she was on the pill. *But contraceptive pills aren't one hundred percent effective*, she thought worriedly. It didn't matter, she reassured herself. Noah's sickly sperm couldn't impregnate her or anyone else. His baby-making days were over.

Drowsy from too much champagne, Noah nodded off in the middle of the celebration.

"You can go home, Irma, the party's over," Milan said in a hushed voice, escorting Irma out of the bedroom suite.

"What you're doing isn't right, Milan," Irma whispered out in the hallway. "Now, I've held my tongue all this time, but I'm gonna speak my mind. You can try to fire me but as long as Mr. Brockington is alive, he's going to keep me on."

Milan glared at the meddlesome woman and shot a look at Noah's closed bedroom door. "Can we have this discussion in private?" She ushered Irma down the staircase. "Now, what does my marriage to Noah have to do with you?" Milan asked when they reached the downstairs landing.

Irma put her hand on her hip saucily. It was a defiant gesture, and Milan was taken aback. The cook hadn't gotten feisty with her since she'd been put in her place. "Marrying that sickly man just so you can get your hands on his money is a sin and a shame," Irma said, her bottom lip protruding in disapproval.

"What's it to you? Really, Irma, how does my marriage to Noah concern you?"

"I'm just trying to warn you. Mr. Brockington isn't right in the head." Irma tapped her temple area for emphasis.

"Obviously," Milan said, and chuckled sarcastically. "Still, I don't see why his mental status would be of any concern to you. Your position here is…what? A cook, a scullery maid? A poorly trained scullery maid," Milan added viciously. "So mind your business. I'm not stupid, Irma. I know where this conversation is going. You want to blackmail me. Again! But there's not a chance in hell that you're getting your grubby fingers on one penny of Mr. Brockington's fortune—"

"Mr. Brockington is so proud," Irma interrupted. "He told me about the contract and the heir he plans on leaving."

Milan smiled. "If it's any of your business, which it's not, we're planning on having a passel of children to carry on the Brockington name." Milan did a wide sweep of her hand.

"Well, I know you're not planning on honoring your contract," Irma blurted. "You're on the pill. I know where you hide them, and I count them every day."

This time Milan did choke. She had a fit of coughing so severe, Irma smacked her hard on the back and then gave her a glass of water.

After Milan settled down, Irma informed her that she'd keep quiet if Milan signed a document promising to keep Irma on after Mr. Brockington's death. Irma expected a pay raise at five times her current salary, and a one-million-dollar bonus when Milan secured her deceased husband's fortune.

"I'm tired, Irma. Can we discuss this tomorrow?" Milan asked wearily.

"All right. But remember, if I don't get what I want, I'm gonna start singing!"

Start singing! Irma sounded like a character in an old gangster flick. It was all too much for Milan. Every time she thought she had things figured out, someone threw a monkey wrench in her plans. She didn't know how much longer she could put up with the insanity in the Brockington household. Noah was looking and acting healthier by the minute, there'd been a reversal of power between her and the nurse, and now Irma's greedy ass was hounding her for a part of her inheritance.

Milan was walking a tightrope; something had to give. Distraught, she wished she could talk to Gerard. Just being near him would be a comfort. But she wasn't allowed to contact him without permission. Desperate for solace and some type of understanding, she picked up the phone and called her sister.

"Hey, Sweetie. Can we get together somewhere so we can talk?"

"Oh, really? You must be in trouble again, otherwise, you'd still be hiding out. It's a shame the way you treat your family, Milan. You won't give out the number to that house you're living in. You don't call nobody and you won't answer your cell. After I didn't hear nothing else from you about the wedding, I got worried. Tried to get in touch with Tookie's mom, but she was on a cruise. When she got back, she had the nerve to be acting all tight-lipped—wouldn't give out that ol' man's phone number or address. Tookie's my girl and everything but her mom made me so mad, I told

Quantez that we might have to get one of them young thugs he works with to go rough Miss Elise up."

Milan laughed.

"That shit ain't funny, Milan. You got family and you're supposed to keep in touch."

"I need to talk, Sweetie. It's serious. Can you meet me somewhere?" she asked her sister.

"How you gon' be calling me from out of the clear blue and expect me to just stop what I'm doing and come running to you. Bring your ass over here. I'm in the middle of cooking dinner for Quantez and the kids."

"Sweetie, please. I can't come over; it's a very private matter and I need some sisterly advice. Please. It won't take long."

Sweetie became quiet. "How come you never call Mom for motherly advice?"

Milan sighed. "Mom doesn't care about me, Sweetie. You know that. She only loves you."

"That's not true, Milan. She loves us both the same."

"No, Sweetie. She hated my father and she hates me. But I didn't call you to talk about that. Are you going to meet me or not?"

"Okay, Milan. I guess Quantez can watch the food. Where do you want to meet? And don't go choosing no high-siddity place because I'm coming as I am; I'm not changing my clothes."

"Let's see…how about that KFC at Sixty-first and Lancaster Avenue? Is that ghetto enough for you?"

"See. There you go, acting like you're better than everyone else. That's what Mommy don't like about you—"

"I was only kidding about the ghetto part. I thought it would make you laugh. And for your information, Sweetie, Mommy doesn't like *anything* about me."

"Whatever. I'll see you in an hour." Sweetie hung up.

Milan checked on Noah, making sure he was still conked out before she slipped out of the house.

chapter thirty-two

Sweetie, plump yet pretty as ever, sat at a table drinking a soda when Milan entered the fast-food restaurant. Sweetie gasped when Milan sat across the table from her. "*You* came out in public without make-up? I guess that's a good thing because me and Mommy always thought you wore too much of the stuff. Still, I'm shocked that you would show your face without it." Sweetie looked Milan up and down. "What's up with your hair?" She eyed Milan's drab ponytail. "Look at your edges—you need a perm, girl!" Sweetie frowned at Milan's appearance. "I thought you were living with that rich man, planning to marry him to get his money to buy all the material things you worship so much. But, um, it looks like he's changing you. I hope this change is for the better," Sweetie said skeptically.

Milan waved her hand. "This has nothing to do with Noah. I stopped wearing makeup because the man I'm in love with said I don't need it. He likes me to have a more natural look."

Sweetie's jaw dropped. With the straw from the soda resting against her bottom lip, she was a humorous sight.

"That's why I called you." Milan beamed. "I'm in love, Sweetie! I'm twenty-six years old and I'm in love for the first time in my life."

Sweetie frowned in confusion. "In love? You fell in love with the old man?"

"No! I hate him!" Milan grimaced at the insult. "I'm in love with my personal trainer. He's gorgeous, Sweetie. He's sexy and smart."

"Okay, slow down. You're in love with your what?"

"I hired a personal trainer to get me in shape for the wedding. But it was love at first sight and that's when I decided I didn't want a big wedding."

"Whoa, whoa," Sweetie said, shaking her head and gesturing with her hand. "You're in love with another man but you're still going through with the wedding?" As if drinking the soda would clear her mind, Sweetie bent her head and took a deep sip from the straw.

"Yes," Milan said, suddenly solemn. "I'm not going to just throw away all that money. I'm going through with the wedding plans."

Sweetie stared at Milan as if she were a total stranger. She drained the milkshake. "And what does your new boyfriend think about that?"

"He doesn't know about Noah," Milan confessed.

"Milan! You always want to lay the blame on other people. But the problem in your life is *you!* Wasn't it bad enough to marry a dying man so you could get your hands on his money? Now you're making the situation even more complicated."

"Sweetie, I'm in trouble," Milan whined. "Don't fuss at me. Not right now. I need your support."

"Oh, here we go again. What kind of support can I give you? You're cheating on your sick-ass future husband. Your new man doesn't even know you're engaged." Sweetie's eyes darted to Milan's ring finger. "Oh, by the way...I really hate your ring."

"I know," Milan responded. "It sucks."

"But back to your sick situation. Why did you want me to meet you; what do you think I can do?"

"Be supportive. That's all. Noah has moved up the wedding date. We're getting married the third Saturday next month."

"That soon. Damn, thanks for taking the time to let me know." Sweetie sucked her teeth. "I guess I'll have enough time to find a dress for this sham of a wedding."

"Oh, don't bother; you're not invited. We're having a private ceremony at home."

Sweetie just shook her head. "Milan, you need help. You're not right. Something tells me this whole thing is gonna blow up in your face."

"No it isn't. I have everything planned out. After Noah dies, I'm going to sell the house and buy a bigger one for me and Gerard."

"Gerard? He's the one you're creeping with?" Sweetie asked.

Milan sucked her teeth at Sweetie's crude wording. "Yes, Gerard is the man I'm in love with."

"Okay, I'm just trying to keep the names straight."

"Here's the problem, Sweetie—"

"You mean to tell me there's more to this twisted tale?"

Milan nodded and then fiddled with her engagement ring, nervously twisting it back and forth. "I suspect Noah is trying to trick me."

"About the money?" Sweetie asked, wide-eyed.

"No, no. He has plenty of money and I'm entitled to a lot of it after we're married. But I'm starting to get worried."

"About what?"

"I'm beginning to think he's not as sick as he says he is. I mean…he claimed he only had six months to live, but lately he's been looking kind of healthy and actually walking around without the help of his nurse." Milan paused, in thought. She didn't notice the look of horror on her sister's face. "I don't have any legitimate proof that he's actually going to die any-time soon. And if he doesn't die right after we're married, I might have to kill his ass." When Milan finally focused on her sister's face, she saw the shock in Sweetie's eyes. "I'm not kidding, Sweetie. I *have* to be with Gerard. I can't sit around waiting forever."

"Are you out of your mind!" Sweetie banged the table with her palm of her hand. Sighing and rolling her eyes in disgust, she grabbed her purse. "I'm leaving. I'm going to pretend we didn't have this conversation."

"Wait, Sweetie. Don't leave."

"I'm out! You done lost your damn mind. I'm not sitting around here lis-tening to you plot murder. That would make me an accessory to the crime."

"I didn't say I was definitely going to do it. I just wanted to run the pos-sibility past you. Since he's supposed to be so sick and all, if I plan it right, I know I can get away with it."

"That's it; I'm out." Sweetie stood up abruptly. "You're nuts and I don't want to hear another word of this. I gotta worry about Quantez and my two kids. You love living on the edge. I don't."

"Sweetie," Milan said pleadingly. "I really need to discuss this with you."

Sweetie wagged a finger at Milan. "You don't need to talk with me. What you really need is a couch and a nice long talk with a damn psychiatrist."

Milan winced. "I'm not crazy and you know it," she said, sounding hurt.

"Well, stop talkin' crazy. And don't look at me as if I should feel sorry for you. Oh yeah, you can keep that money you promised to give me and Quantez. I don't want it. Don't bother to call me; I can't afford to be involved with someone as crazy as you." Sweetie gave Milan a long hard stare and then pushed past her sister and walked out the door.

For a few moments, Milan stared at the door that Sweetie had exited through. Then she shrugged. *To hell with you, Sweetie.* Her sister's departure from her life was for the best. The lifestyle she planned to live with Gerard would be hard to explain to Sweetie and her mother. Yes, it was for the best that she lived in seclusion.

Then sorrow washed over Milan. She didn't want to go home; Noah might be awake. If he was and wanted to play one of his games, there was no telling how she'd respond. And murdering him before the wedding wasn't a good financial decision.

On the way to her car, she slipped her cell phone out of her handbag. She had to talk to Gerard. If he didn't want to talk, he wouldn't answer. If he picked up and chastised her for calling without permission, at least she'd have the satisfaction of hearing his voice. But if he punished her by refusing to see her at her next appointed time, she'd beg and plead, cry, and throw herself at his mercy.

After weighing the pros and cons, Milan went ahead and pushed Gerard's number. Surprisingly, her call was answered on the first ring. But instead of hearing Gerard's deep, sensual voice, Milan was startled to hear the feminine voice of a woman. "May I speak to Gerard?" Milan asked, sounding nervous and perplexed.

"If you don't mind waiting, I'll get him in just a moment," said the overly solicitous voice of the anonymous female. Milan thought she heard several voices in the background. It was probably the television or the radio, she told herself. Whatever the case, she was sorry she'd called him. It was a spontaneous decision and not a very good one, she now realized. Most likely, he was in the midst of a training session. The woman who had answered his phone was probably a paying client. Sorry she'd disturbed him from his work, she feared that she now faced a severe reprimand.

"My pet," Gerard said when he picked up the phone. He sounded cheerful. Milan was relieved. "So, you've decided to break the rules. You know you're not supposed to call," he said, still sounding chipper.

"I'm sorry, sir. I wouldn't have called if it wasn't an emergency…" She heard Gerard breathe out deeply. After several seconds of silence, Milan realized Gerard did not intend to inquire about the emergency, so she pressed on. "The need to see you was so strong, I couldn't help myself." Milan hesitated as the female voices in the background grew closer. Thankfully, neither voice belonged to Ming. Gerard still did not speak.

"After your company leaves, can I come over?" Milan asked timidly.

"You can come over right now," he said coolly. "It shouldn't take more than a half hour to get here. I'll see you soon."

Milan glanced at her watch. It was five o'clock. She'd have to get there at exactly five-thirty if she expected to be admitted. "Thank you, sir," Milan said. Regretfully, she'd have to share him with yet another woman. There was no telling what was in store for her. But what could she do? She was hopelessly addicted to him and there was no limit to what she'd do to be with him.

⁂

Shockingly, Casey, the young snob from the fitness club, opened the door for Milan. And even more shocking, Casey came to the door wearing nothing except a pink leather submission collar fastened around her neck. From the collar hung a gleaming silver engraved dog tag. Fearing that the tag would reveal Gerard as her owner, Milan couldn't bring herself to read the lettering. Slowly and bravely, she brought her eyes up to the dog tag and zoomed in on the fancy script, *Property of Ming*.

Okay, so where was this brat's rightful owner? Then she remembered—Ming was Casey's stepmother. Damn, Ming was doing her thing with the father and his daughter.

Seeing Casey put in her place was uplifting, but it occurred to her that if Casey was Ming's property, then Ming had to be in close proximity. Milan became nervous. She was not in the mood for another scene with Ming. She'd heard another female voice over the phone and now assumed Ming was in the house somewhere. Where was she? Milan wondered. Was she upstairs sucking off Gerard? A hot wave of jealousy hit her like fire.

"Close the door and get back in your cage, Casey," Gerard called from the dining room. *Cage!* Casey humbly lowered herself to the floor and hurriedly crawled across the living room. When she reached the dining room, a wall blocked Milan's view and Casey disappeared from her scope of vision.

Milan had seen a lot of things in her life, but seeing the arrogant heiress degraded to crawling like a dog was totally unexpected. It had to be the most outlandish and thoroughly satisfying sight she'd witnessed in a long, long time.

Milan stood near the front door, not daring to sit or leave the location of the living room until she had Gerard's expressed permission to do so. She could hear the low sexy rumble of his voice and the mingled soft voices of Casey and another female. The other female was definitely not Ming. Milan knew Ming's voice all too well.

She could also hear the sound of clanging metal as the door of the cage was slammed shut. Then she heard what she assumed was a lock snapping into place. Curiosity was killing her, but Milan knew better than to pry.

Holding a leash connected to the pink collar of a gorgeous black woman, Gerard came into the living room. Milan's heart sank when she saw how stunningly beautiful the woman was. Gerard wore a proud expression as he gently tugged the chain. The woman was led into the room walking upright—she wasn't made to crawl like Casey, who had scurried to the cage in the dining room like a terrified terrier. But despite the collar and leash that relegated her to being property, there was a proud sensual sway to the woman's walk. She had a regal carriage that made it hard to fathom how this confident woman could belong to anyone. Her skin was deep, dark chocolate, a darker hue than Milan's. Her body was strong and well muscled; her huge breasts sat upright with large dark nipples that Milan prayed Gerard had not tasted. She was a walking work of art and Milan was hot with envy, wishing it was she who put such joy on Gerard's face; wishing he would parade her around with a leash and collar.

"Milan. Say hello to Nyla."

"Hi, Nyla," Milan muttered uncertainly. The new world she'd stepped into was filled with surprises, but aside from serving Gerard by obeying his explicit command, she'd found none of the discoveries very pleasant.

She'd particularly despised having been made aware of his weird relationship with Ming. Now this. Finding him in possession of Ming's property did not fill her with warm feelings. Ming, after all, tried to tempt him with sharing ownership of her female submissives. Was that the reason her two pets were here with Gerard?

But why, she wondered, was Nyla being granted the liberty of walking upright when Casey was made to crawl? Was there a difference in ownership? Did Nyla belong to Gerard? From a distance, Milan scrutinized Nyla's collar. It was a replica of the one Casey wore. She strained to read the script, but couldn't make out the letters. If the black beauty belonged to Gerard, Milan feared she'd collapse and die instantly from a broken heart.

"I'm taking care of Ming's submissives while she's out of town on a business trip. It's time for Nyla's exercise. Make yourself comfortable while I walk her upstairs." Gerard pointed to the sofa. He led Nyla past Milan. The woman kept her eyes focused on Gerard as he gingerly pulled the leash.

Milan didn't like Gerard's expression. He looked delighted with Nyla. It couldn't have been Milan's imagination. Gerard looked giddy with joy. And he was so enthralled with Nyla, he forgot to give Milan the nod to bow down and kiss his feet.

She couldn't help but wonder what was going on upstairs. Gerard and Nyla were quiet as mice. Milan strained to listen but she couldn't hear a sound. She checked the time. They'd been upstairs for ten minutes. What could be taking so long? She longed to be in Gerard's presence; she hadn't come over to sit on the sofa alone. She wanted some attention, even if it meant being disciplined.

Bored and curious, she crept into the dining room. Maybe Casey would give her some information. She gasped in shock when she found Casey locked inside a large cage and looking completely miserable curled up in the confining space. The uppity redhead had been thoroughly put in her place. Being treated like an animal served her right but, needing information from the young captive, Milan held back a gloating smile.

"Casey," Milan said in a whisper. "Does Nyla belong to Gerard or Ming?"

Casey's face contorted. She shrank back, scooting to the back of the cage as if she'd been splashed with boiling water. Then she let out several small yelps that sounded very much like the high-pitched yap of a small dog.

Mystified by Casey's reaction, Milan stared at her in disbelief. "I just asked you a simple question…" Suddenly Milan felt someone's presence. Casey's terror-stricken eyes shot upward. Instinctively, Milan spun around. With his arms folded, Gerard stood behind her in the doorway. Wearing a terrible scowl, he shook his head.

"Ming tried to warn me. She told me I was wasting my time trying to train you. She said you would never respect my authority, that I could never train you to be as obedient and well trained as her submissives. I guess she was right," he said in a tone that was a mixture of sorrow and anger. He turned a softer gaze down at Casey. "Good girl, Casey," he said. He walked toward the cage and then unlocked it. He reached inside and patted the top of Casey's head. "Good girl," he repeated. "Your bark let me know that there was trouble."

Casey nuzzled Gerard's hand, rubbing her nose and lips against it. Then she licked it, running her tongue appreciatively over his fingers and the top of his hand. Milan wanted to kick the redhead for getting her in trouble.

Gerard reached in his pocket and held out a cupped hand. "Good girl," he repeated as he fed Casey some sort of treat from his palm. "Now, run upstairs and play with Nyla. I'll be up in a few minutes," he told her and lightly smacked her bottom.

As Casey scampered away on her hands and knees, Gerard followed her with fondness in his eyes. His eyes turned cold when they shifted back to Milan's face.

"I told you to sit on the sofa and wait."

"I'm sorry, sir. Please forgive me." Milan dropped to the floor and desperately tried to press her lips against Gerard's feet. He grabbed the collar of her coat and pulled her upright. "I want you to undress and get in the cage," he said through gritted teeth.

Solemnly, she took off all her clothes. "Give me your wristwatch," he ordered. Obediently, Milan took off the watch and placed it in Gerard's outstretched hand.

"Bad girl," he scolded as Milan slowly crawled into the metal crate that was positioned next to Casey's empty cage.

chapter thirty-three

Degraded, humiliated, and alone inside the cage, unable to speak or move freely, Milan had plenty of time to think. She was failing miserably as a proper mate. At this point she'd endured the pain and humiliation of being clamped, burned, and turned into an inanimate object. Now she was locked inside a cage and Gerard still didn't think she was worthy of his ownership. She was out of ideas on how to improve herself.

Time seemed to move in slow motion. Without a watch, she couldn't begin to guess whether hours or only moments had passed. Her body was cramped and sore like she'd been in the small space for hours and hours. Inside the crate, there was just enough room to lie down and crawl around in a circle.

From upstairs, she could hear the soft murmur of feminine voices. Shutting out their sounds of pleasure—of freedom—Milan covered her ears with her hands. In spite of the tight fit of the pet cage and the bloating in her stomach from the urgent need to urinate, she somehow found a comfortable position and nodded off to sleep.

"Milan!" Gerard spoke her name harshly.

Milan quickly positioned herself on her hands and knees. Gerard stood outside the cage. His tone was angry, his expression stern, yet Milan sensed a hint of kindness, forgiveness.

He looked at his wristwatch. "It's been two hours. I'm going to let you out to use the bathroom," he said as he unlocked the cage.

"Get off your knees. Stand up!" Gerard ordered when Milan crawled out of the cage. As she stood upright, Milan smiled to herself. His concern about the appearance of her knees proved he still wanted her as a mate. Additionally, she was grateful to be off her knees because her muscles were so cramped and her bladder was so painfully full, she wasn't sure if she would have been able to manage crawling up a flight of stairs.

Gerard looked pointedly at her vagina. "I see your pubic hairs are coming back in."

"Yes, sir." Little did he know that Ruth the nurse would be wielding a razor the following day at the next turkey basting session. It would take a lot of convincing to get the eager nurse to forgo shaving the tiny out-grown hairs.

"Did you notice that Casey and Nyla are wearing collars?" he asked, looking over his shoulder at Milan as she followed him up the stairs.

"Yes, I did."

"Do you know how they acquired them?"

Milan pondered the question briefly. "By being obedient and loyal to Ming."

"Exactly. Being collared is an extremely high honor, Milan. It's more sacred, more meaningful than a traditional wedding ring. I had hoped to collar you one day." He shook his head. "But I'm not sure if it's going to happen."

"It was wrong for me to disobey you. I'd like another chance."

"I've given you many. Your defiance is becoming an embarrassment."

"I made a mistake…I'm still learning. But I know I can make you proud," she said, sensing that Gerard wasn't ready to give up on her.

"We shall see," he murmured when they reached the top of the stairs.

A door to one of the bedrooms was left ajar. Milan attempted to avert her gaze, but couldn't help taking a peek. The two women were wrapped in an embrace. Milan gazed at them, mesmerized by their contrasting flesh tones, their sensual murmurs, their feminine sexuality.

"Go!" Gerard said, breaking her daze. He pointed to the bathroom at the end of the hall. "After you're finished, you'll be joining them."

Denying her privacy, he walked into the bathroom with Milan and stood impatiently as she urinated. Afterward, he left the bathroom and took long strides toward the stairs. With Milan following closely behind him, he abruptly stopped at the bedroom doorway, leaned against the doorframe, and with his arms folded he watched the dimly lit, writhing bodies of Nyla and Casey. In the shadow of the darkened corridor, Milan remained behind him.

Gerard cleared his throat. The sexual frenzy between the two women ceased. Both women looked at him expectantly. He waved his hand, gesturing for them to continue. As he made steps into the room, the women merged into an embrace and resumed nibbling, licking, and kissing.

"Sit here," Gerard told Milan, patting a spot on the bed.

Milan sat near the edge of the bed but cut her eyes away from the intensely erotic lesbian sex play taking place next to her.

"Move closer."

Doing as she was told, she inched closer.

"Watch and learn. Observe the masterful performance of collared women."

Ordered to look, Milan's eyes moved leisurely from their well-toned lower limbs and up to their breasts, which were pressed together.

Nyla's ample dark bosom pressed against Casey's small boobs was an arousing visual. As if aware that Milan was fascinated by the sight of their contrasting breast size and shades of color, Nyla pulled away, and lowered Casey into a reclining position. She kissed Casey's small nipples until they became demanding and stiff. Milan watched in fascination as the tiny pink nipples grew larger and changed to a deeper hue.

Unwittingly, Milan's clitoris became engorged with passion as she watched Nyla suck Casey's nipples. Casey's open eyes were glazed over, her delicate child-like hands affectionately cupped Nyla's face, holding it to her nipples that now resembled ripened raspberries.

"Switch," Gerard uttered.

Like a tracking device, Milan's eyes followed the movement of the women. Her pussy throbbed with desire as she watched Nyla's two dark hands grasp Casey's shoulders and guide the girl's delicate pale face toward her generously sized breasts. Using her lips and her fingers, Casey excited one of Nyla's nipples to hardness. Nyla purred contentedly.

Oddly, Milan found herself gazing longingly at Nyla's unattended breast. "Go ahead," Gerard told Milan. "Join them."

Feeling self-conscious and unsure of her ability to stimulate another woman, she hesitantly caressed Nyla's firm nipple with her tongue. Her tongue slid over the unfamiliar texture of the hardened nugget, timidly at first. Then, emboldened by the unexpected pleasure she derived from tonguing a woman's nipple, Milan parted her lips. Hungrily, she drew in Nyla's dark jewel and sucked. Nyla moaned in bliss.

Distracted by the murmurs of pleasure that Nyla emitted, Casey released the dark nipple from her mouth and observed Milan's impassioned participation. After a moment or two, Casey repositioned herself and lay on her belly with her face between Nyla's parted legs. Milan worked on the nipple in her mouth but kept a curious eye on the action below. Propped up on her elbows, Casey spread the folds of Nyla's pussy, probing inside with a slender finger.

Seeing what Casey was doing to Nyla made Milan's inner muscles tighten. She stifled a small groan of pleasure. During that instant of intense arousal, Milan's eyes fluttered shut. In that brief moment, Casey abandoned Nyla and scooted over to Milan. Casey's tongue explored Milan's wet creases. She nibbled on Milan's pussy, taunting her gaping wet hole with gentle licks and soft bites. Milan bucked and spread her legs as wide as she could, trying to give Casey more access, but Casey's mouth suddenly deserted her as she returned to Nyla's gleaming opening.

Yearning for Gerard to assure her that her sensitive pussy would receive more of the attention it craved, Milan threw a panicked look in his direction.

Fully clothed, Gerard regarded the three naked women. Then he narrowed his eyes slyly. "You'll do *anything* to please me?"

Warning alarms went off inside Milan's head. Sure, her pussy had been licked by the anonymous women at Tryst, and without a doubt, Casey's tongue had turned her on, but Milan had never tasted another woman's juices; it wasn't something she'd ever dreamed of doing. Yet, she knew she'd have to sacrifice her principles and surrender her tongue to pussy if Gerard commanded her to.

"Yes," she finally answered. "I'll do anything to please you."

Gerard clapped his hands. Casey's head jerked up, her pink lips glistened with Nyla's thick nectar. "I want Milan to lie on her back." The two women made room for Milan to lie prone. "Casey, I want you at the top." He looked at Nyla and motioned for her to move down to the foot of the bed.

Nyla and Casey didn't need further instruction, they knew exactly what Gerard expected. Nyla straddled Milan, rotating her womanly hips until their pussies rubbed together, until they were locked, clit to clit.

Milan had just begun to get into the rhythm and enjoy the hot friction created by Nyla's rotating pussy when Casey suddenly squatted over her face. Amazingly soft, red pubic hairs grazed her lips, inviting her to indulge her taste buds—to treat herself to a different kind of flavor.

Knowing Gerard expected an inspired performance, Milan reluctantly opened her mouth and bravely plunged her tongue deeply into Casey's willing slit. Casey moaned as Milan's tongue pressed against the flesh of her pussy walls. Rather quickly, Milan got over the shock of the salty taste and musky scent of the female genitalia and fully threw herself into the ritual of pussy eating.

Milan lapped and sucked lustfully, as if she were an experienced slit-licker. Meanwhile Casey slid her clit up and down Milan's tongue until her juices trickled down the sides of Milan's face.

Spent, Casey dismounted from Milan's face. Nyla rotated her hips fast and furiously, grinding her pussy against Milan's hairless mound. Milan became so pleasantly caught up in the excitement of pussy bumping, she was taken completely off guard when Nyla, without missing a beat, reached behind her back and furtively inserted a finger into her wet hole. Milan sighed deeply and bit down on her lip as Nyla's finger slipped in and out, soon joined by a second finger. Milan welcomed the intrusion of the two-digit finger fuck. Her hips swayed, involuntarily keeping up with the rhythm of the finger thrusts. Then the room began to spin as she felt the beginning of an explosion firing inside her pussy, followed by body shudders and moans of gratitude.

Basking in the afterglow of desperately needed sexual release, Milan closed her eyes contentedly and snuggled next to Casey. Under normal circumstances she wouldn't have gone anywhere near the uppity little fitness heiress without an explicit order from Gerard. But the scent of pussy hung in the air, thick and intoxicating. So intoxicating, Milan was persuaded to overlook the fact that she viewed Casey as an adversary, not a lover.

From the corner of her eye, she noticed Gerard reaching a hand to Nyla. He gently pulled the dark beauty from the bed. With Nyla standing in front of him, her proud buttocks pressed into his groin, Gerard embraced her from behind, squeezing and kneading her magnificent bosom. He'd never touched Milan that way, in fact, he'd always been emotionally distant with her. But Milan was in such a serene place, she didn't feel a bit envious of Gerard's affectionate interaction with Nyla.

"Milan and Casey," he called and snapped his fingers twice. Milan and Casey jumped up from their languished positions.

Snatched from her post-orgasmic stupor, Milan now saw Gerard and Nyla with new eyes. Seeing his hands all over Nyla enraged her. The heat of jealousy scorched her cheeks. Knowing there'd be severe consequences if she displayed her emotions, Milan didn't allow her anger to show.

"Nyla needs to be serviced. I want you two to do her at the same time." He gave Nyla a love bite to the neck and then alternately pinched her nipples and fondled her enormous breasts. "Get on the bed," he told Nyla and gently nudged her toward the bed.

Nyla situated herself in the center of the bed, on her knees with her legs spread wide, ass raised, pussy exposed.

Grasping Milan's shoulders, Gerard guided her face between Nyla's legs. Casey didn't need any prodding. In an instant, she moved behind Nyla, probing the ebony-colored woman's anus with her tongue.

For Milan, performing cunnilingus was a forbidden pleasure she'd recklessly indulged in while caught up in the throes of wild passion. But now, after climaxing and fully regaining her senses, being forced to eat pussy was particularly appalling.

She hadn't suffered Gerard's abuse to end up eating pussy on demand. She wanted dick. She'd been willing to do almost anything for it, but she now realized she'd been wasting her time. Gerard was stingy with the dick because it was already spoken for. It belonged exclusively to the woman with fat pockets—Ming.

"What are you waiting for? Do her!" Gerard's voice was commanding. "Get back in position and service Nyla." He checked his watch. "Ming should be here soon. For your impudence, I'm going to send you home with Ming; I'll keep Nyla until you're properly trained."

She jerked her face away from the dark vagina. Had she heard Gerard correctly? Had he just threatened to send her home with Ming? The spell was broken. Milan looked at Gerard as if he'd completely lost his mind.

"Do not ignore an order."

"I have to decline," she said firmly.

Nyla uttered a soft cry of shock at Milan's bold rebelliousness. But Casey, performing as a well-trained slave, continued licking Nyla's ass.

"Then leave my house," he said.

She knew Gerard expected her to bend to his will at the threat of being banished. Instead of cracking under pressure, she shrugged and said, "Not a problem." As she eased off the bed, Milan caught a glimpse of something she'd never seen in Gerard's eyes—respect.

But it was too little, too late. She'd desired Gerard more than she'd ever desired another human being. Up until now, she'd done everything she could to please him. She'd willingly allowed herself to be debased, bowing to him, kissing his feet, and sniffing him like a lovesick puppy. But eating one pussy after another was not what she'd bargained for. If she continued to follow Gerard's lead, she'd wind up being a human footstool beneath Ming's feet. It was obviously Ming was the real dominant in this relationship. Gerard was nothing more than the wealthy Asian's trainee. Most likely, he was training Milan to share her with Ming. Damn, she'd been so enamored of him, she hadn't recognized that she was being deceived.

Downstairs, Milan dressed at a leisurely pace. She collected her watch from the coffee table, took one last glance at the home she'd hoped to share. "I'll let myself out," she whispered to herself as she solemnly opened the front door.

She thought about the money she'd paid Gerard...Oh well, she shrugged, accepting the loss. There was plenty more money at home in the trunk, and in Noah's bank account.

chapter thirty-four

At three in the morning the city was asleep. On her way home, deep in thought, Milan drove well below the speed limit. An occasional commercial truck zoomed past as her car crawled along City Avenue. But for the most part, Milan had the road to herself.

She needed to hatch a plan, come up with a believable explanation for her nearly twelve-hour absence. It was foolish to risk Noah's ire so close to their wedding date. In retrospect, she realized she should have stayed home and kept an eye on him—on her assets. The prize was so close at hand and she'd invested far too much of herself to lose out now.

Suppose he'd keeled over and died while she was out playing the role of submissive? Being a mere fiancée, she wasn't yet entitled to any portion of Noah's vast fortune. It would be just her luck to get home and find him dead as a doornail. The thought gave her a shudder and prompted her to press down on the gas.

Instead of running out and wasting her time on a man who obviously didn't want her, she should have been at home doting on the ol' fool. As an act of good faith, she could have volunteered to inject herself with a batch of Noah's useless semen. Making the gesture might have gained his trust and it definitely would have earned her some extra cash. But she'd lost control of her emotions and had gone running to Gerard.

Gerard. The thought of him hurt her heart. But the time had come to face some hard facts. Sure, her trainer was one of the most handsome men on the planet, and yes, he exuded sensuality. He had turned her out, had whipped her with just the promise of dick. The lifestyle Gerard offered was kinky and sexually arousing, but no matter how docile she was, how well she behaved, her loyalty and obedience would never be enough. Most likely, her collar would have said: *Property of Gerard and Ming.* Gathering the strength to leave Gerard had been a wise decision. It was time to get back to the business of money and marriage.

Finally home, Milan pulled into the long driveway. Believing her eyes were deceiving her, she blinked rapidly to clear her vision and then gawked at the white stretch limousine that blocked the entrance to the garage. *What the hell?* Then it hit her. Her worst fear had been realized. Noah had been secretly conversing over the phone with distant relatives and now his impoverished country cousins had shown up. And they had the audacity to arrive in style. While she was away, they'd pounced upon him and at this very moment were probably forcing a pen into his hand, persuading him to include them in his will.

Livid, Milan was ready to wage war with the interlopers. Unable to maneuver around the long and impressive vehicle, she left her car idling as she stormed over to the driver's side of the limo. The expensive purr of the limousine's engine infuriated her. Noah's relatives had a lot of nerve carousing around with a hired chauffeur. She imagined they were gearing up for the high life they intended to live after they got their grubby fingers on Noah's money.

She knocked sharply on the tinted window. She could see the shadowy silhouette of the driver who sat behind the wheel. He didn't turn his head an inch, just looked straight ahead, deliberately ignoring her.

How dare he! Enraged, Milan pounded on the smoky glass. Finally, the window eased down. "Yes?" The driver's pudgy face was creased in annoyance.

"Move this *thing*—" She looked disgustedly at the elegant limo as if it were a battered pick-up truck. "You're blocking me; I'd like to park in *my* garage if you don't mind."

"No, dice," the driver said, shaking his head. "Park over there." He inclined his head toward an area near the garage.

Milan could feel the heat of rage. She was tired and irritable and close to slapping the rude driver. Weren't limo drivers required to be courteous and solicitous? Most likely, his boldness reflected the entitled attitude of the people who hired him. Noah's relatives had a lot of gall instructing the driver to take up half a mile of the driveway. Noah wasn't even in his grave and already they were behaving as if they had the privilege of running the Brockington estate.

Milan cut off her engine and left her car parked crookedly. With anger boiling over, she hurried to the front door, intending to cuss out Noah's country cousins. She wouldn't be the least bit surprised if all her ghetto ways resurfaced and she came to blows with the money-grubbing relatives.

With her key, she hastily unlocked the front door, but stopped dead still when she heard the voice of a man. He was upstairs yelling at Noah. "I can't believe you'd do such a dishonest and despicable thing!" shouted the British-sounding voice.

Milan arched a curious brow. That couldn't be a relative—not with an English accent. It had to be Noah's best friend from England. What the hell was he doing here, weeks before the wedding?

"What did you expect me to do, wait forever?" Noah responded, his arrogant tone overlaid with a whiny pitch.

Wondering if she should race up the stairs and demand an explanation, Milan stared at the staircase for what seemed like endless moments. There was more than a touch of authority in the Brit's tone that kept her frozen in place. She needed more information before barging into Noah's suite, so she decided to listen in silence for a few more minutes.

"I certainly didn't expect you to throw a temper tantrum and disperse my money as recklessly as you would if you were playing a game of Monopoly."

At those words, a sharp sense of dread knifed through her. Milan swallowed in apprehension. *Dear Lord! It can't be true. Please tell me that scumbag did not give me money that didn't belong to him.* She tasted salty bile that rose up her throat and forced it down. She couldn't have a total meltdown. Not yet. She had to get to the bottom of this disastrous situation.

I shouldn't jump to conclusions. I didn't hear the entire exchange; I entered the house mid-conversation...I obviously misinterpreted their words. Yes, that's what happened, I misunderstood.

Moving with a daring she didn't possess in her heart, Milan swiftly climbed the stairs and barged into Noah's bedroom. "What's going on, Noah?"

"Hello...uh, my dear," Noah said tensely. "Where have you been? You look terrible. Were you accosted?" He was sitting up in bed, cushioned by his mountain of pillows. His complexion had lost its recent healthy appearance, he was back to his former withered appearance and unhealthy pallor.

Milan took a quick glance in the bureau mirror. She looked a haggard wreck; her hair was tousled as if she'd just rolled out of bed. She attempted to smooth back her hair but gave up; there wasn't much she could do with her appearance. "No, no. I wasn't accosted; I was, um...I spent some time with my family. I'm sorry, I should have told you," she explained with a curious eye fixed on the stranger.

The visitor, a grim-faced, expensively attired white man, sat erect in a chair across from Noah's bed. He seemed to sneer at Milan. He had aristocratic, handsome features, thick salt-and-pepper-colored hair, and brown eyes. Angry brown eyes that shifted in Milan's direction. There was tension in the room that stretched Milan's nerves taut; she wished she had delayed her entrance until the air had cleared. Swallowing the knot of fear in her throat, she asked, "Is something wrong, Noah?"

"No, no. Of course not," he stammered. "I'd like you to meet Hayden McIntyre, my, uh, dearest friend from London," Noah said with an uneasy chuckle.

"I'm not your friend; I'm your *employer* from London," the Brit interjected spitefully.

"His employer? What are you talking about? Noah is an independently wealthy man," Milan protested, gawking at Noah and waiting for him to chime in and agree with her.

"Allow me to correct myself," Hayden said and then ceremoniously cleared his throat. "Noah Brockington is my *former* employee. He's currently unemployed. He's now a penniless pauper," Hayden McIntyre said with a ruthless narrowing of his eyes.

A penniless pauper? The fateful words dropped from the British man's lips seemed to echo. Milan's mouth gaped open. "Noah isn't rich?" Her eyes darted questioningly from Noah to Hayden.

Noah gave Milan a sheepish *"he's just kidding"* smile.

"Noah doesn't have a pot to piss in." Hayden bent over in malicious laughter.

Noah's smile twitched and then faded. It was replaced with an unhappy expression.

Milan's temples throbbed. Her heart rate accelerated.

"It appears you've been taken for a ride," Hayden taunted. "And you won't be getting another red cent of my money," he said with bitterness.

This wasn't possible. It was a bad dream. It had to be. She was not a stupid woman. She was far too bright to have endured Noah's absurdities and perversions only to end up getting stiffed.

But the pompous tilt to Hayden's chin, the scornful glint in his eyes, told her that she had indeed been duped. Anxiety welled up inside her. The overpowering sense of dread sharpened to the point of physical pain. She clutched her chest and sagged against one of the pillars in the vast bedroom.

"How could you do this to me, Noah?" she asked in a raspy voice.

"I—I was trying to hurt Hayden."

"Well, it worked. You hurt me deeply," Hayden responded.

"Hurt him? Why?" Milan wanted to know. "And what does your hurting him have to do with, um, your finances?" she stammered, unable to concentrate because her mind kept replaying the words, *Noah doesn't have a pot to piss in.*

"Put yourself in my place," Noah appealed to Hayden, looking anguished. "What would you have done if you were made to wait as long as you've had me waiting?"

"I left you with several million dollars in cash for your comfort and to prove my intentions—" He stopped talking, took a deep breath. "That was money my wife didn't know about and couldn't touch if she involved me in a bitter divorce." Hayden sighed loudly. "But my good intentions weren't enough, were they, Noah?" he continued, shaking his head regretfully.

"Every time I called, all you did was whine and complain about your health."

Something really strange was going on here. Something more than an employer/employee relationship. And that something didn't bode well for Milan. A new sense of dread crept up the back of her neck. Thoughts flitted to the secret phone calls she'd overheard. She'd thought Noah had been having clandestine telephone conversations with distant relatives—bemoaning his fate, but he had actually been talking with Hayden McIntyre.

From his bed, Noah groaned. "Hayden! Try to understand—"

Hayden held up a hand. "There's nothing to understand. You betrayed me. You violated my trust," Hayden accused. "I allowed you to live in the lap of luxury, provided you with credit cards, a personal cook, and household staff…" Hayden uttered a disdainful sound. "Now I see you with clearer vision. I see you as you really are—you're nothing more than a servant. *My* manservant."

Noah gasped. "How could you throw that in my face…after all we've meant to each other." His demeanor and vocal delivery were suddenly quite feminine, Milan noted with an arched brow.

"I was foolish to expect a domestic to behave as a gentleman." Hayden smiled sardonically. Weeping, Noah pulled a handkerchief from his pajama pocket and covered his face.

Milan's mouth went dry. She could actually feel her heart plunging into her stomach. Noah wasn't even employed in a dignified position. He was a servant. *A manservant!* Being a manservant sounded worse than being a butler, for Chrissakes!

"What's he talking about, Noah? Do you work for this man? Are you his servant?"

Noah uncovered his face. He didn't speak. He just looked at her and there was something in his pathetic face that made the answer all too clear. She was engaged to marry a pauper. Milan was shocked speechless. She could have kicked herself for ignoring the warning signs.

How could she have been so gullible to believe this fool—this manservant—was a wealthy person? No wonder she couldn't find any information about the Brockington family when she searched online. He probably came from a long line of freakin' sharecroppers. Employed as a manservant, Noah was probably considered the family's success story!

"You bastard!" she shouted at Noah. "I should sue you for false representation."

"It serves you right, you gold-digging little trollop!" Hayden spat, standing up combatively as if prepared to get physical with Milan. "That ring you're wearing is a family heirloom." He glared at Noah. "I can't believe you gave her my Aunt Gwyneth's ring!"

Milan gawked at the hideous ring and then jerked her head in Noah's direction. "Does my ring belong to his aunt?" she asked, knowing the answer.

A troubling thought in the back of her mind demanded attention. She grimaced in discomfort and replayed Noah and Hayden's conversation in her mind. As the fuzz cleared, their emotional exchange finally became obvious: Noah had been a kept man. He and Hayden McIntyre were involved in a homosexual relationship. *Oh God!*

Noah nodded. "Yes," he sobbed. "The ring belongs to Hayden." He cried openly, tears streaming down his cheeks. Milan detested him; she'd never despised a human being more than she despised Noah. His emotional display was so gay. And revolting. She had nothing against homosexuals but she certainly didn't appreciate being duped into a twisted sexual relationship with a man who presented himself as straight. A red flag should have waved like crazy the very first time he requested anal penetration. But blinded by greed, she'd ignored it. Now she was left to deal with circumstances that she refused to even ponder at the moment.

Needing to hear Noah admit his homosexuality, she asked, "Are you and he...?"

"Yes," Noah answered before she finished the question. He uttered a pitiful cry and then wept like a woman. "Hayden and I are lovers," he said through sobs.

She steadied her footing and took a deep breath before asking the next question. "Are you dying, Noah?"

"No." He shook his head vehemently. "That was a lie as well. I pretended to be deathly ill, feigning a terminal illness as a scare tactic to coerce Hayden into leaving his wife."

"You're not terminally ill?" Milan screamed with wide, incredulous eyes.

"Of course not," Hayden said disgustedly. "Aside from starving himself like a lovesick schoolgirl, Noah's in perfect health."

"I'm sorry, Hayden. But you must know that every deceitful action was intended to get your attention," Noah told Hayden, sounding contrite.

"Your little scheme has backfired, hasn't it? After getting your wedding invitation, I pressured Emma into a trial separation. I was beside myself with grief. I thought you had thrown in the towel and was hell bent on finding some semblance of happiness even if it meant suffering through a loveless marriage with a *woman*," he said, turning up his nose. "At first I was going to do the honorable thing, put up a brave front and attend the wedding with Emma." Hayden gave a snort. "But I changed my mind. Silly me, I came here to surprise you with the news that I've decided to ask Emma for a divorce. I was going to beg you on bended knee to accept my hand in a commitment ceremony. But now that I've discovered your treachery, I don't want anything more to do with you." Hayden stood with his arms tightly folded. He breathed in deeply. "Noah, I want you to pack your bags. Leave the premises immediately."

With unexpected agility, Noah leapt from the bed and clutched at the front of Hayden's shirt. "Please! Don't do this to me. I was mean and spiteful. I admit it. But I did it for love. I love you with my whole heart; you know I do."

Noah's admission of love was sickening. Milan doubted if she'd ever hated anyone as much as she hated Noah in that instant. Could her existence get any worse? From the moment of her unwanted conception, her life had been nothing more than a comedy of errors. And it wasn't fair. The illness, the engagement, the pending marriage, the insemination had all been nothing more than a game to Noah. A vicious game.

She'd put up with Noah's sickening fantasies and perversions, had even been injected with his foul sperm. What he'd done to her was despicable; she deserved to be compensated for her duress. She glanced at Hayden. It would be tough to get him to see things her way, but she'd use every tool in her arsenal to convince Hayden to compensate her for the time spent and trouble endured with his down-low paramour.

chapter thirty-five

"**M**iss Nelson…," Hayden said, startling Milan by using the alias she had briefly used while dodging the law. His harsh tone and dark, unforgiving eyes pinned Milan in place. He resumed his seat, reached over, and picked up a stack of papers from a nearby table.

So much drama had unfolded, so many secrets revealed, Milan hadn't noticed the ominously official-looking paperwork the Brit now waved in the air. "It is Miss Nelson, isn't it?"

Trouble was brewing. She felt her blood surging in response to being called by the alias she'd completely forgotten about.

"Or should I call you Miss Walden? It seems you have several aliases. Which name do you currently go by?" he asked with a pompous tilt to his head and a malicious smile as he rustled through the papers.

Milan gulped. "Uh, my name is Milan Walden. Noah knows that." She shot Noah an evil look. But Noah was knelt before Hayden, clinging to him with his head placed in Hayden's lap.

Revealed as an imposter himself, Noah refused to meet her gaze. She wanted to yank Noah from Hayden's lap, and collar and bitch slap him. It took every ounce of restraint not to pounce upon Noah and strangle him until his tongue lolled and his eyes bulged in death.

"Whatever your name is, I have evidence that you have taken well over a half million dollars of *my* money. I could have you arrested for theft." He pointed to her left hand. "Your acceptance of this ring could bring on an additional charge—receiving stolen goods!"

In light of the fact that she had only eighty thousand squirreled away in her hidden stash, the amount he accused her of taking was ridiculously excessive. Sure, Noah had paid her large sums of money, he'd even liberated her of her financial grief with Pure Paradise, but it still didn't add up anywhere close to half a million dollars.

Hearing the word *arrested* issued from the lips of an affluent man was disconcerting, to say the least. It was clearly time to cut her losses and make a speedy exit. "Look, I don't know what you're talking about. I worked for Noah. I made an honest living here," she said, yanking off the ugly engagement ring. "Here's your property. Sorry for your trouble," she said and turned to leave.

"Not so fast!" Hayden watched Milan with unwavering eyes. "I can see that you're an opportunist. You obviously took advantage of poor Noah," Hayden informed her and then tossed Noah a sympathetic smile and gave him tender pats on the head.

Apparently all was forgiven, Milan surmised with a *tsk*. The two creeps deserved each other.

"If you don't return every single dollar you stole from me I'll have no choice but to notify the authorities."

Noah lifted his head from Hayden's lap. "He's right. You took advantage of me. I was distraught and in an unhealthy mental state…"

"Shut up, you pervert. Did you tell your boyfriend what I had to do for that money?"

"Please. Spare me the sordid details," Hayden said snidely. "Young lady, at this point I have no interest in your tawdry love affair. I'm only interested in regaining the money you stole from me."

"I didn't steal anything. Noah paid for my services. The money he paid me didn't come close to a half million."

"I agreed to pay for the services of a companion for Noah." Hayden shuffled through the pages. "Yes, here it is," he said, peering at a computer-generated spreadsheet. "Companion fee—two hundred and fifty dollars a week including room and board and full use of all the amenities." His focus reverted to Milan. "I offered to pay for a companion for Noah, someone to keep him company until I could resolve my situation. I never intended to maintain the lavish lifestyle of a gold digger."

Milan didn't flinch. The personal affront was the least of her worries. "Noah led me to believe that he was independently wealthy," she said, defending herself while wondering if she could possibly bargain her way out of the predicament. "As you know," she said, speaking quickly, "we were planning to be married. Imagine how shocked I am to learn that Noah— my fiancé—is on the down low."

"He's on the what?"

"He's a gay man pretending to be straight," she explained to Hayden, who obviously had not heard of the expression. "He's bisexual. On the down low, like you," she added matter-of-factly, but hoping to somehow use Hayden's hidden sexual orientation for leverage. "No, he's probably worse than you. He's such a freak, he likes to pretend that I'm a little schoolgirl."

Stone-faced, Hayden did not react to the incriminating insult. "An attempt at blackmail is not a wise move. Now tell me, exactly how much of my cash did you siphon?" he asked bluntly.

As if the answer lurked in a hidden corner of Noah's bedroom, Milan looked in every direction as she tried to come up with the type of lie that would declare her innocence and allow her to escape this house of inquisition with every dollar she had earned. She'd sold her soul to a nutcase homo pervert and she'd be damned if she'd leave empty-handed. The situation reminded her of the ordeal with Pure Paradise when she was railroaded by the members of the board. Being accused of fraudulent behavior was like a recurring bad dream. She resolved that this time, she would not go out without a fight.

Feeling invigorated and determined to keep most of the money, she told Hayden, "I only earned about ten thousand! Noah said my elegant room and board was sufficient for now, that I'd be handsomely compensated after our marriage."

"I said no such thing!" Noah objected.

Milan opened her mouth to respond, but struck with an excellent idea, she instead assembled a speech. "I'm saddened by this dreadful turn of events, Noah. I've spent hours celebrating with my family—my mother and my sister," she lied. "Celebrating the new life that you and I are bringing into the world."

Noah frowned. Hayden turned as white as the papers he held in his hands. "You had sex with her?" Hayden recoiled visibly.

"Never!" Noah said firmly.

"He's telling the truth," Milan said. She narrowed her gaze and studied Hayden's expression, watched his features soften with relief. Then she went in for the kill. "We never had sex, not in the conventional sense, but I am most definitely carrying his child. The advances in technology are amazing and I was able to use an early detection at-home pregnancy kit. I'm approximately ten days' pregnant. Isn't that wonderful?" Milan asked, beaming.

"An immaculate conception, I presume," Hayden said. Judging by his doubtful expression and the sarcasm in his tone, he obviously didn't believe her.

"Noah hired a nurse to inject his sperm into my uterus. Check your records, you'll see that he doubled the hours of Ruth Henry from the Mobile Nurse Agency."

Hayden quickly leafed through the pages. Spotting the incriminating evidence, his body stiffened. "You did pay extra hours for this nurse."

"I admit it," Noah said quietly.

"She used a turkey baster to do the deed," Milan chimed in. Hayden grimaced.

"I didn't have possession of my rational mind," Noah whined. His panicky eyes flicked over Hayden's rigid form. "I thought I'd lost you; I wanted to hurt you as much as you hurt me. Bringing my own progeny into the world was an act of defiance—a ludicrous notion. I'm so sorry, Hayden. Darling Hayden, please forgive me."

"I do forgive you, dearest, but this is quite an awful mess."

Milan wanted to throw up, but doing so would interfere with the flow of the plan she'd put in motion. "Seems you two have an additional problem now that I have a little Noah on the way."

"How do I know that what you're saying is true?" Hayden asked, his voice rising angrily.

"You don't," Milan replied in a calm tone. "My attorney will handle all the details of the paternity suit."

"Sue!" Hayden said challengingly. "As I've told you, Noah doesn't have a plug nickel to his name."

"That may be true, but I'm going to have to find a way to support myself during my pregnancy…" Her voice trailed off. She inhaled blissfully. Wearing a serene smile, she caressed her stomach.

Noah and Hayden shared expressions of revulsion.

"Mr. McIntyre—may I call you Hayden?"

Hayden grunted a response.

"I don't know what you do for a living or your social ranking, but Noah spoke of you as if you were royalty."

"Believe me, I have no ties with the royal family." Hayden gave a nervous titter.

"Well, you strike me as a rather prominent person—a well-connected man with strong social ties. I'm sure my story will make great fodder for one of those British tabloids. And with all Noah's bills being funded by your account, I can assure you that you will indeed be dragged along with Noah through the court system. I plan to divulge everything I know about your homosexual relationship with Noah, your manservant." Milan snorted. "I'll provide graphic details of Noah's ruthless and twisted revenge tactics that resulted in the conception of an innocent child. You two," she said waving a finger at the two men, "will be held in scorn by the masses. I see a book deal and a film offer in my future. Yes, this awful mess might work out just fine for me," Milan said brightly.

"How could you get me involved in such a scandalous disgrace?" Hayden shouted at Noah. "I can't have my name dragged through the courts and sensationalized in the tabloids. Why, Emma will never get invited to another social function, the poor dear will have to hide in shame. I can't let this happen," Hayden avowed as he slammed the heap of documents on top of the table, then pounded the pile with a balled fist.

When he'd arrived, Hayden had been ready to divorce his wife, according to him. Now he had a change of heart. Milan suspected he'd been stringing Noah along for years with the divorcing and un-divorcing of his wife. But what did she care? She was too close to the prize to concern herself with the twisted love triangle of Noah, Hayden, and Emma, the unsuspecting wife.

She hadn't stolen one dollar. The money she had stashed was hard earned and she wasn't about to take a fall for the misdeeds of the group of thieves Noah had hired. Milan didn't have a problem dropping names, including that of Tookie's mom. For all Milan knew, Elise could very well be the thief. Hell, if it wasn't Elise than it had to be Irma, Greer, or even Ruth Henry—any of those women could have stolen the money. She'd be damned if she was going to be left holding the bag.

"Listen, I'm going to cut to the chase," she blurted. "I don't know what happened to your money. Noah had a companion before I was hired. Her name is Elise Corbett and I heard she's sitting pretty—doesn't have to work another day of her life. He also had a traveling nurse from down South, Greer Wilson. Greer made out like a bandit too. Check your records—you'll see she charged a king's ransom for every sugar pill she dispensed. Noah paid for her family's vacation. And that cook…" Milan sighed. Irma had obviously been in cahoots with Noah. Her thoughts traveled to the many lies Irma had told her and focused on the most recent: *The jeweler was here…*" No jeweler had delivered the ring. Milan shook her head. More than any of the others, she particularly wanted Irma to go down! "Don't get me started about Irma," Milan said, sucking her teeth. "She bought food for her family and charged it to Noah's grocery bill. At one point, the freakin' cook had a key to the trunk where the cash is kept! Now that's the person you should have been interrogating, not me."

Hayden nodded wearily. "Miss Walden, I've had a change of heart. I'm not interested in pressing charges against the cook or anyone else," he said softly. "I want this entire matter to go away. I plan to sell this house as quickly as possible. Noah, you're returning to London with me. I don't want an ocean to separate us ever again. We'll work out our problems together. Do you agree, dear boy?"

"Yes!" Noah said emphatically. "Yes, without a doubt. I'll wait for you for-ever if I have to; I'll be your manservant again. To be back in your good graces, I'll even put up with your marriage to Emma. Whatever you desire."

"Yes, you'll return to London as my manservant. Emma will be happy to give my current servant the boot. He's not as polite and polished as you," Hayden said, giving Noah a nod.

Hayden turned his attention to Milan. "I'll have my attorney draw up the paperwork. Of course, you'll state that Noah is not the parent of your unborn child. I'll pay you one million dollars with the expectation that you will go away and leave us alone. Forever."

Milan stroked her chin as she pondered his offer. Hayden could afford to pacify Noah with several million. She didn't see why she should she settle for only one mil. Her pain and suffering was worth much more than that. "Make it five million and I'll sign anything you want."

Hayden bristled. He raked his fingers through his thick hair, breathed in deeply, and finally nodded. "I'll have the papers drawn tomorrow," he said resignedly.

chapter thirty-six

Some would call it a coincidence, others would say it was just a stroke of good luck, but Milan knew it was true kismet that brought Maxwell Torrance into her life.

From the haughty air he exuded and the boisterous manner in which he barked orders to his hired lackeys, no one would have ever guessed that a powerful man such as Maxwell Torrance would have responded to the ad Milan posted on the internet: STERN MISTRESS SEEKING WEALTHY PLEASURE TOY.

Her involvement with Gerard had provided an outlet to explore her sexuality and embrace her submissive nature. Transitioning from submissive to dominant had not been a simple undertaking; her finances, however, had demanded that she do so. She'd treated herself to every imaginable luxury, including forking over a hefty monthly mortgage on a two-million-dollar mini mansion, a personal chef, a gardener, a housekeeper, and she'd bravely gone under the knife for breast implants, which were a magnificent work of art.

Milan purchased new homes and cars for her mother and sister. Her mother cautiously accepted Milan's gifts with the dire warning that Milan's new-found wealth just wasn't right—she was headed for trouble and needed to get married, settle down, and have kids.

She'd bought Sweetie's family a roomy home and new SUV and also financed a take-out restaurant for Sweetie's husband, Quantez. And recently Sweetie, who suddenly had no problem accepting money that she wasn't sure Milan had killed Noah to acquire, was trying to hit her up for even more money to open a day care center. Thinking of her sister's selective moral values made Milan smile and shake her head.

Milan possessed a powerful fear of poverty and in light of her spending habits, which were admittedly out of hand, taking on a wealthy submissive was a wise financial move.

Having no idea how much longer the remaining money she'd swindled from Noah's boyfriend would last, it made good financial sense to step up to the plate and sexually dominate a wealthy man who could easily afford to maintain the lavish lifestyle she'd become accustomed to. And billionaire Maxwell Torrance was a serious upgrade from the impoverished imposter, Noah Brockington.

❦

The chauffeur, a tall broad-shouldered, black man, parked Maxwell Torrance's Rolls-Royce at the curb near the Broad Street and Lehigh Avenue subway stop. The declined inner-city neighborhood bustled with commuters and other pedestrians of meager means who ogled the nineteen-foot-long luxury automobile.

Milan, relaxed in the rear seat, read the financial report she'd recently received from her acquisitions attorney. Cool as a cucumber, she didn't lift her gaze when the chauffeur reported, "There he is!"

"Hmm," she uttered. Disinterested, she continued reading.

Accustomed to taking orders from the man who had just emerged from the bowels of the subway station, the driver was ill at ease. "Should I open the door for Mr. Torrance?" he asked. Creases of concern marked his forehead but did not distort his rugged good looks.

"There's no hurry; let him wait," she said casually.

"You think it's safe out there for Mr. Torrance?"

"Maxwell Torrance needs a reality check; let him wait!" she said firmly.

Milan enjoyed the performance as she watched the smartly dressed business mogul hurry to the driver's window. To no avail, he urgently rapped on the tinted window. Amidst the scoffing laughter of the onlookers who were amused by his humiliating predicament, Maxwell Torrance made even more of a spectacle of himself as he rushed from one side of his Rolls to the other, desperately jiggling the handles of the locked front and rear passenger doors.

It was an unsafe neighborhood. It was risky business for Milan to force her rich benefactor into such a potentially dangerous situation, but throughout her life, she'd been a risk taker. Pushing the limits and leaving the powerful deal-maker exposed and vulnerable would remind him who called the shots in their relationship. This exercise in degradation would motivate him to promptly obey her future orders without question. From now on, Maxwell Torrance would respectfully affix his signature to any document she ordered him to sign. And he'd do it without the benefit of reviewing the material. If he knew what was good for him, he'd sign whatever she commanded him to sign, without hesitation.

Five minutes later, she instructed the driver to open the door. The chauffeur was a big man, but he moved with the grace and agility of an NFL player, which was his occupation before a knee injury cut his career short.

Milan paid no attention to the beleaguered older caucasian man who fell into the back of the car and dropped his briefcase heavily to the floor. Gasping and panting, the harried man mopped his brow as if he'd narrowly escaped the bullet of a paid assassin.

"Are you ready, Mr. Torr—" The driver caught his error and respectfully corrected himself. "Excuse me, are you ready, Miss Walden?"

"Yes, I'm ready, driver," Milan said, shifting her gaze to the tinted passenger window. The Rolls always attracted a lot of attention, but parked in this low-income district, the car was as out of place as a spacecraft. Milan could see curiosity in the eyes of the swarm of North Philadelphians who gawked at the time-honored symbol of success. She knew they wondered which celebrity or which wealthy socialite on the other side of the tinted glass had taunted the obviously affluent businessman.

"How was your commute?" she asked in a ridiculing tone as the Rolls glided into Broad Street traffic.

For a few seconds, Maxwell Torrance was silent. To blurt out the truth—that utilizing public transportation from his posh corporate headquarters to this frightening urban neighborhood was a stiff and humiliating experience—would result in even harsher consequences. Milan swelled with pride as the powerful and obscenely wealthy tycoon mentally scrambled to come up with just the right words.

"Riding the subway was interesting. If it pleases my mistress," he said sincerely, "I'll repeat the humbling travel arrangement tomorrow."

Milan snorted. "Whether or not you travel on public transportation depends on you. I gather you've reviewed your behavior and have learned a valuable lesson."

"I have, mistress. I will never again hesitate when you command me to do something. Unquestioningly, I will obey you." His worshipful eyes were damp with earnest tears.

Disrespectfully, Milan smacked his face with the pile of legal papers. The sound echoed. "Your words don't impress me," she snarled.

The billionaire flinched, and then cowered awkwardly when she threateningly raised the papers again. "Do you fear me?" she hissed.

"Yes," he told her, his voice an annoying whine.

"Good, now sign the last page of this legal document."

Groping inside a concealed pocket of his Armani jacket, he searched for a pen.

Seconds later, Milan gazed happily at his scrawled signature. "Now, sign this!" She presented another form to him. "Do you agree that you're unworthy of having a chauffeured automobile?"

"I agree wholeheartedly, mistress," he said, exuberantly pressing the tip of the pen against the paper.

"Do you regret relinquishing your car and your driver to me?" Milan directed a triumphant glance at the rearview mirror where she locked eyes with the chauffeur.

"No. I have no regrets, mistress. I'm honored to bestow you with this car and my driver. It's my duty as your slave to make your life one of leisure, to indulge your every whim."

Using both hands, she gave her lap several audible pats, queuing Maxwell to kneel before her in the spacious accommodations in the rear of the car. She hitched up her dress and parted her legs. "You've pleased me, slave. You may eat."

With his head bowed reverently, he whispered, "Thank you, mistress." With long and fervent strokes, he licked her labia exactly the way she'd taught him. When her brown thighs clamped firmly against his pale cheeks, he was trained to extend his tongue and enter her. Milan moaned softly as his tongue slid in and out of her vagina. Her eyelids fluttered open and she found herself looking into the hungry dark eyes of the handsome driver.

Milan winked at the driver, sending him a silent message that the services of his stiffened dick would be required immediately after they dropped Maxwell off at the gate of his palatial mansion—a sprawling stone structure that Milan also intended to acquire in due time.

⚜

A week later, swathed in black silk, her face concealed by tinted sunglasses, Milan was escorted to the board room by a gaggle of attorneys as well as Maxwell Torrance, whose reputation as a ferocious businessman preceded him.

It had been a hostile takeover. Shareholders had been duped into selling their shares and the board was now comprised mainly of members that the attorneys had put in place, with only three of the former board members remaining.

Assuming Maxwell Torrance to be the new owner of Pure Paradise, the members of the board all directed head nods and glowing smiles in his direction. The chairperson, Dr. Kayla Pauley, stood respectfully and wore a warm, extra wide smile. However, when Milan Walden removed her shades, Dr. Pauley's smile converted to a jittery contortion and then a full-scale grimace.

Milan took the empty seat at the head of the conference table. Maxwell Torrance took a seat facing her at the far end of the table.

Dr. Pauley, seated next to Milan, gawked at the young black woman and then swung her neck in the opposite direction and stared questioningly at Maxwell Torrance. Her confused eyes, mixed with a hint of hostility, implored Milan to state her business. "What are you doing here, Milan? Uh, I believe you're sitting in Mr. Torrance's chair," Dr. Pauley said nervously. "Are you Mr. Torrance's assistant?"

"Ms. Walden is the new owner of Pure Paradise," one of the attorneys chimed in. "Mr. Torrance, a friend and a business associate of Ms. Walden, has invested in the company. I guess you could say he's here to meet the people responsible for making sure his investment turns a very lucrative profit," the attorney said with a confident chuckle. "He's also here to support Ms. Walden." The attorney threw Milan a broad smile. "Not that she needs any assistance… A few of you already know Ms. Walden and are familiar with her business savvy. She's a shrewd businesswoman with sound judgment. So let's give your new leader a welcoming round of applause."

Dr. Pauley, wearing a strained smile, clapped her hands together listlessly. Apparently, the news had hit like a bombshell. She tried to make eye contact with Walter Billings, one of the remaining original members who had played a part in Milan's untimely dismissal, but Billings disassociated himself, clapping soundly and looking straight ahead.

Near hysteria, Dr. Pauley sucked in air, touched her chest, and rubbed it in circular motions as she struggled to wipe the horrified look off her face. "Milan, uh, Ms. Walden— welcome back to Pure Paradise," she said, stuttering. "We had no idea you were the new owner." Dr. Pauley drew a deep, calming breath. "We're all looking forward to a healthy fiscal year," she announced, sounding fully composed now. "We know that under your new leadership, Pure Paradise will blend contemporary amenities and technologies with old-fashioned courtesy to cater to the well-being of our guests—"

"Oh, cut the crap, Kayla. Oops! " Milan covered her mouth with her hand. "Forgive me for calling you by your first name; how presumptuous of me." Milan feigned an apologetic expression.

"Oh no, I'm not offended at all. Call me Kayla. Please."

"Okay, that's fine. However, I expect to be addressed as Ms. Walden. Is that clear, Kayla?"

"Certainly, uh...Ms. Walden. Absolutely," Dr. Pauley gushed, wearing a solicitous smile.

Milan fluttered her hands impatiently, indicating that the members seated closest should move down to allow her attorneys to flank her. The board members, including Dr. Pauley, quickly scooted down several chairs.

"Kayla, the words you're mouthing off sound familiar. If I'm not mistaken, didn't I express those exact sentiments in a brochure I created for Pure Paradise last year? Yes, I believe I did," Milan answered herself, nodding. "I'm sure you recall the gleaming brochure I produced right before I got canned..."

Dr. Pauley, now five chairs down from Milan, winced and then looked around at the lawyers and other board members, her face red with mortification.

"Refresh my memory," Milan demanded. "Why did you give me the boot?"

"I didn't personally have you terminated. It was decided by the entire board..." Dr. Pauley's head swiveled toward Walter Billings. Leaving Dr. Pauley hanging, Billings kept his eyes focused on the new owner.

"Whatever!" Milan said, holding up her hand to silence the woman.

For several uncomfortable moments, Dr. Pauley's mouth hung open. Every eye in the room was on her when she finally embarrassedly closed it.

"I have innovative plans for Pure Paradise," Milan revealed in a hushed tone that persuaded everyone in the room to lean forward expectantly. "Pure Paradise will no longer limit its services to women only. We will not discriminate based on gender identity. We're also going to expand our scope of services to meet the sexual urges and desires of our clientele." Milan paused. "Why? I'll tell you why." Her audience waited with bated breath to be informed. "Why do we strive for beauty and health?" she asked. "Because we want to look attractive and feel good in order to attract sexual partners. Humans are sexual beings who possess an innate desire to express their sexuality. Here at Pure Paradise, clients will enjoy a safe and judgment-free environment that allows them the freedom to explore all aspects of their sexuality. Pure Paradise will be a cutting-edge sex center for consenting adults. Don't let the boldness of my claim concern you. What goes on behind the closed doors of this facility will be kept confidential and is completely legal."

"Brilliant, absolutely brilliant," Dr. Pauley emoted, nodding her head vigorously.

"Brilliant," the other members agreed, clapping their hands enthusiastically. The room was filled with the thunder of applause.

The tables had turned, one-eighty. It was amazing how easily she had reduced the arrogant chairperson to a groveling peon. She would have never expected Dr. Kayla Pauley to kiss up with such enthusiasm. Obviously, it would be just a matter of time before the woman was literally kissing her ass. Yes, there was a thin line between submission and dominance and Milan looked forward to training the insufferable Dr. Pauley.

After a lifetime of sexual confusion, Milan had finally discovered her true nature. She was a fem/dom. *I'm a fem/dom diva*, she thought to herself, expounding on her identity.

There'd be no more bottoming for her. She promised herself that she'd never again take an order from anyone. She wished Gerard much success with his and Ming's training center, but she doubted if their facility could begin to compete with the enhanced version of Pure Paradise once it was up and running.

She made a mental note to check out their training center. If it struck her fancy and if it seemed worth her while, she'd engage in yet another company takeover. In the meantime, she'd content herself with running her business, amassing wealth and building a stable of willing human property.

After Milan dismissed her attorneys and the members of the board, she gazed at Maxwell Torrance, who sat at the far end of the conference table.

"Are you happy, mistress?" he inquired, loosening his tie and unbuttoning the top buttons of his shirt. His collar, a thin platinum band with a dangling tag that proclaimed Milan to be his owner, glimmered brilliantly.

"Come to me," Milan said breathily. Aroused by the collar, she raised her skirt and slid down her panties.

Maxwell stood at her command, caressing the collar.

"Crawl," she ordered.

Wearing a look that was a mixture of devotion and gratitude, he dropped to the plush carpeted floor. As her devoted property crawled toward her, she took in a satisfied burst of air. It didn't get much better than this—sitting at the head of the conference table waiting for the man who'd made it possible, crawl to her and lick her pussy in gratitude at being owned by her.

Undoubtedly, she had it all. Her sister had once claimed that no man would ever find her loveable. Milan shrugged as she inched her naked ass to the edge of the resplendent board room chair and pointed a leather boot. Next, she gave a strong yank to Maxwell's hair, prompting him to open his mouth. "Remove my boots...with your teeth."

Instantly, he opened his mouth. Expertly, he did as he was bidden and used his teeth to unzip his owner's two-thousand-dollar Manolo Blahnik stretch leather boot. Without needing further instruction, the billionaire on the floor—a respected CEO of several Fortune 500 companies, clamped his teeth around the heel of Milan's boot and tugged it until he worked the boot off her foot. Milan smiled contentedly. She didn't need a man to find her loveable when she owned a filthy rich man who worshipped her totally.

Yes, her life was completely fulfilling—it was grand, indeed. While her other boot was being unzipped, Milan's mind drifted to her to-do list. The only thing still pending was the writing of her how-to-book, *Weekend Escape: Your Spa at Home*. She made a slight frown. At this point, she really had no interest in writing *that* book.

"I've got a great idea," she said, as she rubbed her now bare feet playfully through her property's hair and across his face. He responded by kissing her feet adoringly. "I'm going to write a book," Milan exclaimed. The working title is: *Train Your Man in One Weekend: He'll Service You for the Rest of Your Life!*"

"Genius, Mistress. Pure genius," Maxwell Torrance agreed.

Aroused by the idea of a potential bestseller, Milan pulled her feet away and nudged the head that was bowed in reverence. At her signal, Maxwell lifted his head and pressed his lips against her vagina. Moans of contentment escaped his throat as he flicked his tongue back and forth across the labia and clit he adored.

When Milan gave the next signal, he probed inside with a curled tongue, sending jolts to her system, making her draw up her legs to receive deeper tongue penetration.

⚜

Later, when Milan and Maxwell exited Pure Paradise, the broad-shoul-dered driver promptly opened the door for the attractive pair.

At first sight, curious eyes would see an impeccably groomed power couple. The platinum collar of ownership hidden beneath Maxwell's tightly knotted tie declared him Milan's property as did the slowly healing burned skin on his forearm where he'd been branded with her mark of ownership.

"Let's take Maxwell home," Milan told the driver.

The driver and Milan made eye contact in the rear view mirror. Her eyes told him she'd had an arduous day; she'd experienced the kind of stress that even the most skillful tongue could not begin to relieve. What ailed her lay deep within and only a long dick with sizeable girth could make contact with the soft spots that were clenching and demanding satisfaction.

She leaned back against the posh interior of the Rolls Royce and closed her eyes. She instantly saw a visual of Kayla Pauley's attractive face buried between her legs, Kayla's slender neck graced by a platinum ownership collar. The visual was arousing as hell.

Hornier than ever, Milan leaned forward. "Speed it up, driver."

"No problem." He pressed down on the gas pedal. One hand held the steering wheel while his other hand stroked the dick that pulsed until it became lengthy and thick. The car, the driver, as well as the driver's over-sized appendage belonged to Milan now, a very extravagant gift given to her by the man who sat contentedly in the rear seat beside her. For Milan, life had become a series of sexual conquests—numerous men and women angling to lap the nectar from her honey pot.

But tonight would be a special treat: no lips, no tongues, no fingers. Milan was ready for the kind of release that those body parts could never induce.

Very soon, she'd feel the driver's raw meat pushing inside her, indulging her with its thickness. She'd ultimately receive a powerful orgasm that only a skillful big dick could generate. But she'd have to be careful—she'd have to keep her guard up. For she knew that a man packing a good-sized dick could lead the most focused woman astray.

She gazed in the mirror again and gave the former NFL player a sultry smile. He winked at her and grinned. It was the kind of cocky grin that reflected the major come-up he expected after he successfully dick-whipped Milan.

But Milan knew better than to give another man the upper hand. Gerard had taught her well. She smirked at the driver's stupid self-assurance. *Let the sex games begin!* Smiling smugly, she envisioned the macho ball player being led around on a leash.

She eased back and gave a satisfied sigh. It was her world and life was grand, indeed.

about the author

Allison Hobbs was raised in suburban Philadelphia. After high school she worked for several years in the music industry as a singer, songwriter, and studio background vocalist. She eventually attended Temple University and earned a Bachelor of Science degree. She is the national bestselling author of *Pandora's Box, Insatiable, Dangerously in Love, Double Dippin'* and *The Enchantress.* Hobbs currently resides in Philadelphia. Visit her at www.allisonhobbs.com and www.myspace.com/allisonhobbs or email her at pb@allisonhobbs.com

SNEAK PREVIEW! EXCERPT FROM

THE CLIMAX: INSATIABLE 2

BY ALLISON HOBBS

AVAILABLE FROM STREBOR BOOKS FEBRUARY 2008

CHAPTER 1

To the observer, it seemed Terelle Chambers was unaware of her surroundings, locked inside herself. Her caregivers at Spring Haven Psychiatric Hospital hand-fed her, manually moved her limbs and even toileted her, but they treated Terelle dispassionately as if she were an inanimate object—*something* that required care. Her affliction, Persistent Catatonia, had robbed the twenty-three-year-old of even a glimmer of her former personality.

Aside from occasional sorrowful whimpers, anguished moans—fleeting echoes of a tormented inner world—Terelle had not uttered a coherent word in two years.

Although she appeared to have retreated from the outside world, Terelle, however, was keenly aware of touch, taste, smell, and sound. Her thoughts and memory were jumbled and disjointed but she was able to distinguish between the smells and voices and even the touch of the doctors and nurses who briskly performed their duties on her behalf without emotional attachment.

Awakened by the sound of footsteps approaching the bed where her rigid body lay, Terelle felt instantly comforted by the feelings of compassion and love that emanated from the person who had entered her room and was now standing over her.

Saleema, she thought as a smile formed in her mind. She would have greeted her dearest friend with a hug if her unmoving arms and clenched, contracted fists would agree to such a gesture. She wished she could remember how to speak the word, *hello,* but the technique required to form clear and audible words escaped her.

Terelle inhaled deeply, trying to draw in her best friend's fragrance. But instead of the pleasant hint of Saleema's perfume, Terelle recognized a masculine scent. She gasped in alarm.

Long thick fingers tenderly stroked her cheek, calming her. The fingers inched upward and caressed the soft hair that curled at her temples. Terelle knew this man; she recognized his touch—his essence. Was she still asleep? Was she lost inside a dream?

The squeal of the bedrail being lowered sounded all too real for this to be a dream, but in her heart she knew a dream was all this could be. Terelle's lashes fluttered as she struggled to raise eyelids that felt much too heavy too lift. The struggle to open her eyes ceased when she felt the weight of his chest pressing down upon her breasts. He kissed her cheek.

"Terelle," he whispered her name. "You gotta get better, babe." He squeezed her closed fist. "This ain't the way it was supposed to go down." His voice caught. She heard him taking in deep breaths. She felt his raw emotions. His sorrow. And his love. "I miss you."

Terelle wanted to look in her man's face, but she knew if she opened her eyes, he'd disappear as he did at the end of every dream. She could only be with Marquise during slumber, so she allowed herself to relax, praying to remain blissfully asleep forever.

"I know you got the strength to come up outta this," he said, stroking her hair. "You can't give up. We still can have a future together. Me, you and Keeta."

Markeeta! Oh God, my poor baby. She'd been enjoying the time spent in dreamland with Marquise long enough. It wasn't right for her to remain in her inner world just to be with him. She had to get well for Markeeta.

"You can't give up like this." He caressed her arms and her hand and then leaned down and kissed her lips. The sensation of their hearts beating together nearly took her breath away. When she felt his lips touch hers, Terelle easily accepted that her life on earth had ended and she was finally reunited with her beloved. No dream kiss could feel like this. Had she died—was she in heaven?

"All that shit with that other broad wasn't about nothing. Didn't you listen to the message I left on your voice mail?" His voice sounded choked. "I gotta go," he said abruptly and then pulled away.

Wait! Don't leave me, she wanted to scream but couldn't get the words out.

"I love you, girl. But I can show you better than I can tell you," he told her, speaking words that were uniquely his.

Oh Marquise. It's you. It's really you! Tears moistened and unsealed Terelle's closed eyes. In an act of sheer determination, she willed the muscles in her neck to cooperate. She turned her head and caught a glimpse of a very tall man pacing quickly toward the open door. *Marquise!*

From the depths of her soul, she drew on the memory of the mechanics required to produce coherent sound. She tried to shout his name, but the sound that issued from her lips was an unintelligible whimper. Determinedly, she tried again and this time his name came out in a loud and clear shriek. *Marquiiiiiiise!*

But instead of being comforted in Marquise's loving arms, Terelle was held down by several pairs of strong hands, trained to restrain the chronically mentally ill.

❂❂❂

The next day Saleema Sparks sat at Terelle's bedside. Saleema's anxious eyes stared at her best friend but Terelle did not acknowledge Saleema. As usual she was mute and wore a blank expression.

Holding Terelle's limp hand, Saleema pleaded, "Talk to me, Terelle. Why won't you say something? The charge nurse called last night. She told me you spoke. She said you screamed for…" Saleema swallowed. "She said you screamed for Marquise." She squeezed Terelle's hand imploringly and gasped when she felt a slight movement in Terelle's fingers. Saleema's eyes, shining with hope, flashed upon Terelle's face.

Terelle's vacant look was replaced by a grimace as she struggled to emit sound.

"Terelle! You're back! I know you are. Oh my God; I gotta get a nurse," Saleema said excitedly as she pushed herself forward, prepared to rise. Terelle's fingers wiggled urgently.

"No?" Saleema asked. "You don't want me to get the nurse?"

One side of Terelle's face twitched as she uttered a gurgling sound. Saleema looked into Terelle's eyes. Terelle blinked rapidly. "Okay, I understand. You don't want me to get a nurse. But I don't know what to do. Are you in pain?"

"Maaar," Terelle uttered with great effort.

"Markeeta?" Saleema said, nodding. "She's fine, Terelle. Keeta's beautiful. Four years old and smart as a whip. I've been taking real good care of your baby. I love her like I would my own but I make sure she knows you and…" Saleema's voice faltered. "I show her pictures of you and her daddy," she said in a voice filled with emotion.

Tears slid down Terelle's cheek. "Oh my God. You're crying. But that's a good thing," Saleema said as she snatched a tissue out of a box on Terelle's bedside stand. She wiped the tears from Terelle's eyes. "Your tears mean that you hear me. You understand everything I've told you." Tears now welled in Saleema's eyes. "Oh, Terelle. I missed you so much." She bent down and gave Terelle's prone body an awkward hug. "I'm so glad you're back." Then Saleema, unable to keep her emotions in check, began to sniffle. She reached over and grabbed another tissue to wipe her own eyes.

"Maaarq…," Terelle said again. And Saleema realized her friend was referring to Marquise. But instead of acknowledging Terelle's attempt to speak her deceased fiancé's name, Saleema spoke animatedly about Terelle's daughter, Markeeta.

Exhausted from the effort of trying to speak, Terelle closed her eyes. Saleema sat holding Terelle's hand until her friend drifted off to sleep. Looking back at Terelle with concern, Saleema quietly left the room.

Saleema barged into the charge nurse's office. "I want Terelle to have speech lessons."

"Well, she's been evaluated and unfortunately—despite her breakthrough last night, Terelle's still not responsive. I'm sorry;" the nurse said sincerely. "Terelle is not a candidate for speech therapy."

"Excuse me!" Saleema held up her hand in an exaggerated motion, which informed the nurse that she was not pleased. "The last time I checked, my name was written at the bottom of the check this hospital gets for taking care of Terelle Chambers. Don't get it twisted; I'm not *asking* for anything. If she can't get speech therapy here, then I'll take her to another hospital—a better one." Saleema whirled around and strutted away.

"Ms. Sparks, "the nurse blurted. "I didn't mean to offend you. I'm only reporting what the speech therapist wrote in her evaluation note."

Saleema stopped abruptly, turned around. "You people told me that Terelle would never have meaningful or conscious interaction with her family or friends. That's what the doctors said, right?"

The nurse nodded.

"Wrong! My girl is interacting her ass off—blinking, moving her fingers— trying to communicate with me. So do your job. No more tests. Call in a speech therapist who knows what the fuck she's doing—"

"Ms. Sparks, that language isn't…"

Saleema held up her hand. "Don't be criticizing my language. I can talk any way I want. The way y'all misdiagnosed Terelle, you shouldn't be concerning yourself about no cuss words. You better hope I don't call my attorney and have him slap this place with a malpractice suit."

"I'll have another speech therapist evaluate Terelle."

"No, I'm not trying to hear that," Saleema said, wagging a finger. "No more evaluations—no more tests. The next time I come up in here, that therapist better be doing her job; I want her working with Terelle and giving her some real speech lessons. Ya heard?" Deliberately intimidating the now obviously frazzled nurse, Saleema threw out her arms in a flagrant combative gesture, glowered at the nurse and then sashayed out the door.